What People Are Saying About 'The Project'

"A fast paced and entertaining story, a provocative read showing potential consequences from the continuing spread of nuclear weapons technology. First three pages just blew me away."

Captain Richard Rodgers
U.S. Navy (ret.)

"A captivating and well told story of intriguing events in the Middle East."

Muhammed Al'Rahaief
Subject of the book, *Because Each Life is Precious: The Story of Saving Private Jessica Lynch*

The Project

Richard Folsom

ISBN: 978-0-9843008-1-5

ELEVENCO ENC, Blount's Creek, NC

The Red Phone

CNN Broadcast Studios, Atlanta, Georgia
3:30 AM Eastern Standard Time

THE EARLY MORNING ANNOUNCER pressed a hand to the side of his head, listening in an earphone as he glanced up at the control booth with a puzzled look on his face. "Excuse me," he said to his television audience, "but we're receiving breaking news of an event taking place in the Middle East." He paused. "Two events... no three, I'm being told."

He looked around the newsroom as if to ask could anyone confirm the story when he saw his director pointing to a live feed of an aircraft flying above Jerusalem. "Ladies and gentlemen," the announcer continued. "We're receiving information that at this very moment, 10:30 AM Middle Eastern Time, three aircraft, armed with nuclear weapons, are flying above the cities of Mecca, Tehran, and Jerusalem."

He stared at the quad screen on his teleprompter, watching satellite feeds of military jets flying above the three cities. The images were being transmitted live from the BBC in London, and through Al Jazeera in Qatar.

"According to the pilot of the aircraft flying above Tehran, who contacted the BBC via satellite phone, each jet is carrying a three megaton thermonuclear weapon, that he claims is the equivalent of an American ICBM warhead, more than enough to destroy the three cities and kill millions of people.

"Demands are now being made to the governments of Iran, Saudi Arabia and Israel, and they have only one hour to respond." He glanced up at the control room and made an ad-lib comment rarely heard on broadcast television. "Holy shit! This thing could be over before America even wakes up. Does the President know about this?"

A light on a red phone began blinking then buzzed twice in quick succession. The President rolled toward the nightstand lifted the receiver and heard the anxious voice of his National Security Advisor. "Mr. President, could you please come down to the Situation Room? We know the locations of the hijacked Saudi F-15 Strike Eagles."

He listened a moment longer then tried to respond with a calm voice. "Make the calls to the Israeli and Saudi embassies, and the Special Interest Section for Iran. Ask the ambassadors and envoy to arrive at the White House in twenty minutes for an emergency meeting. And get all the senior staff in as soon as possible."

"Yes, Sir, Mr. President, right away."

Video of nuclear-armed jets streamed through satellite networks around the world. Television news celebrities interrupted regular programming bringing live coverage of an event that was certain to bring the world to the brink of nuclear disaster. "Nothing like this has occurred since the Cuban Missile Crisis in October of 1962," a BBC announcer said. "And as far as we know, nuclear weapons have never been deployed over major population centers. This is an unprecedented moment in history."

Chinese officials in Beijing sat in front of huge digital screens, considering the massive financial investments recently made in the oil fields of Iran, and what a disruption of supply could mean to their economy. In a quickly calculated strategy they began applying their enormous financial reserves to bid up oil futures.

Western economists watched in fear as the price of oil in spot markets spiraled beyond anything ever seen. "At this pace," an analyst shouted, "if something is not done quickly, we could slip into economic recession before the end of the day!"

"Who are these people and what do they really want?" a French television announcer shouted into her microphone. "Do they want to create a nuclear disaster, or is this just another Islamist plot to throw the world into chaos so that Sharia Law might seem like a pleasant alternative to the madness sure to follow?"

"If these weapons detonate," a calmer voice in Germany predicted, "only decisive action by western governments will be able to resolve this crisis and stabilize oil production in the Middle East. And the nations of the Persian Gulf may find themselves once again occupied by military forces from around the world."

"The immediate questions on everyone's mind," an analyst for CBS news in New York asked, "Who are these people, and how did they get their hands on fissionable material? How did they get it processed into nuclear weapons without anyone in the world community knowing about it, and just what is it they're trying to accomplish?"

"Oh, my God!" shouted the commentator in Atlanta as he listened to a message coming through his earphone. "There's been a nuclear detonation in Saudi Arabia!"

Al Haram

Ten Months Earlier
Al Haram Mosque in Makkah, Saudi Arabia

PRINCE MUHAMMAD ABDULLAH BIN Ghazi, summoned to a secret meeting in the holy city of Makkah, stepped carefully down the narrow staircase of his private jet into a bright blue sky. The Saudi Ambassador to the United Nations stood for a moment to straighten his fashionable grey dishdasha, a long wool dress that covered his ample body from neck to feet. A cousin to the King, Muhammad gently stroked a blackish beard that covered his sanguine face, while his dark eyes searched the tarmac. He saw a black Mercedes driving toward his plane and walked with a regal air toward the vehicle.

As the limo wound through the narrow streets of the city on its way to the al-Haram Mosque, bin Ghazi noticed merchants tending kiosks on every corner. They were hawking the wares and souvenirs of the hajj, a journey that devout Muslims try to make at least once in their lives. He knew that nearly all of the 1.3 million citizens of Makkah made their living providing services to visiting pilgrims. *I wonder what our Prophet would think?* he asked himself.

The faithful arrived not only during the great December Hajj, but also throughout the year to satisfy the Fifth Pillar of Islam. Inside al-Haram they would perform the Tawaff, walking seven times around the Ka'ba, which Muslims all over the world face five times each day, in prayer.

At the eastern entrance to the mosque an Imam met the limo and escorted the prince to the Hateem, the original rectangular footprint of the now curtained Ka'ba. Like all Muslims fortunate enough to make the pilgrimage, bin Ghazi stood in wonder of the small building shrouded in a massive black and white cloth. He paused to listen as a group of Turkish pilgrims passed, nodding attentively toward their effusive guide. The men lined the front wearing their finest white thoubs and gutrahs, while the women stood behind shrouded in long white abayahs, with hejabs covering their heads and faces.

"It is a thirteen by nine meter cube, thirty-nine feet, six inches tall," the host wailed in a practiced delivery. "The walls contain 1, 614 polished stones that are one meter wide, and inside there is a room with a floor, two meters higher than where we now stand.

"The Ka'ba," he continued, " has been rebuilt as many as a dozen times since the Prophet Adam first built his house for all humanity to worship Allah. And our Prophet Mohammad, peace and blessings be upon him, once helped with a reconstruction after a flood destroyed much of the City of Makkah. It was during the rebuilding that he was chosen to place the Hajar, the sacred Black Stone, here on the corner where you see it now." The pilgrims sighed with admiration and surged toward the wall, hoping to kneel and kiss the silver framed black stone, but they were gently held back.

The Imam leaned over and whispered in bin Ghazi's ear. "Follow me, a great man awaits you." The prince was pleased the Imam recognized that the emissary waiting for him was also a man of position and prestige. As they began walking toward the only door leading inside the Ka'ba, the pilgrims paused in astonishment. They recognized the royal insignia embroidered on the front of the prince's long sleeved dishdasha.

Opening a ground level door the Imam pulled a white cotton gutrah across his face. The prince did the same, releasing a black braided ogal that held his three-piece head cover together. When the shumag, a traditional cool weather red and white-checkered cloth, used to protect one's face from the cold and sand, was loosened he fastened it to cover all but his eyes.

Nodding toward the door the Imam led his guest up a small set of stairs inside the Ka'ba. Two large oil lamps hanging from a high windowless ceiling provided a dim glow that shimmered over the polished marble floor. The room could hold fifty standing adults, and was sparsely furnished with only a small wooden table near the rear wall and tall marble pillars standing on each side.

A white embroidered cloth hanging above the table revealed the words of the Kalimah, the simple phrase uttered by every person who becomes a Muslim. "There is no deity worthy of worship except Allah, and Mohammad is the messenger of Allah." But the prince was staring only at the magnificently robed figure standing behind the table. "Could it be?" he asked himself in astonishment, without noticing the Imam had disappeared down the stairs and out the door.

"Muhammad Abdullah bin Ghazi," the man announced with open arms. "Do you know me?"

"Yes," the prince responded with bowed head. Even in the darkness, and with the red and white shumag across his face, he recognized the portly figure. "You are Khalid Abdullah ibn Saud, King of Saudi Arabia."

The King raised his hands and looked around the room, "It is I, bin Ghazi, and it is good to see my cousin. May the blessings of Allah be upon you."

"May Allah grant you wisdom in all things, and a long life, my King."

"Wisdom," the monarch smiled curiously. "Yes, we will need much in this endeavor." There was nowhere in the small room for either man to sit. They stared at each other across the small wooden table as the king pulled the simple red and white cloth from his face. "I have a grave and dangerous mission for you."

Khalid reached out and picked up a golden burner with several small pieces of Aoud in the bowl. When burned, the perfumed wood surrendered a sweet and delicate aroma, but it was not lit and he poured the bits of fuel on the table. The King spoke in a whisper as he set the burner down. "You are the only man I can trust with this project. The risks we are about to take are significant. It could cost us everything, even the monarchy. But if we succeed, the reward is even greater."

He looked softly into the eyes of the Saudi ambassador, as if sharing a burden with a compassionate friend. "A dangerous wind now blows across the gulf that will soon challenge the balance of power between Sunnis and Shiites in the region. It is that small cartel of Shiite Mullahs, and their Revolutionary Guards. They are on the verge of creating a crisis in the Islamic world. If Iran becomes a nuclear power, then every Sunni nation in the Middle East must respond, and that could be even more dangerous."

The King lowered his brow. "I have consulted with other Sunni leaders, and it is our opinion this must not happen. Bold action must be taken now, before the Iranians start a nuclear arms race in the Persian Gulf. He looked into the eyes of his cousin. "I have a plan to address Iran's nuclear ambitions."

The prince stared down at the polished marble floor. He had little choice. His position, power and wealth had all come from appointments by the royal family, and now Khalid was taking him into his confidence. "But," the diplomat responded cautiously, "we have asserted all nations have the right to pursue peaceful uses of nuclear energy."

"Peaceful yes, but that is not what the Mullahs are doing. They are enriching uranium fuel for reactors that will later be turned into weapons grade plutonium, and they are building missiles that can deliver these weapons to any city in the Middle East.

"They are trying to develop weapons that cannot easily be challenged, but what Iran will eventually do is destabilize the Persian Gulf in a way that two wars in Iraq have yet to accomplish."

Khalid arched his brow and snarled. "If they continue on this path, they will provide the excuse for Israel or America to take dramatic action against Iran, and possibly destroy all the progress we have made with 'The Project,' our plan to peacefully settle western democracies."

A lingering silence settled between them as bin Ghazi considered the words of his King. "If the Iranians wanted nuclear energy to generate power, the West would provide technology and support. But from the beginning their nuclear program has been shrouded in secrecy, and there is much to suspect regarding their intentions." He sighed heavily, "What would my King have me do?"

"Apply diplomatic brinksmanship, to the point of catastrophe."

"And if diplomacy should fail?"

The King's gentle countenance disappeared. "Then we must be prepared to apply the sword."

"What kind of sword?"

"A nuclear sword," the King replied.

"But we do not have such weapons."

"Not yet, but soon we will."

Muhammad was shocked by the audacity of his King. "We have always relied on the Americans, with their great military. What will they do if we acquire nuclear weapons?"

Khalid rested his hands against the edge of the table and stared thoughtfully at the golden burner. "America was once a great nation, but they have transferred much of their wealth to others to satisfy an insatiable appetite for oil, and with their unilateral military initiatives across the globe, they have over extended themselves.

"To many observers, America is weakening, and the balance of power in the Middle East is shifting in Iran's favor. So, we can no longer wait for the Americans to do for us what we must eventually do for ourselves. We must deal with Iran now, before they acquire nuclear weapons."

The King reached inside a hidden pocket, retrieved a single folded sheet of paper and stared at his disbelieving prince. Khalid reached forward with the small piece of paper in hand. "Here is my plan to obtain viable nuclear weapons. You must memorize everything, including the names you see here. Then I will burn the paper."

As Muhammad studied the few paragraphs, the King continued. "When you return to America, a man called Jake Eastwood will contact you in New York, and you may also speak with his leader, Nalum Taylor. Another man, Robert Faircloth, will soon be speaking on our behalf in the Middle East. After you meet with Mr. Eastwood, you will transfer the first installment of twenty million dollars into their Swiss account. The NDR will then begin to implement our plan."

"The NDR?" his cousin asked.

"Perhaps you have heard of them? They call themselves The New Democratic Right. They are a highly regarded paramilitary group with a history of efficiency that al-Queda would envy. These rogues will carry out our mission."

The Prince studied the words on the paper. "Peaceful Eagle, this is your plan?"

"Peace is our goal, Muhammad, and the eagle is a symbol of strength and courage, like the aircraft that will deliver our bomb to the Mullahs, if they do not rid themselves of their nuclear weapons program." The King spoke softly, "It is an opportunity for stability in the Middle East."

"Or nuclear destruction," the prince said cryptically.

"Muhammad!" the King shouted. "You know what will happen if the Iranians acquire nuclear weapons. The radical Mullahs will eventually allow smaller versions to pass into the hands of their surrogates in Lebanon and Gaza. Then what? A nuclear holocaust will follow, and it will be the irrational followers of Islam who have been first to use such weapons in the modern era."

He glared at his cousin. "We, the keepers of the Sunni faith, cannot allow this tragedy to be visited upon the world at the hands of the Shiites. It must be dealt with now, before the Iranians acquire such weapons."

"And what of the radical Sunnis, the Wahhabists, al-Queda, Hamas, the Taliban, the Muslim Brotherhood, and those who support them, including some of the younger members of the royal family?"

The King looked thoughtfully at his cousin. "Our young extremists are very impatient. They want everything to happen in a hurry, and now seem to have little regard for 'The Project,' our plan that has been working so well for the last thirty years.

"After the first Infintada, in 1987," the King continued, "the Iranians shunned our 'Project,' and now they proceed with the development of nuclear weapons."

"My King," Muhammad interrupted, "their UN ambassador has confided that the Mullahs no longer trust the Sunni plan. They believe that Shiites will not have a future in a Sunni world created by such a strategy."

"Such a remarkable plan," the King mused, "a holy cru-sade by Muslims, that may accomplish by peaceful means that which could never could be done through war. And hopefully it will lead to a gradual and balanced shift away from the deca-dent values of western nations to governments based on Sharia law.

"Just imagine," Muhammad said proudly, "Islamic centers throughout Eurabia, where the process of Islamification con-tinues. And one day, perhaps Amerabia, where Sunni Islam will become rooted in the souls and lives of the Americans and Canadians."

"Go and teach all nations. Isn't that what the Christian book teaches?"

"Yes," the prince agreed. "We are simply doing what Christians have done for centuries, sending missionaries into the world to spread the word of our prophet, Mohammad, the true messenger of Allah."

"Missionaries," the King said, "reproducing like Bedouins of the desert wherever they settle. By this one method we have increased the population of Sunnis everywhere in the west, and constructed our mosques in their communities. As the Sunni presence has grown we have permeated the echelons of their social, political and economic institutions, including their military."

Khalid looked at his prince with a knowing smile. "Perhaps in another generation, we may supplant some western governments with Islamic theocracies, but for now," he added with resignation, "we must find a way to reign in the Iranians. If not, they will way-lay 'The Project' and may even destroy much of Islam with their nuclear agenda."

Muhammad studied the sheet of paper in his hand. "We would use such a weapon against the Shiites of Iran?"

The King's chin fell, and he sighed heavily. "If this hazardous course against the government of Iran leads us to the brink of catastrophe, then we must be prepared to follow through with the sword, and allow the world to learn a terrible lesson about the grave dangers of nuclear proliferation."

The prince looked past his King. "But what if we are discovered?"

"We, the King said emphatically, "cannot be discovered, and this is the most difficult sacrifice I must ask you to consider. If this plan is revealed, only you can be discovered. Saudi Arabia and the monarchy must go on. The royal family must have complete deniability of any involvement in this."

"But what of me and my family, if I am… "

"The Royal Family will find itself in a delicate position in the court of world opinion. So, you, Muhammad, will be presented as a ruthless scheming prince who used your position as a senior diplomat to develop such a project, to ensure your succession to the Saudi throne."

"My project," the prince repeated with a laugh, "but your majesty, I have never aspired to the throne. I am satisfied to be of service at the United Nations."

"And that is why you are such a rare man, one who can be trusted, to serve with dignity and do his utmost to complete such a difficult mission."

"And my family, if I should fail?"

"Your wives and children will live in comfort and privacy for all their days."

A slight smile creased the lips of the prince. "But if we should succeed?"

"Then you, Muhammad, will be the unsung hero of the Sunni Muslim world. Only you and I, and Allah, will know of your glorious service to Islam. But I will never forget, and I will reward you and your family as only a king may do."

The prince laughed. "As you said, Peaceful Eagle has many risks, but also great rewards. May Allah place his blessings upon a peaceful outcome."

The King took the small sheet of paper with the names of the prince's contacts inside the NDR, crumpled it on the small golden incense bowl and lit the paper on fire. As it burned completely Khalid reached inside his left pocket and retrieved a small envelope. "This contains the number of a Swiss account in which two-hundred million dollars has been deposited. Each month transfer ten million dollars into the NDR account, and spend as needed to ensure the success of our plan. When you return to New York, Mr. Eastwood will contact you to explain the details.

"This is your project now, Muhammad," the king announced solemnly. "Your responsibility is to discreetly fund the operation, make sure that everything goes according to plan, and ensure that it remains a well guarded secret."

"I understand, and as you have said, I can be trusted to carry out this mission."

"Very well, and from this moment I can have no further direct contact with you." Khalid bowed before his prince. "May Allah bless and keep you safe." The King pulled the red and white shumag across his face to help conceal his identity as he walked down the steps and slipped out the door.

Muhammad remained inside the Ka'ba to give Khalid time to reach his car and leave al-Haram. While waiting he looked slowly around the empty room and considered the great task before him.

"My project," he whispered with a coy smile on his face. "Great risk for even greater rewards." He bowed before the Kalima then covered his face and walked slowly out the door into the bright sunlit day.

"Another one!" shouted a small group of Indonesian tourists, pointing at the royal emblem on the garment of the prince. The pilgrims smiled then turned away and continued on the fourth of seven circums around the holy Ka'ba.

Nahunta

Faro, NC

"YOU SURE THERE'S A nuclear bomb out there?" Rufus Leach asked, glancing over at Jake Eastwood, Operations Director for the New Democratic Right. Jake was staring thorough the windshield of the pickup truck, toward a field overgrown with knee-high grass and briar thickets, that led down to Nahunta Swamp Creek.

Rufus was the leader of the NDR cell in North Carolina. He was also a civil engineer, and in charge of the project to recover the nuclear warhead. He liked to wear an outside engineer's uniform, baggy tan pants, a long sleeve blue shirt that covered years of comfortable living, a pair of sturdy brown work boots, and a broad-rimmed canvas field hat that sat beside him on the front seat of the truck.

Jake lifted his right arm and pointed toward the field. "See all those little white pipes sticking up out of the ground?"

"Looks like some kind of science experiment."

"Yeah," it does," Jake responded with a grin. "That's where the warhead has been buried since 1961."

"Why didn't they dig it up back then?"

"They tried, Rufus, but it's one-hundred eighty feet down in the Castle Hayne aquifer. They dug about fifty feet, but all they got were some tail fins from the bomb, a parachute that didn't open, and a huge lake that kept filling with water."

"You're sure about that, Jake?"

The NDR leader lifted a three-pound master's thesis. "According to this it's out there, and our people in D.C. went through agency channels to verify it. So, it's there, Rufus, just waiting for someone to get the right kind of equipment on site and dig it up."

Eastwood was a lean six-footer, with grayish brown hair and sparkling blue eyes, a Viet Nam 'Silver Star' veteran, and survivor of a dozen black operations for the Central Intelligence Agency. He had been wounded several times, but nothing like the burns he suffered during a bumbled rescue mission in the desert of Iraq in 1980. It took three reconstructive surgeries and years of therapy for him to recover, and thirty years later, Jake still carried himself like a seasoned warrior.

"I don't have time to read that thing, Jake. Tell me what happened. Why did that B-52 crash here in '61?"

Jake laid the weighty tome in his lap. "It was back in the Cold War days with the old Soviet Union, when Seymour Johnson, just south of Goldsboro, was an Air Force SAC base."

'Strategic Air Command," Rufus added with a smile. "Remember all those 'duck and cover' drills we used to do in school, in case there was a nuclear attack? The intercom would squawk "Air Raid Drill," and everyone would line up and go out in the hallway, boys on one side, girls on the other, then kneel down on the floor and cover our heads till the "All Clear" sounded."

"Yeah, I remember those drills, like an old black and white movie, because we didn't have color television in those days."

"Or air conditioning."

"How did we ever survive with just window fans?" Jake asked with a laugh then continued with the story of the crash. "It was part of America's military strategy during the Cold War to keep a bomber airborne at all times, nuclear armed and ready to retaliate against any surprise attack.

"On January 24th 1961, a B-52 took off from Seymour Johnson. It was supposed to fly up the coast toward Newfoundland then back down toward Miami, and meet a KC-135 off the coast of North Carolina. The bomber met the refueler near Wilmington, and topped off the bladders in the left wing.

"When the boom operator moved the fuel nozzle to the other wing, there was unexpected turbulence that separated the two aircraft, jerking the nozzle out of the right wing of the B-52.

"When the nozzle slammed back down it missed the fuel opening and punched a hole through the wing and bladders on the right side. JP-4 began spewing out, covering the belly and tail section of the bomber."

"What the hell did they do?"

"The pilots knew that after the jet fuel emptied out of the right wing, they would have an unbalanced aircraft. So, for several hours they flew the unstable bomber in a hundred mile circle over the Atlantic, burning off most of the fuel in the left wing. Then they headed back to Seymour Johnson, and that's when it happened.

"They were coming in from the northeast at eight thousand feet and had to make a right turn to line up with the runway, some twelve miles from the base. As the aircraft banked to the right it just kept rolling, past vertical, and shaking so hard the right wing sheared away. Most of the crew was able to bail out, except for two that weren't in ejection seats. They went down with the fuselage."

"What about the bombs, Jake?"

The NDR leader stared out at the brush-covered field in front of the truck. "The parachute on the first bomb opened after it fell out of the bay. It floated down into some trees, nose up, only eighteen inches in the ground. It was recovered the next day.

"The second parachute didn't open, and the three and a half ton weapon fell to earth at the speed of sound. Buried itself right out there, one hundred eighty feet deep in the ground. And that's what all those little pipes are for, Rufus, water quality testing. If the Secondary Encasement Vessel ever ruptures, the entire Castle

Hayne, the largest underground aquifer in North Carolina, could be contaminated, and that would be a disaster of another kind."

"So, if we remove the warhead," Rufus said thoughtfully, "we'll actually be helping the people in this part of the state."

Jake almost smiled. "That's right, but we have another use for that warhead."

"Two hundred million dollars worth, wouldn't you say?"

The NDR leader looked back out toward the field. "Know anything about nuclear weapons, Rufus, about the yields of atomic versus hydrogen bombs, kilotons versus megatons?"

"Not really, but I know the bombs dropped on Hiroshima and Nagasaki, at the end of World War II, were small ones."

"Little Boy and Fat Man," Jake whispered. "Each one yielded fifteen to twenty thousand tons of dynamite going off all at once, not much more than a firecracker compared to what's buried out there."

"But they ended World War II pretty quick."

"Yes, they did, but by 1961, we had weapons that yielded megatons, a million tons of dynamite. The Mark 41 that's buried out there was one of the highest yielding weapons ever produced by America. It had a two-stage thermo nuclear segment, plus a new third stage plutonium section, that together could yield twenty-four million tons of dynamite going off all at once."

"Wow!" Rufus exclaimed. "So, there's a twenty-four megaton warhead still in the ground out there, and that's what we're going after?"

"That's right," Jake said calmly. "The Secondary Encasement, with one-hundred ten kilos of enriched uranium and thirty-six kilos of plutonium is still out there, just waiting for anyone who can dig it up."

"Or tunnel under it," Rufus added with a wry grin. He pointed up the hill toward a forest line. "A quarter mile beyond those trees is the farmhouse and new outbuildings on the old Davies farm. We've estimated two and a half days for the Tunnel

Boring Machine to reach this location, one day for retrieval, then another two back to the farm. All together, the dig should take about six days."

"Sounds like a good plan, Rufus. The technology to tunnel under, and up to the warhead didn't exist in the 1960s, but since then, new Tunnel Boring Machines have been developed that can churn right through the limestone of an underground aquifer."

"Or solid rock like they encountered while digging the Chunnel under the English Channel," Rufus added. "It's pretty damn expensive to transport and assemble one of the smaller TBMs, but with it we should be able to access the containment vessel and retrieve the warhead." He pointed to a pipe on the far left side of the field with a red cap, and three more that formed a large rectangle in the field. "Know what those are for, Jake?"

"Security?"

"Sort of, each one marks the location of a remote seismograph. It's about the only security they have out here. They prefer to keep a real low profile."

Jake glanced at him with a curious look in his eyes. "How's the TBM supposed to dig a tunnel without the seismographs registering?"

"It's just technology, Jake. No problem. Flip up the solar powered head and there's an on-off switch. The day the dig starts, we sneak out here and turn them off."

"But won't they know the seismographs are turned off?"

"Nope," Rufus responded confidently. "This model only sends out an RF signal if it detects seismic activity. It's a power saving device. Otherwise, it remains dormant. So it will work out just fine for us to dig for a few days, after we turn them off." A curious look came over his face. "What about the people who lived around here back in '61, Jake? Weren't they concerned about a nuclear bomb being left in the ground?"

"Four months after the crash, the Air Force issued a news bulletin saying everything that could be recovered from the crash site had been recovered. Then they stamped 'Top Secret' on the file so nobody could get any more information about the Broken Arrow, what the Air Force calls a lost and un-recovered nuclear weapon.

"You remember how it was back then, Rufus? Most Americans still believed their government officials. But I bet a lot of the farmers around Faro were whispering among themselves about what the Air Force might have left buried in the ground, down here by the creek on Big Daddy's Road."

The Man of Peace

Bayssour, Lebanon

ROBERT FAIRCLOTH, AN AMERICAN of medium frame and ashen gray hair, walked outside of the Hotel Phoenicia into a glaring blue sky. Mamoud, the always-cheerful shuttle driver, was waiting for him. The Shiite guide knew the destination of the foreigner, out of the relative safety of the Mar Mikhael area in downtown Beirut, and up into the southern hills controlled by Hezbollah militias.

Mamoud greeted his passenger, wondering why anyone would ask to be driven to such a dangerous place. "Good morning, Mr. Faircloth. You are ready to go?" he asked in French tinged English.

Robert opened the passenger side door and sat up front. "Yes," he said with an uncertain sigh. "Do you know how to find the Café Fatima in Bayssour?"

"Of course, I have been there many times, but never with an American. You are certain this is where you need to go?"

"Everything has been arranged for me to meet with an important person."

"And you do not wish for me to wait for you?"

"Not this time, Mamoud. If things go well, I will be there several hours."

"And if things do not go well?"

Robert took a slow deep breath and exhaled briskly. "Either way, just drop me off and you may return to the hotel."

"But, Mr. Faircloth," the driver pleaded. "This is an unsafe area for foreigners, especially Americans. If I were not a Shiite Muslim, I would not go there myself."

"Thank you for your concern," Robert said with a conciliatory smile, "but this is something I must do for the good of many other people."

Mamoud nodded. "Sometimes courageous men must do dangerous things," then he pressed his foot on the gas pedal and the small orange van lurched forward.

Ten minutes later they were driving beyond the Rafic Hariri International Airport where Robert had flown in two days before. They turned southeast and up into the hills, toward the old city of Bayssour where he was to meet a Hezbollah militia commander. If the leader believed Robert's story of an impending nuclear disaster in Iran, then he would be taken to an Imam who had direct access to the Shiite Mullahs of Iran.

The thirty-minute ride offered Robert time for personal reflection. He reminisced about his previous life with a pretty young blonde from Myrtle Beach, SC. In a surge of youthful enthusiasm they had run away to Dillon and gotten married. *She was perfect,* he remembered with eyes closed, a smile spreading across his tanned aging face.

He recalled the terrible accident in Charlotte, NC, in which his wife and son had died, and the crippling injuries suffered by his daughter, Libby. He also remembered being initiated into a secret paramilitary organization, the New Democratic Right, by his best friend from high school, Jake Eastwood. *All those years we thought Jake was dead, and all that time he was running black operations for the CIA.*

It was Jake who had convinced Robert that the NDR needed a public voice then informed him that he was being drafted for the task, because of his legal background and effective communication skills. *Not hired, but drafted,* Robert recalled with a smile. *To get you out of the funk,* he remembered Jake saying, *to get back in the game where you can do some good.* And then Jake sealed the deal. *It's what Dare would want you to do.*

It had been exciting, dangerous and deadly. The body count during the NDR's initiative to purge America of its most egregious cultural offenders had risen quickly, and soon overwhelmed Robert. He wanted to escape but feared what might happen to his daughter. So, he determined to write the story of his involvement with the NDR and its leadership, and use it as leverage to ensure her safety.

With eyes still closed and a slight smile on his face, Robert thought to himself. *Who could have imagined that it would work out so well?* Libby met and fell in love with Early Williams, a member of the California NDR cell, a young man that Robert had come to admire and respect.

Robert's thoughts drifted to more recent events, the day Jake had called and revealed the NDR had been engaged by a Middle-Eastern monarch to retrieve a nuclear weapon buried in the ground in North Carolina. Jake explained that it was a risky peace initiative, and that it required his unique communication skills as a potential peacemaker.

Robert's part of the operation was being initiated long before Peaceful Eagle would be put into effect. If he could find a way to convince the Shiite Mullahs to dismantle their nuclear weapons program, the nuclear option would not be necessary. *But first,* Robert thought as he squinted his eyes together and grimaced, *he had to find a way to make contact with the Mullahs, and meeting with the Hezbollah militia commander was a first step in that direction.*

* * *

"So you are the man of peace," the commander said, greeting Robert in the café.

Robert extended his hand, but the militia leader refused it. "Liar!" he screamed in Robert's face. "Do you not think we have seen this kind of treachery before? CIA! That's what you are, Mr. Faircloth." The meeting in Bayssour was not going well.

Before Robert could respond a black hood was thrown over his head and his hands restrained behind his back with plastic ties. He was taken out the door of the café and stuffed in the back seat of a vehicle, then driven to another location in the small southern town where his interrogation began.

"Allah Akbar!" they screamed, and pushed him down to a kneeling position on a grainy tile floor. They beat him with long wooden sticks. "Allah Akbar!" they shouted over and over.

"If God is so great," Robert yelped between strokes, "then why are you beating me? I am a man of peace, trying to help resolve the crisis in your country."

"CIA!" they shrieked at him. "All Americans are spies for the great satan of your government." The beating continued for several minutes, until a boot struck him hard in the back and knocked him sideways to the floor.

Pain racked his body from the slap of wood against his back and legs, and he felt a suffocating desire for fresh air from having the cloth bag over his head. The pressure of his arms being held together in one position caused his shoulders to ache and throb, and he could feel the plastic ties slowly eating into his wrists.

He was dragged into a small room where his head struck something hard and he heard the sound of a toilet being flushed. He was lifted up as a hand on the back of his head pushed his face into the bowl and dipped his nose into the swirling water. The men laughed as he pursed his lips together, struggling to keep the smell of urine from running inside his nostrils.

"Again!" someone shrieked in English after the tank had refilled, and most of them shouted and cheered in Arabic, a language he barely understood. Over and over they flushed the toilet as Robert spurted water from his mouth and nose feeling like he was drowning. Finally, they dropped him on a hard tile floor and retreated into another part of the house. One guard remained and removed the soggy wrap from Robert's head saying, "You must pay, man of peace. American spy, you must pay."

He was beaten that morning and interrogated all afternoon by a dizzying array of men he had not seen before. All of them were convinced he was working for the CIA or the Israelis, but Robert never strayed from his mission, that he needed their help to get a message to the Mullahs of Iran.

After two days whether they believed him or not, the beatings finally stopped. The quality of food lowered in a basket through a trap door in the floor above him improved. Rather than stale bread and cheese he was now eating lamb stew and potatoes with an occasional pastry. And the plastic bottles of water, along with the basic necessities of personal hygiene, were like manna from above.

At the beginning of the third day another captive was thrown into the cellar. In the dim light from the two small foundation-level grates above their heads, Robert could see the Lebanese man had also been beaten. The guards above would yell down to him in Arabic repeating something over and over that seemed to instill terror inside the man.

He was shorter than Robert with a slim physique. His dark hair was matted with sweat and his face puffed from beatings. Robert could only guess at how he must look to the other man who stared for a moment then screamed back up to the guards. The men above stomped on the floor and shouted threats and the poor beaten man cowered against a wall.

They sat on the hard dirt floor of the cellar staring at each other. Robert wanted to ask him questions; who he was and why he was put in the cellar, but he did not speak the language. Finally, the man addressed him in perfect English. "My name is Yusef. I am here to teach you the recitations of the Qur'an, and convert you to Islam."

Robert was dumbfounded. *Teach me? Convert me?*

"If I do not succeed, they will kill me. Do you understand?"

Robert could barely believe the man's words. *How brutal were these men who claimed God was great, if they would kill one of their own for something like this?*

"Please help me," the man pleaded. "I have a wife and children."

"Who are you?" Robert asked.

"I am a theology professor at the American University. That is all I can tell you. Please, call me 'teacher.'"

It was an astonishing turn of events that would haunt Robert afterwards. He could not perceive of converting to the Islamic faith, at least not at the point of a gun. Still, he felt compelled to assist the man who implored him to help save his life.

Robert's understanding of Islamic traditions began with a simple question to his teacher. "Can you tell me why I'm being held against my will?"

"The fidyah," his teacher responded as he called up to the men guarding the house. The food bucket was lowered, this time with two books inside, English translations of the Qur'an. The professor reached in and took them, holding each one reverently, and handed a copy to Robert.

Though he felt some relief in the teacher's words, Robert did not understand. "What is a fidyah?"

"It can have many meanings, but in your case it is a ransom." The teacher took a halting breath and began the first of many lessons. "Once it was the jizah, a tax paid by foreigners in lands conquered by Islamic armies. It began shortly after Muhammad's death in the year 632.

"Omar, the second Caliph of the Muslim world, issued a proclamation defining the rights and obligations of Christians and Jews in lands conquered by Islamic armies. One of those was to pay a tax to local Muslim leaders, for the privilege of living under the protection of Islam.

"Today it is part of the time honored tradition of fidyah, paying to right a wrong. After your ransom is paid you will be set free, but first, I must teach you what I can of Islam."

The Farm

Faro, NC

"IS THE TUNNEL BORING MACHINE READY?" Jake asked in an edgy voice as they drove on a gravel road through the galvanized steel farm gate.

"Just about," Rufus responded with the enthusiasm of an engineer who had nearly completed a project. "All that's left is to connect the air compressor lines to the operator's cabin and the water hoses to the slurry box. We should be ready to start the dig pretty soon after you give the go ahead."

"And the Russian?" Jake asked, referring to Vladimir Petrovski, the Soviet era scientist contracted to build three nuclear weapons. "Is he prepped and ready?"

"For a million bucks he'd better be," Rufus added. "That's a lot of money for an unemployed nuclear weapons specialist."

"Does he have everything he needs in the lab to disassemble the old weapon and build new ones?"

"I took care of everything, Jake; built the underground bunker to your specs and personally installed the equipment. I even got a case of his favorite Russian vodka. He says it takes a liter a day to calm his nerves after working with enriched uranium." Rufus laughed to himself, but got little response from Jake.

"How about the Pakistani, is he ready?"

"Yeah, Dr. Khan's in an apartment over in Goldsboro. Our guys are keeping a tight leash on him, but he's driving the boys crazy with those tiny cups of espresso and stinky little Turkish cigarettes. He smokes 'em down till they burn his fingertips."

Rufus looked curiously at Jake. "He says he's related to the guy in Pakistan that sold nuclear technology to North Korea and Iran. That true?"

Jake nodded his head. "They're cousins, both nuclear scientists. Ironic that one sold to North Korea and Iran and the other is selling to us. Our guy wants a million bucks and a U.S. green card to validate the Russian's work.

"His cousin, Abdul Khan, was the leader of Pakistan's effort to be the first Islamic country to have a nuclear weapon. It was supposed to be a deterrent to the bomb developed by India. In 1998, after Abdul succeeded he was a national hero in Pakistan, but then he began secretly selling the technology.

"In 2000, he sold used P-1 centrifuges to North Korea and Iran to enrich yellow cake uranium into weapons-grade material. It was a little nuclear technology neither of them had at the time. At first he said he did it on his own without any help from the Pakistani government, but later he claimed Musharff, head of Pakistan's army, knew all along what he was doing."

"Well that son of a bitch sure upset the world's nuclear apple cart," Rufus said with disgust. Then he changed the subject to matters at hand. "When we retrieve the encasement container I'll have Vlad working an eight-hour day and Khan the night shift. So far, Vlad's finished one containment vessel and a firing tube for the test fire and he doesn't know that Khan comes in at night to check his work."

Rufus was still grinning proudly as they pulled up to the old farmhouse and he could sense Jake's approval of the scene before him. Two huge aluminum buildings lined end to end nearly consumed the field beside the old farmhouse. Each measured forty by eighty feet and were connected by a smaller twenty by thirty foot building.

"Good Lord, Rufus, they're huge."

"Had to be if we wanted to assemble the TBM inside away from prying eyes. That monster's a hundred sixty-five feet long and we had to dig a twenty-foot trench at the south end just to give the disc cutters a six percent grade to start digging. This is a big undertaking, Jake," and then he grinned. "Sure am glad the prince has got a lot of that Saudi oil money cause this is gonna be one expensive bitch."

Jake glanced at Rufus with a knowing half smile then stared at the impressive buildings and sheds with several monster-sized tractors and attachments parked nearby. To anyone who might drive up or fly over it appeared to be just another huge corporate farming operation.

Schism

Beirut, Lebanon

WHENEVER FOOTSTEPS APPROACHED THE door in the ceiling they would quote Qur'anic verse, but most of the time the professor seemed resigned to allow the discussions to take any course Robert chose. "It was like a fight in one of your Christian churches," Yusef explained, "between those who want to keep the leader they have, and another group that breaks away to begin a new church."

"Too simple," Robert responded. "The Sunnis and Shiites have been killing each other for a thousand years and for what, a fight over who has the better preacher?"

"Yes," the professor responded with a laugh. "That is too simple to explain this," and he paused for a moment in thought. "The great schism in Islam occurred over twelve hundred years ago, only twenty-five years after Muhammad died."

"That long, huh? Better than a lot of Southern Baptist churches," Robert said recalling the small church he attended while growing up.

"It is written," Yusef continued, "that in the year 610, Muhammad received the first of over 600 revelations from the angel Gabriel. He was thirty and living in Makkah, and at that time local tribal leaders were very jealous of anyone who might try to convert their followers from established tribal culture to a new religious teaching.

"But Muhammad had a protector, his uncle who was also a tribal leader. After the uncle died Muhammad feared for his safety and fled from Makkah to Medina, 280 miles to the north. After a few years his followers numbered around three thousand.

"In the year AD 627, the tribal leaders from Makkah led an army to attack him, but Muhammad was also a very good military leader. His army fought off the invaders. That is when he converted his followers into the umma, a religious theocracy that became an Islamic army.

"By AD 630, Muhammad had attacked and taken Makkah. His army then began conquering neighboring cities and then countries. Even after he died the Caliphs continued fighting, capturing Palestine and Syria from the Byzantines; then Iraq and Persia, and in AD 639, they conquered Egypt.

"Many of Muhammad's revelations had been written down by that time. By AD 650, all his revelations from Gabriel had been codified into our sacred text, the Qur'an, which you may know as the Koran."

"Religion at the end of a sword," Robert said curtly. "Just like the conquistadors in Mexico and Peru."

"And like Charlemagne during the Dark Ages of Europe," the professor added with a shrug of his shoulders. "Did you know that in all the lands he conquered he gave the people a choice, convert to Christianity or die? And that, my friend, is why Europe became a Christian continent."

"But," he said, getting back to his narrative, "Muhammad didn't live to see much of the conquest of his armies. He died in AD 632, in the arms of Aisha the youngest of his many wives. Then a very contentious process of naming his successor began."

"Let me guess," Robert said. "That's when one group wanted their preacher to take over and another group wanted their guy in power, just like the Baptists."

"Not exactly," Yusef said with a smile. "It was a tradition among the Bedouin tribes that the new leader be appointed by a consensus of elders. The Arabic word for tradition is 'sunnah' and the traditionalists became know as Sunni Muslims.

"There was also a large minority that listened to the pleas of Muhammad's daughter, Fatima. She declared that the successor should come from within the prophet's own family. She wanted her husband, Ali, who was also Muhammad's cousin to be the next leader. This group was known as Shiat Ali or Partisans of Ali. These became the Shiite Muslims, the dissenters."

"Sounds like the Democrats back in America," Robert said.

The teacher responded with a grave expression. "There are no democratic institutions in an Islamic theocracy. The law is whatever the Caliphs, Imams, Mullahs and Ayatollahs interpret it to be." Then he continued. "The Sunnis, being the most populous, chose Abu Bakr and later Omar, two of Muhammad's lieutenants, as the first and second Caliphs to lead the expanding Muslim world. The third Caliph, Othman, was murdered by rivals in AD 657, and when it came time to name the fourth, that's when the great schism occurred."

Robert smiled, "Now it sounds like the Republicans and Democrats back home."

"But at least in America political partisans aren't killing each other. Shortly after Muhammad's death fighting broke out between supporters of Fatima and those of Abu Bakr. Later these street brawls evolved into full battles with traditional Sunnis on one side and revolutionary Shiites on the other.

"It was during the Battle of Damascus against the Byzantines, in AD 657, that the fourth Caliph, Ali, agreed to have an arbitrator settle the issue to stop the bloodshed. Because the Sunnis were much more populous they became the majority and the Shiites became the minority. But after Ali, the Shias would accept no other Sunni caliphs. From that day to this, they choose to be led by their own mullahs and ayatollahs.

"And that is how it is, even now, the struggle for power and influence in the Islamic world between the Sunnis who comprise nearly 85% of all Muslims, and the Shiites who make up 12%."

"Who are the other Muslims?"

"Mostly Sufi mystics and a few other lesser sects within Islam."

Robert nodded. "Well, it seems like the cold war between the Sunnis and Shiites is about to get a lot hotter."

"It is with the rise of Shiite dominated Iran, an oil rich nation that is building its military resources including a nuclear capability. Now the Sunnis feel compelled to respond. Also by invading Iraq, America has exposed a second more sinister war in the Middle East.

"What began as Osama bin Ladin's regional al-Queda spawned into a network of radical fundamentalist organizations that believe Western nations have become weak and vulnerable. They see an opportunity to impose Sharia Law on the world, one country at a time, as they believe is already happening in Europe. And as we have seen, they will sacrifice anyone and everything to impose their radical interpretation of the Qu'ran."

Robert shook his head. "I've heard this before from U.S. and British intelligence agencies, and now from you," then he shook his head in disbelief, "in the cellar of a house in Lebannon!"

The professor leaned in, "You should know, even I have heard that Persian chauvinism is on the rise. Many Iranians have a nostalgic desire to once again be a super power as in the days of Cyrus and Darius in the 6th century B.C. The Ayatollahs of Iran want their country to become the major Islamic power in the Middle East."

He glanced up to where the guards sat above them, and realizing they were paying little attention, the teacher whispered to Robert. "Do not be fooled by the claim of my Shiite brothers who say they only want to enrich uranium for peaceful purposes." At the mention of nuclear material Robert's attention was riveted on the professor.

"The Mullahs of Iran will lead a covert war through proxy Islamic armies against Western interests all over the world. Al-Queda only got things started. Now all the oil producing nations, most of which are in the Middle East, understand the true Achilles Heel of the West, their addiction to oil.

"The Iranians who are predominantly Shia Muslims do not consider themselves Arabs. In truth, they are insulted to be called such. With their ancient and noble history, they believe they are far above the Bedouins of the Arabian Desert who overran their country and converted them to Islam."

The information was an epiphany for Robert who was beginning to understand that the Ayatollah and Mullahs of Iran, as much as the Sunni fanatics of Al-Queda, were responsible for much of the terrorism in the Middle East. "Do you think the people of Iran understand what their leaders are really up to?"

Yusef shrugged his shoulders. "I believe they can be as easily manipulated by their government as you Americans have been by your own. But you must know not all Iranians embrace the extremes of Sharia law being forced upon them.

"It is like when the Cubans embraced Fidel Castro. How many of them understood that he would convert Cuba into a Communist nation? It was the same with Khomeini. How many Iranians understood that when the Shah was deposed an extremist group would convert their country into an Islamic theocracy? Initially, the people welcomed the Islamic government as a change from the Western ways of the Shah. But too late, they discovered the Ayatollah and Mullahs had taken control of every segment of their economy and government."

"The leaders of Iran run things much like an old communist nation. Everyone and everything is monitored. People spy on each other including parents, friends, and co-workers. Stalin, the dreaded master of the old Soviet Union, could not have instilled a more rigorous control over the people than have the small cartel of fanatical Mullahs and Revolutionary Guards who now control everything. It is the first time in the history of Islam that clerics have become the rulers of a Muslim nation."

The teacher shrugged his shoulders and stared off toward one of the grates in the ceiling above them. "It seems the lovers of peace are always the last to understand. They sit silently by while a small aggressive minority takes over the institutions of government. It happened many times in the 20th century where the peace lovers became irrelevant because they remained silent. They did not speak up until the fanatics had taken over, then they, too, were murdered into submission.

Robert stared thoughtfully at the clay floor considering his next question. "What about the Saudis? How do they feel about Iran's nuclear ambitions?"

"They're Sunnis. They stand against the Shias of Iran, and their allies in Syria, Iraq, Yemen, Pakistan, and Afghanistan; and also Iran's surrogate armies, Hezbollah, here in Lebanon, and to a lesser degree, Hamas in Gaza.

"From my point of view, the major concern of the Saudis is that American influence is weakening in the Middle East and the balance of power is shifting in Iran's favor. Still, the Saudis need a strong America as their ally or they may be forced to take desperate measures themselves, but I don't think they would ever take that risk."

The look on Robert's faced unnerved the teacher. "What is it? Do you think the Saudi's will try something?"

"Have you ever heard of Peaceful Eagle?"

Fire in the Hole

Faro, NC

THE RUSSIAN SCIENTIST BACKED away from the well as he played out an electrical line connected to a detonator. A drilling rig had been used the day before to bore a two-foot wide, thirty-foot deep dry hole behind the out buildings. A new test containment vessel, a one-foot by two-foot long titanium cylinder, with cordite explosive from 105mm artillery shells attached at each end, had been lowered to the bottom and was now ready for test firing. The trigger was hard wired to a handheld detonator.

"How will we know if it works?" Jake asked.

"The ends of the cylinder will be destroyed by the energy released from the primary," Rufus answered. "And without any nuclear material inside the force will either blow it apart, which we don't want to happen, or it will blow back out both ends. Either way, we should see dirt fly out of this hole. Then we'll retrieve the vessel and check its integrity. If it holds together then we know we have a successful test."

As Rufus finished the explanation, Jake's head turned to catch the sound of a pickup truck rumbling up the driveway. "Who in the hell is that?" he asked tensely.

"Hold on, Jake," Rufus said calmly. "The front gate may have been left open and you know how curious neighbors can be. Let me go talk to him."

"Okay, but if not... " Jake's voice trailed off as he reached for a side pocket patting a hawk bill knife, one of his favorite weapons.

"I know, Jake. I understand."

Rufus walked casually over to the house and up to the truck as a local farmer got out. They shook hands and the older man introduced himself. "My name's Vernon Whaley. Just stoppin' by for a neighborly visit. Got a place down the road a bit. Heard the boy done sold his grand pappy's place to a bunch of foreigners, but you don't look foreign to me."

Rufus answered and with as straight a face as possible told his lie. "No, I'm not. My name is Fred Jones and I work for Italia, the corporation that bought this place. Say, you wouldn't be interested in selling your place, would you? We're setting up quite a farming operation here and it would be nice if we had a few hundred more acres."

The farmer shook his head. "Can't help you with that, but I know if anything ever happens to me, my boy would sell in a heart beat. He never liked it here on the farm; went off to college and don't come back much," then he craned his neck looking over Rufus' shoulder at the huge aluminum buildings. "Gotta lot of equipment, do ya?"

Rufus turned to look at the buildings and waved at the men beside the hole in the ground letting them know that everything was fine. "Yes, we do. It's been our experience on other farms that it's better to keep everything out of the weather. Equipment lasts longer and works better when it's taken care of that way."

"Yeah, you got a point there but most of us small farmers can't afford such stuff." Then he looked over at the derrick. "Diggin' a well?"

"Yes sir, we need a good source of water for our operation. But we have a little problem. We hit some hard rock down about thirty feet. We're just getting ready to drop a few sticks of dynamite in the hole to loosen things up so we can keep drilling."

The old farmer grinned, "Well, guess it won't hurt to have a few fire crackers goin' off in the ground."

Rufus laughed with the older man. "Guess not," and he politely added. "I'd love to talk with you about your farm, that is if you're ever interested in selling, but right now I have to get back to work on the well."

"Can't say I wanna sell any time soon, but I'll keep it in mind."

"I understand, Mr. Whaley. Well, gotta get back to work. It was nice meeting you. You'll have to come back some time when everything is set up and let me give you a tour of the place."

"Yeah, I'd like that," the farmer said as he opened the door to get back inside his truck. "I'll let the boys down at the store know that you fellas are gonna be doing a little blasting out here so's none of them will get too worked up about it."

"Thank you, Mr. Whaley. I appreciate that. And as soon as the well is in we'll be bringing in some heavy equipment to move some more dirt around."

"Gonna expand the pond?"

Rufus looked around at what he had been calling a lake. "Yeah, we're gonna make the pond bigger," he said, spreading his arms wide.

"Well, you boys have a nice day. And come join us one mornin' for a cup of Joe down to the store. Bunch a nice fellas around here and they would enjoy meeting you."

"One morning I will, real soon," Rufus said as the farmer began backing away. He waved again as the truck pulled off then walked back over to Jake. "Right after this test would you mind taking my truck and running out to the road and make sure that gate is shut and locked? We don't need any more company."

"You handled that well, Rufus."

"Nice and neighborly works real good," then he looked over at the Russian. "Is everything ready?"

"Everything is in position," the scientist said holding up the detonator.

Rufus shouted a warning to those around him. "Fire in the hole." Then he gave a thumbs-up to Vlad who squeezed the detonator. An electrical impulse traveled down the wire to the blasting caps on the ends of the cordite packages. A loud, muffled explosion was heard and soil blew skyward from the hole then settled gently over the ground.

Rufus motioned for the derrick to move back over the pit and retrieve what was left of the experiment. As the containment vessel was pulled up everyone could see the ends of the cylinder had borne the brunt of the explosion, but the Secondary Containment Encasement vessel remained intact.

"A successful test," the Russian shouted with a cunning grin on his weathered old face. "I take my vodka, now."

Heron Point

Beaufort County, NC

RUFUS DROVE HIS BLACK Ford F-150 north on Highway 17 toward Washington, NC. "What time does the prince get in?"

Jake stared out the side window. "Should've arrived at ten o'clock at the airport north of town. The Vice-President of Sales for Lightning Power Boats was to meet bin-Ghazi there, take him for a tour of the plant, then a test ride in one of their new forty-eight foot Speed Masters."

"Damn, Jake, those things are nice. I couldn't afford to keep gas in a boat like that. How many three hundred horsepower motors do they have on the back?"

"Four."

"Holy shit, that's like 1200 horsepower."

"We don't need the engines, Rufus, just a big lead keel."

"That's right," the engineer added with a grin. "That model's got the biggest keel Lightning puts in a power boat. Gosh, never met a prince before. We gonna meet him at the plant or wait till we get to Duke's house on the Pamlico River?"

"We're staying out of sight, Rufus. We'll meet bin-Ghazi at the new guy's house. What's his name, DisSisto?" Jake had not met the newest vetted member of the North Carolina cell of the New Democratic Right. "Doesn't sound like an Eastern North Carolina name."

"It's not," Rufus responded as they drove through Chocowinity. He glanced over at Jake, impeccably dressed in a navy blue suit with a white shirt and yellow striped tie that complemented his graying brown hair. He rubbed his large balding head and tugged gently on thick-framed glasses wishing he had worn something more suitable than engineer's attire: tan slacks, open-collared shirt with a plastic pack of pens in the pocket and a polyester navy blazer to cover it all up.

"Duke's mother was Christa Davies, daughter of the farmer who owned the land where the B-52 crashed in 1961. After she graduated from Appalachian State, up in Boone, she moved to Washington, D.C. and went to work for *National Geographic*. She met one of their photographers, an Italian kid from Long Island. They had a whirlwind romance, she got pregnant, they got married, and three years later he took off with another woman. She pretty much raised Duke on her own and he spent summers with his grandfather on the farm outside Faro."

"So, Duke inherited the farm from his mother's side of the family?"

"That's right," Rufus answered as he looked carefully for the signpost where he would turn onto the river road. "Her brother was in the Navy. He died back in 1988 in the Philippines. It was a terrorist attack at a bar outside a U.S. base near Manila. At first they thought it was a nationalist group sending a message to the U.S. military to get out of the Philippines, but later they discovered it was a radical Islamist group."

"Is that why Duke wanted to sign on with the NDR?"

"Partly, but also the death of his wife and daughter back in '99."

Jake looked over with piercing blue eyes as if demanding to know the story and the look on Rufus' face let him know it would not be a pleasant tale. "His wife was visiting her parents over in Tarboro. She went into a drugstore to get a prescription filled for her mother, left the car unlocked with the air conditioner running and the baby strapped in a car seat."

"Unlocked?" Jake asked.

"Small town America, Jake. People used to do that sort of thing. When she came back out and got in her car, a gang-banger jumped in the back seat and pointed a gun at her head. A witness said she drove away with that gun stuck to the side of her neck. Next day a farmer found the car behind one of his old tobacco barns. She was laying on the ground in front of the car, naked, shot twice in the head."

"What about the baby?"

"She would have been fine except the car doors were shut and the temperature got above ninety that day. Baby girl died of heat exposure in the car seat. The killer raped Duke's wife, shot her then just walked away leaving the baby to die."

"Did they ever catch him?" Jake asked solemnly.

"Someone did!" Rufus exclaimed. "After police matched fingerprints on her discarded purse with those of a local gang member, he was found strung up by his feet like a fresh-killed deer gutted from asshole to chin. After they pulled the duct tape off his mouth his penis fell out, sure sign of a revenge attack."

Jake looked hard at Rufus. "Did the North Carolina NDR have anything to do with it, something I wasn't told about?"

"Nope, not us, Jake. But I wouldn't be surprised if Duke wasn't the one who took that bad guy down. He won't even tell me for sure."

Jake's normally intense visage seemed to relax a bit as he realized that Duke DisSisto was a man that could keep a secret. "Terrible thing to happen to a young man, lose his family like that, but thanks for sharing the story with me."

"I was gonna tell you, Jake, but it just hadn't come up yet. Any way, the Davies' family pretty much stopped farming after their son died and leased their four hundred acres to other farmers in the area. The grandfather died in '91, the grandmother in '94, and Christa inherited everything. She continued leasing the property hoping that one-day Duke would take over the farm, but not him, he's into computers and electronics."

"So, how did he get the property?"

"Christa went on a *Geographic* assignment to Ireland in 2003 and met a sheep farmer who swept her off her feet. She's still living with him somewhere north of Galway. She wanted Duke to have the family farm, sold it to him for a dollar and he's been leasing it out ever since."

"Until we made him an offer he couldn't turn down," Jake added.

"It's not the money, Jake. Duke's a good man and he's on our side. He attended NC State, played football, and graduated with a Mechanical Engineering degree. And I guess all those stories his grandfather told him about the B-52 crashing on their property must have gotten him interested in flying, because a year later he was commissioned in the Air Force and became an F-15 Strike Eagle pilot. Like I told you, Duke flew in the first war with Iraq, and he's willing to fly again for us. But for now he loves tinkering with fast boats."

"Is that why he works for Lightning Power Boats?"

"Oh, no, he doesn't work for them," Rufus responded. "He's too independent for that. He has a shop just down the road from the boat manufacturing plant and he does all the electronic detailing work for every boat manufactured by Lightning."

Jake realized they were gaining four valuable assets with Duke DiSisto. An Italian farming corporation, affiliated with NDR, had recently purchased Duke's farm where the bomber crashed fifty years ago. And soon they would retrieve the Secondary Encasement vessel containing the uranium and plutonium. Duke had also offered his shop as a location to install the enriched uranium inside the lead keel of the Lightning Power Boat, effectively concealing its radioactive signature, and Duke was a trained F-15 Strike Eagle pilot.

"Here we go," Rufus said as he turned slowly onto a road that would take them down to the river. They drove parallel to the water for half a mile, behind a row of elevated homes till they reached a large double security gate with Blue Herons carved into the doors.

"Heron Point," he said as he pulled out his cell phone and pressed a speed dial number. "We're here," he whispered, then flipped the phone shut.

The gates slowly opened revealing a lush green lawn and a beautiful waterfront home raised ten feet to accommodate seasonal storm surges. They drove along a short concrete driveway under a dozen tall pine trees swaying gently above the manicured grass, and realized Duke's home sat on a bulk-headed peninsula next to a large canal flowing out into the Pamlico River.

"Check it out," Rufus said, pointing toward a huge boathouse on the canal side. A sparkling black 'Speed Master' was hanging in the lift of a covered boathouse. It was forty-two feet long with three brand new three hundred horsepower Mercury engines hanging from the rear. "That's not the one the Prince will be buying?" he asked.

"No, that's Duke's boat. The Prince will be buying one like it, only a forty-eight foot model with a bigger keel and every bell and whistle you can put on a power boat."

Jake stared at the sleek vessel. "Bet that monster sucks some gas!"

"Duke can afford it," Rufus replied. "He makes good money with Lightning, then makes a killing on aftermarket modifications. A third of the boats purchased from the factory eventually find their way back to his workshop for some extra tweaking of the electronics and engines, whether inboard or outboard."

Jake admired the glistening craft. "What will that boat do in a straight-a-way?"

"I've been with Duke when he's had it up to one hundred thirty miles per hour on a nice day with flat water and calm winds. But it can be pretty scary when you run a boat that fast. People who don't know what they're doing get killed in high-speed turns. Maybe after we're done Duke will take us out for a test drive."

"Yeah," Jake said, his mind drifting back to the meeting. "That would be nice."

Rufus pulled his old pickup to a stop behind Duke's sporty white Toyota Tundra. As they got out a youthful looking forty-year-old came bouncing down the steps. He looked every bit the line backer he had been on the NC State football team in the late 1980s, six-feet three, a trim two hundred pounds with a head full of bushy brown hair and a huge smile on his face. He reached out with his right hand toward Rufus, but never took his eyes off Jake.

"This is Duke DiSisto, the man I've been telling you about."

Duke swung his hand around applying a firm but gentle grip to Jake's hand. "I'm very pleased to meet you, Mr. Eastwood."

"Call me Jake. All my friends do. May I call you Duke?"

"You bet," he responded with a southern twang. "After Rufus brought me in and got me oriented, he told me a lot about you and the NDR, what you've accomplished here in this country and what you plan to do in the Middle East." Then he looked into Jake's steel blue eyes and said calmly, "I'm on board for the full ride, Jake, whatever it takes to get this job done."

Jake stared back for several seconds convinced that even if Duke didn't know all that he might have gotten himself into, Rufus had found just the right man. "Is the Prince here?" he asked

"Inside. He took a Speed Master out for a test run then pulled up to my pier out front. The sales guy, two body guards and a couple of blondes are hanging out by the boat. The Prince told them he was coming up to the house for a discussion about some after-market modifications and that he might be a while. So he's alone in there, knocking down some Crown Royal over ice."

Jihad

Bayssour in Southern Lebanon

EACH MORNING AFTER PRAYERS, Robert observed his teacher as he prepared for the discussions of the day. Yusef carefully wiped dust from the covers of both copies of the Qur'an then flipped through the pages, shaking them gently to remove any lingering particles. Then he looked at his student and said, "Allah, Akbar," in a comforting tone.

Robert smiled back at him. "Yusef, I would like to know why some Muslims believe they are supposed to kill infidels?"

"Infidels!" screeched the professor and he laughed out loud. "That is not even an Arabic word, nor does it appear in the Qur'an."

"It's not?" Robert asked in surprise.

"No, it comes from the Latin word *infidelis*. It was used first by Europeans in the Middle Ages to describe Muslims, who they believed were non-believers. Kafir is the Arabic word for non-believers."

"So, Muslims first heard the term in Europe and when they left they carried it back to…"

"Muslims didn't exactly leave," the professor continued. "They were forced out. Do you recall that when the king and queen of Spain sent Columbus off to search for a sea route to the riches of the Orient, Ferdinand also issued an edict requiring all Jews to convert to Christianity or be expelled from the country?"

"I remember reading something about that," Robert replied.

"Those poor Jews who converted and remained were then exposed to the terrors of the Spanish Inquisition, to determine if they were Christian enough to be allowed to live at all. Many were tortured, some to death, and because they were accused of crimes against God all their property was forfeited to the church." The professor leaned in to emphasize the next words. "The Catholic Church became very rich during the 500 years of the inquisition."

"Did it go on that long?"

"From the mid 13th century until it was officially abolished in Spain in 1836, but in 1499, it was the turn of Muslims who remained in Spain after the *Reconquista*. Ferdinand issued another edict requiring them to also convert to Christianity or be expelled, and after witnessing what had happened to the Jews most of them chose to leave. There is much misinformation in history," the professor added while shaking his head, "but now, back to your question about jihad and *The Verse of the Sword* which is being misapplied to advocate violence against non-believers.

"The Qur'an is divided into suras, Robert, like chapters, but it is not classified by subjects. Muhammad's words were copied down as he spoke them, and in various suras he often spoke on topics he had previously mentioned. In fact, in order to interpret what he meant, the process of abrogation is applied to clarify his meaning."

"I don't understand."

"Essentially, it means that if the Prophet had spoken on a subject previously and if his most recent words conflicted with anything he had said before, then the newer meaning would abrogate, or replace the previous understanding of his words."

"Oh, I get it. If something mentioned in sura 2 is mentioned again in sura 4, then the later interpretation would apply."

"Yes, Robert, and this is a very important thing to understand when it comes to jihad. The concept of holy war is not mentioned in the Qur'an until Sura 9 and the radical Islamists are misapplying the principle of abrogation."

Robert shook his head. "I'm not following this."

"The process of making war is mentioned several times in various suras, but war against Christian non-believers was not mentioned until Mohammed was preparing to fight against the Byzantines in AD 630.

"It was part of the preparation for The Battle of Tabuk, that never took place, because the Byzantine warriors had withdrawn before the Muslim army arrived. The night before they reached Tabuk Mohammed gave a speech to his army, like Alexander would have done in Persia, or Patton in North Africa.

"In this speech he issued a proclamation that was recorded in Sura 9:5, that has come to be known as *The Verse of the Sword.* Before the battle he encouraged his followers to act with aggression against the non-Muslims they would be fighting. And in Sura 47:4 he also said, "When the holy months have passed and you encounter the unbelievers, strike off their heads, until ye have made a great slaughter among them."

"Well, that sure sounds like..." but before he finished his thought the professor raised his hand and cut him off.

"If you take it out of its historical context you can misapply it that way, Robert. Our Prophet Mohammed issued those statements before going to war, but the question Muslims must ask themselves today is, were they to be applied only during that period of history, or toward all non-Muslims during any period of time? Or, were they only to be applied by Muslims in self-defense?"

"Hmmm," Robert said thoughtfully. "Statements can be taken out of context and twisted to mean..."

"Exactly," the professor said with a wave of his hand, "and to properly evaluate any subject in the Qur'an, all the verses on that subject must be gathered then analyzed in both the historical context and interpretive manner. This allows one to resolve any contradictions that may seem to exist between any two verses."

"But wouldn't that be difficult for lay Muslims to do?"

"Indeed, Robert, more than half of all Muslims are poor and uneducated. They have to rely on clerics to interpret the Qur'an for them."

"So, if their trusted religious leaders read them *The Verse of the Sword* and tell them it is time for jihad, they have little choice but to believe them."

"That is correct. In countries where Muslims cannot read and interpret the Qur'an for themselves, or where their children have been indoctrinated with a radical interpretation of the words of our Prophet Muhammad, they can easily be led into jihad, convinced they are serving Allah by wrapping themselves in an explosive vest and detonating among those they have been told are the enemies of Islam."

"Even if it means killing other Muslims?"

"Sadly, this is true," the professor said. "Over ten thousand Muslims have been killed by other Muslims since the spectacular terrorist attacks of '9/11.' Please, Robert, understand that moderate peace loving Muslims have been just as affected by those tragic events as have you Americans.

"And because of the way the Qur'an is organized it is easy to isolate one or two verses on holy war and apply them to a purpose out of context to the original meaning. In this," he added softly, "Muslims, Christians and Jews are alike. We can evoke from our scriptures whatever serves our purpose.

"I believe the worst thing for seekers of knowledge to do is approach their religious text with the purpose of finding only verses that confirm what they already believe, and turning a blind eye to anything that does not support their pre-conceived beliefs and biases."

"So you're saying that only a minority of Muslims are invoking *The Verse of the Sword* to make war on non-believers?"

"Very few, Robert. If all Muslims had believed this throughout history then fighting between Muslims and Christians would never have stopped. Today Sura 9:5 is primarily invoked for nationalistic purposes. It is neither holy nor sanctioned by the Qur'an, and most Muslims, both Sunni and Shiite understand this."

"But why do so many Muslims appear to support the jihadists?"

"Some may feel that what is being done may be good for Islam, but the rest of the Muslim world is fearful of speaking out."

"Fear?"

"Yes, Robert. Moderates who speak against the evil fanatics are being killed. In more peaceful times most of these so-called jihadists would be no more than everyday street criminals, but in jihad they appear to have legitimacy. They are like the mafia in an old American movie, but very real and very deadly.

"I wish you to know that only a few passages in the Qur'an address making war. The rest of our holy book speaks of how to live a good and proper life and how to live in peace with others under the guidance of Allah. For instance, one of my favorite verses is from Sura 60:8-9. 'God does not forbid you respecting those who have not made war against you on account of your religion, or driven you from your homes; that you show them kindness and deal with them justly, for God loves the doers of justice.'"

Robert smiled at the dignified man who spoke with eloquence and concern for the proper interpretation of the words in his holy book. "You have a more enlightened interpretation of the Qur'an, than some other Muslims I've recently met," and his eyes lifted up to the ceiling.

"Well, you need to make some new Muslim friends," the professor responded with a sheepish grin and both men broke out in laughter.

The Diplomat

Heron Point on the Pamlico River

THE SAUDI PRINCE WAS leaning back on a soft white leather sofa in Duke's home on the Pamlico River. He didn't bother standing to greet the men as they came into the room. Bin-Ghazi was short and thick, with a full head of graying hair and a dark neatly trimmed beard. He was fashionably dressed in western attire, slacks and a golf shirt, instead of the elegant white robes and head cover he wore at the United Nations. "Ah, Mr. Eastwood, a pleasure to see you again."

Jake stepped smartly in front of the prince, recalling other occasions when his enemies had temporarily become friends. "Good to see you again bin Ghazi." He looked over at Duke. "I assume you have met our host?"

"Ah, yes, the young genius who knows how to make wonderful things happen inside these magnificent powerboats."

"And this is my associate, Rufus Leach, coordinating our venture at the farm and also here at the boating facility."

The Prince nodded his head and held up his glass to acknowledge the engineer. "You see, Mr. Leach, that I have been enjoying the fine whiskey I miss so much in my own country." He smiled. "It seems that neither Allah nor the King will allow it," and laughed to himself the way a man does who may have filled his glass once too often. "Quickly, now, let us get down to business."

As Jake and Rufus sat down on a small white leather sofa across from the Prince, Duke left to prepare drinks for his guests. The prince addressed Jake. "You have recovered the warhead?"

"Not yet, but very soon."

"When?"

"A few more days," Rufus replied. "The tunnel boring machine is on site but it's taking longer to assemble than we thought. Digging will begin soon."

"I trust you are spending my money wisely," the Prince added. "And this tunnel machine can do the job?"

Rufus leaned forward. "It's a German engineered LOVAT Series 165 with twin 4.0 meter disc cutters that can crunch through limestone at the rate of twenty feet per hour, leaving a perfectly round twelve-foot tunnel."

"Ah," the Prince responded, "but you mentioned this tunnel will be in an aquifer, so will it not be filled with water?"

"Not a problem," Rufus added. "The LOVAT is a self-contained TBM operated by three men working inside a sealed compartment thirty feet behind the disc cutters. The crushed limestone is channeled down to a slurry box behind the boring machine where it's mixed with water and pumped out a ten-inch pipe to the surface."

"And how will the warhead be retrieved?" the Prince asked.

"The operators will bore to a depth of one hundred eighty-five feet then tunnel two hundred feet to the left of the containment vessel. They'll circle back, activate their ground penetrating radar to locate the warhead, position themselves directly below and use an extension arm to bore up and around the SCE. It should drop like a baby into their waiting arms."

"But it will be very heavy, will it not?"

"At least a thousand pounds," Rufus answered.

"After so much time in the ground," the Prince whispered, "is there any chance of an explosion?"

"Not according to our nuclear experts," Jake said in a firm tone. "One is from the old Soviet Union, the other from Pakistan. They'll be on site to monitor everything and rebuild the working mechanisms."

"In a nuclear detonation," Rufus added, "the one million degree heat from the fission reaction fuses the hydrogen isotopes in the lithium deuteride, and that will create tritium and a thermonuclear fusion explosion."

Jake noticed the Prince's head lift slightly and his eyes roll upward with an informed *aha* expression indicating enough of the nuclear details. The Prince leaned forward, placed his elbows on his knees and brought his hands together. He tapped his fingertips for a moment and asked, "One of these bombs will fit inside the belly tank of a Saudi Air Force Strike Eagle?"

"Yes," Jake responded. "Duke will engineer everything to fit inside the belly tank of an F-15. Then it will be disassembled and stored inside the lead keel of the Lightning Power boat you order. Later, the boat will be transported to the port at Morehead City for shipment by freighter to Jeddah, Saudi Arabia. It should arrive by the early December."

"And Mr. Eastwood, you will see to it that this gift is immediately demonstrated for our friends in Tehran?"

"My team will be there to see that a weapon is loaded below a Saudi F-15 Strike Eagle and that your pilot will know how to detonate the package," Jake answered.

"See to what?" Duke asked as he returned with a round of four Crown Royals, but the Prince just sat back thinking with his arms spread across the back of the couch.

"One last sinful beverage before I go," bin-Ghazi said as he reached for another whiskey with a hand that seemed to tremble slightly.

The prince grew somber. "We must acquire these weapons and dissuade the Iranians or a nuclear arms race will take place in the Persian Gulf, and eventually such a weapon will reach the terrorists. This cannot be allowed to happen," he said firmly as he pulled the drink to his lips. "Even if it means that all of us must learn a terrible lesson about the spread of such weapons," then he slammed the glass down on the mahogany coffee table.

"You must understand," he added. "Something like a cold war has existed in the Middle East for centuries between Sunnis and Shiites. If the Mullahs of Iran are allowed to build nuclear weapons, they may use their proxy forces to make sure it is the end for the other side and anyone else caught in the way. They will promise them anything, virgins in heaven and wealth for their families, if they strap such weapons to their bodies and go into the cities of their enemies and detonate their bombs."

He looked into the eyes of the three men sitting across from him. "Iran must be given this final choice. Either give up their nuclear weapons program or learn a terrible lesson before it is too late for the rest of us."

"Once the Iranians realize Saudi Arabia has its own nuclear arsenal and that we are willing to give up our weapons if Iran will do the same, then the balance of power between Sunnis and Shiites will be restored." He slumped back on the couch.

"You see," he added with a smile, "peace is about to break out in the Middle East. Khalid, my new King, is what you call a progressive, and he wants to give this peace a chance, but he fears Iran's nuclear ambitions will derail the process."

"What peace are you talking about?" Rufus asked.

"Have you not heard about the new Arab world full of young Muslims with cell phones, Facebook and Twitter accounts? They talk constantly among themselves about jobs and emigrating to the west where there is opportunity, stability and peace. But now the conversation has changed to 'Why can't we have peace in the Middle East so that we can stay here?' Now they are asking what must be done in their own countries so that peace can prevail?

"They are saying 'Get rid of the old farts and their ideas that have not worked. No more terrorism.' They want to establish western style democracies in which people have a say in how their governments will be run.

"Of course, our intelligence agencies are monitoring all of this, and the al Queda terrorists and their Wahabbist clerics are dumbfounded by this change among young Muslims. King Khalid believes in the change and that it should occur in an orderly fashion, but he fears the Iranian nuclear program will not only stop the process, but will create a nuclear arms race.

"He also believes that most Sunni leaders, in response to the Iranians, will try to squash the hopes and dreams of their young people as they pursue nuclear weapons of their own. And that, gentlemen, will create a scenario for Armageddon that all nations have hoped to avoid since the first nuclear detonation in 1945."

Jake's eyes narrowed as he questioned whose side the prince and his King might really be on. "Your government is playing both sides of the fence, bin-Ghazi. You show one face to America as our friend, our largest supplier of crude oil, and as an ally in the war on terrorism. But you also have a darker face as financial sponsor for the spread of militant Wahhabism?"

"Yes, the Wahhabists," bin Ghazii sighed with a practiced diplomatic smile, "the ultra conservatives of Islam with their own extremist interpretation of Sharia Law. It is an odd symbiotic relationship the monarchy has had with the Wahabbists since the founding of the Saudi nation in 1932, and one that now impedes progress. Khalid is well aware of this I assure you."

"They operate the radical madrassas in Saudi Arabia," Jake added, "teaching and spreading their militant version of Islam and they are the parent of Sunni Islamist terrorist organizations in the Middle East. Anywhere in the world there is a Sunni presence your government is using oil money, through your international charities, to finance the construction of mosques and providing financial support for Muslim clerics who teach Wahhabist fundamentalism. So, by supporting the Wahabbists in your country and financing the spread of their madrassas in other countries, the Saudi Royal Family has allowed your nation to become the epicenter for the spread of global terrorism."

The diplomatic smile vanished from bin-Ghazi's face. His eyes closed as he considered the means to mitigate Jake's interpretation of the Royal Family's support for Wahhabism. "It is not terrorism that we are exporting, it is the peaceful spread of Sunni Islam to western nations and this is no longer a secret to any of your governments.

"In 2005, a document called 'The Project' was taken from the apartment of one of our diplomats in Bern, Switzerland. It was a detailed explanation of our mission to spread Sunni Islamic culture to the west, but it was no more than a plan of goals and objectives, much like that of your Christian missionary organizations used for decades to proselytize throughout the world.

"And yes, I acknowledge that we have an internal problem with the Wahabbists, but for many decades there was a peaceful relationship between the monarchy and their clerics. Since the end of the Second World War, however, there has been a growing frustration with western governments and their treatment of Muslims.

"The young Wahabbists want to address the crimes being committed by Israel against the Palestinians. They also want to purge Islam of outside influences and have all Muslims return to a strict interpretation of Sharia Law.

"It was the Wahhabist clerics that rejuvenated the militant practice of jihad. They interpreted the Qur'anic verses to rationalize holy war to suit their own purposes against anyone they claim as non-believers. This includes *kafirs*, foreigners with other beliefs, and any Muslims who stand against them. Some of the most radical even speak of recapturing the Iberian Peninsula of Spain and re-establishing the Islamic Empire of old." Bin Ghazi paused and smiled to himself. "But this is not the way of the new Islamic world.

"There will always be terrorists just as there are extremists in Western nations, like the men who blew up your federal building with such great loss of life. But you must know that young Muslims have realized that terrorism and destruction have not worked, and they are turning their backs on the extremists to pursue another direction.

"It is our young with their education and technical skills that are leading this new revolution, and Khalid wishes to see an orderly transition into a modern world in which our Islamic traditions are respected and maintained.

"So," bin Ghazi continued, "radical Islamists must never acquire weapons of mass destruction. No country in the Gulf region or the Middle East need ever have such weapons, and the first thing that must be done is to prevent the Shiite extremists in Iran from making their country into a nuclear nation."

Bin-Ghazi picked up his glass and gulped heartily swallowing every drop of the whiskey. "Now I must go, gentlemen, my friends await," then he pointed out the rear window toward the topless blondes sunbathing on the rear deck of the Lightning boat.

"One last thing before you leave," Duke asked. "What happens if the Mullahs agree to stop enriching uranium?"

"Then it is over. Iran and Saudi Arabia will abandon their nuclear ambitions and the stage will be set for the young people of Islam to pursue their new direction."

"But the plan to detonate a bomb in the Saudi desert, that part will remain?"

The prince looked at Jake. "Have you not explained to him that this is essential?"

Jake responded flatly. "As I've said before, the details of Peaceful Eagle are compartmentalized, on a time and need to know basis." He looked over at Duke.

"Our job is to deliver the weapon and make sure it is properly set up on an F-15 Strike Eagle so that a Saudi pilot can fly into the desert for a demonstration detonation. That way the Iranians and the rest of the world will be convinced that Saudi Arabia has gone nuclear. Then an offer will be made to Iran. If they agree to dismantle their nuclear weapons program with International Atomic Energy Agency inspections to verify the process, then the Saudis will surrender their remaining nuclear bombs."

"Yes, that is the plan," the Prince added, and as lucid as his comments had been only moments before, he rose unsteadily to his feet and began wobbling toward the door.

As he tenuously walked down the rear steps Duke said, "Okay, I get it. The Saudis will appear to have an arsenal and that may be enough to keep the Iranians from going nuclear."

"Don't count on it," Jake added as they watched two body-guards run to catch their swaying patron. "I don't believe the Iranians will ever forget that the Saudis detonated a nuclear weapon."

They watched a moment longer as the two men steadied the Prince and walked him toward the end of the pier. "Is everything he told us for real?" Duke asked. "Is the prince on a noble mis-sion, or is he…?"

Jake glanced at Duke and Rufus with a sardonic grin. "He's a professional diplomat skilled at pumping sunshine so far up your ass that it'll warm your heart, but don't think for a minute that he's not part of a Sunni strategy to Islamize the west and create a new world caliphate." Jake took another sip of his beverage. "But for now we need his contacts and credentials to get the bombs to Jeddah, then set-up a Saudi F-15 for the nuclear detonation."

Jake heard a familiar tone chirping from inside a briefcase beside the coffee table. It was his satellite phone. He walked over, reached inside, and was pleasantly surprised to hear the voice of his fiancé, Annalisa Bertola, but shocked at what she told him.

"Jake, we need you back in Paris," a despairing tone linger-ing in her voice. "Hezbollah has Robert. He's somewhere in Southern Lebanon and there's a ransom demand, a big one."

Jake sighed heavily. "Yeah, I was afraid something like this could happen. How long will it take to fly over and pick me up?"

"I can leave Paris in a few hours," she said. "I should arrive at the New Bern airport around eight o'clock in the morning, eastern time."

"Okay, I'll be there. Tell Nalum to keep me informed of any new developments."

"I will, Jake. See you in the morning." Then she paused and whispered softly, "I miss you so much. Paris just isn't any fun without you."

He smiled into the phone. "I miss you, too, Annalisa." After he said good-bye he turned toward Rufus. "You'll have to take over the dig in Faro. I have some urgent business in Paris."

New Hope

Bayssour, Lebanon

LATE IN THE DAY, long after the food basket had been lowered, the trap door opened above Robert and Yusef. An aluminum ladder was inserted into the hole and clanked noisily down until its black rubber feet settled on the clay floor. A man in a dark suit backed slowly down the rungs, planted his polished black shoes and turned toward the prisoners.

He wore a slight beard and mustache with wire rimmed glasses and spoke in English. "Mr. Faircloth, you will be leaving tonight. Say your prayers and gather your things. I will come for you at midnight."

Robert glanced at Yusef. "What about my teacher? Will he also be leaving?"

"Perhaps," the man said as he looked around the cellar. "I hope your room has been comfortable and that you will return for another visit in better days."

He turned away and began climbing the ladder leaving the captives sitting in their chairs, stunned at the news of possible release. Robert stood and walked nervously around the cellar as if measuring the space in which he had been held.

"Come, Robert, please sit down," the professor said. "There is a final lesson I have been saving for you. It is something that few leaders in the west have yet to realize. The Islamic world is going through a difficult period of change, more so than ever before in its history, and this change is being driven by young well-educated Muslims. It involves great excitement and confusion. There is even a growing movement against increasingly irrelevant fatwas, a sort of jihad against jihad."

"Anti-jihad?" Robert asked with a surprised expression as he returned to his seat.

"Yes, since the end of World War II, many Arab nations have been trying to find a way to enter the modern world without giving up their Islamic heritage and culture.

"In some, where more enlightened leaders have stepped forward the transition is being made, but in others backward thinking clerics and despotic autocrats hold back their people by adhering to a strict interpretation of Sharia Law. It has had the unhappy effect of ensuring that many Muslims continue to live in ignorance and poverty.

"Let me explain, Robert. In 1917, after World War I the League of Nations allowed Britain to administer the territories that had been rested from the empire of the Ottoman Turks. This included the land historically known as Palestine and before that it was the home of the ancient Israelites. Almost immediately the British ignited the modern crisis in Palestine when Lord Balfour issued his famous declaration."

"The Balfour Declaration... I've heard of that," Robert responded. "Wasn't it the document that declared that the Jewish Diaspora would end with the establishment of a homeland in Palestine?"

"Very good, you are a good student of history, Robert. But as you know, after the scattering of the Jews the land between the Jordan River and the Mediterranean Sea was settled by the ancestors of the Palestinians, and it had been that way for over a thousand years when Balfour issued his infamous decree.

"At first, Haj Amin al-Husseini, the revered Sunni Mufti of Jerusalem, was not as concerned with the small number of Jews immigrating to Palestine as he was about the territorial ambitions of his Muslim neighbors. Soon, however, the number of Zionist Jews increased to such a level that fighting broke out between Israeli and Palestinian farmers. As a protest, the Mufti encouraged his people to stop paying taxes to the government and openly strike against British interests. In a sense, Robert, that struggle has continued to this day.

"The first Arab Revolt, 1937 to 1940, was a three-year campaign against the portioning of Palestine to include a homeland for the Jews. Unfortunately, during World War Two, the Mufti openly sided with Italy and Germany against the allies which included Britain. He thought that if the Nazis gained control over Palestine they would eliminate his problem with the Jewish settlers and the Palestinians would re-gain autonomy over their homeland.

"But it didn't work out that way."

"No, Robert, it did not and the Mufti had to seek asylum in France, and later in Beirut where he died in 1974. His place was then taken by one of his relatives, a young Arab Nationalist by the name of Yassir Arafat. I'm sure you remember him as leader of the Palestinian Liberation Organization during its violent campaigns of the 70s and 80s.

"So that's how Arafat became leader of the PLO!" Robert exclaimed.

"Yes, and perhaps now you can understand that in spite of any peaceful words he may have uttered during all those peace conferences, sponsored by a series of American presidents, that as PLO leader Arafat would never have agreed to a peace that included Israel as a permanent homeland for the Jews."

"So it was all about diplomacy for Arafat, he never really considered a peaceful settlement to the Arab-Israeli conflict?"

Yusef laughed to himself. "He probably would have been assassinated by his own colleagues if he did, Robert. So, during the 1980s there was significant growth in radical Islamic groups that embraced violence and martyrdom as a means of achieving their political goals. You recall the truck bomb that destroyed the U.S. Marine barracks in Lebanon in 1983?"

Robert's face grimaced in memory as the professor continued. "This type of violence continued until September 11, 2001. That is when the entire Muslim world began to realize that Islam was being tainted by the mass killings of al-Queda and all the other extremist groups. We began to understand that militant Islam was only good for destruction, that it had no solutions for the daily problems of poverty and ignorance, and we began to turn our backs on terror. The violence has not yet ended but young modern Muslims are repudiating the tactics of terror.

"This is the last lesson I have for you, Robert. A real shift is taking place in the hearts and minds of young Muslims, from bombs to ballot boxes, from violence to active political groups, and these young people are the ones leading the way for change in the Islamic world. They are sick of fat old men with tired ideas that seek to hold back progress and enrich themselves in the process.

"Al Queda's day has come and gone. The transition is now underway from fundamentalism to modernization. One third of the Arab world is between the ages of 15 and 29, and these young people are weary of the endless fighting. They want solutions, jobs, opportunities for a better life and to find a rational way to live peacefully with their neighbors in the east and west.

"What I'm saying, Robert, is that there is new hope for Muslims in the modern world where we can find a way to modernize without sacrificing our Islamic heritage. Even though there is still real conflict between fundamentalists and those who wish to change, young Muslims, both Sunnis and Shiites, are pursuing a new path within Islam, but their new world will not be exactly like western democracies.

Robert leaned back in his chair marveling at the education he was receiving from his teacher. "This new opportunity needs a chance to grow," Yusef added, "and that is why Peaceful Eagle must be stopped before it is too late. No one in the Middle East needs nuclear weapons, Robert. So, I will do my best to convince our friends upstairs to help you."

Fidyah

Late August
Beirut, Lebanon

JAKE EASTWOOD STARED OUT the darkened windows of a black Suburban while the burnt orange hues of an early morning sunrise filled a dawning sky. The stifling heat of southern Beirut had not yet engulfed the city as a white Range Rover drove slowly along the quiet empty street.

Jake studied the lone vehicle. He leaned forward as a bound and blind folded prisoner was deposited on a nearby corner and the SUV sped away.

The transfer of a million dollars of the Prince's money from a Swiss account in Bern, Switzerland, to a bank in Damascus, Syria, had been verified. The fidyah had been paid. Robert Faircloth, held by Hezbollah radicals for nearly two weeks, was a free man and within an hour he was on a private jet bound for Paris.

Sacre Coeur

Monmartre District of Paris

LATER THAT EVENING ROBERT AND JAKE were sitting near the summit of a marble staircase in front of a beautiful white Byzantine church with an impressive view of the lights of Paris. The steps ran from the hilltop sanctuary of Sacre Coeur down to the Rue du Chevalier de la Barre.

"I've been here many times," Jake confessed. "It's one of my favorite views in the city. Look at all those narrow winding streets down below. In the late nineteenth century they were home to local artists, shopkeepers, prostitutes, and lots of bawdy can-can houses like the Moulin Rouge."

"Really," Robert sighed.

"According to what I've been told," Jake continued, "Monmartre became a trendy tourist destination right after World War II, full of boutiques, cafes, art houses and lots of fashionable young ladies of the evening. They say very little has changed around here except the rents. Did you know that a hillside loft with a view of the city can rent for nine hundred euros a week?

"Every morning, Robert, just after sunrise joggers sprint up this staircase to the terrace behind us, rest a while then jog back down. And every evening just like tonight, romantic couples sit arm in arm on the stairs drinking wine and spreading cheese on loaves of French bread while they enjoy this view."

He leaned against his old friend. "That was a close call in Beirut. Hezbollah could have killed you."

"I know, " Robert whispered while massaging a bruised shoulder. "It was risky, but I had to make contact with someone who could put me in touch with a Mullah in Iran." His captors had beaten him on the back and legs to ensure that, if needed, his face could still appear in a propaganda video.

"At first they wouldn't listen… "

"Hezbollah doesn't want peace," Jake said with skepticism. "The only thing they care about is a Shia Muslim government dominating Southern Lebanon. Violence is the means they've chosen to reach their goal no matter how many of their people they have to sacrifice." He paused, "But you know, Robert, without the Syrians and their contacts inside Hezbollah, along with some serious money, I'm not sure we could have gotten you out of there."

"I know," Robert said quietly, recalling the fidyah that had been paid. "I appreciate what you and Nalum did to get me out of that house." He looked out over the city with an embarrassed smile. "Did I tell you about Yusef, the poor fellow they put in the cellar with me to teach me about Islam and to convert me?"

"They wanted you to become a Muslim?" Jake asked in a shocked voice.

"Yeah, they wanted the world to see that even their enemies when presented with the wisdom of the Qur'an would submit to Islam."

"Did you?"

Robert shook his head. "I couldn't, Jake, not even to save that poor man's life. And he did try, that's for sure. He could only tell me his name, that he was Shia Muslim and that he was a theology professor at the American University in Beirut."

"What was it like in that cellar?"

"Warm during the day, cool at night, but not too bad. Each of us had a foam mat for the ground and a blanket and pillow. And the sound of that wooden door opening in the ceiling above us was..." he paused in mid-thought. "We were like trained mice, Jake. Every time it opened we stood in hope that something good would either fall or be lowered down in a basket. That's pretty much all we had to look forward to. Other than the professor's lessons every day was pretty much like the one before."

"Was he a good teacher?"

"Excellent," Robert said with enthusiasm. "Yusef helped me understand a lot about the history and politics of the Middle East beginning with the Bedouin tribes in Saudi Arabia, and of course, the life of the Prophet Muhammad. He continued through the days of early Islamic empire building, then the Ottoman Turks and finally, dissolution of their empire after World War I because the Turks had sided with the Axis powers. Many of the Middle Eastern nations we know today either came into existence at that time or were created based on whatever historical record there was.

"I also learned something very important. If you want to talk with the Mullahs in Tehran, you have to find another friendly Mullah to help you. And thanks to Yusef the Hezbollah militia commander finally agreed to do that."

Robert looked calmly at his old friend. "I have to go to Baghdad, Jake. They told me that a very important Shiite cleric that may be willing to meet with me and he has direct contact with the leaders of Iran.

"But you just got away from Hezbollah!" Jake exclaimed in an excited whisper. "I don't think you need to stick your neck out again, so soon I mean. At least in Beirut we could work through the Syrians, but in Baghdad we don't have reliable contacts."

Jake placed his arm around Robert's shoulder. "It could be even more dangerous there, don't you understand?"

"That's why I'm here," Robert said quietly, trying not to raise his voice so that anyone sitting nearby could hear. "What if I reach the Mullahs in Tehran and get them to understand that the Saudis are about to threaten them with a nuclear weapon? This whole thing could be avoided, don't you see? Peaceful Eagle wouldn't have to fly."

Jake looked away from his old friend and turned his gaze toward the lights below. "I believe in you, Robert, and if going to Iraq is what you have to do to get through to the Mullahs, then… " Jake didn't finish the sentence. He just squeezed the back of Robert's neck with his left hand.

The LOVAT

Late August, Faro, NC

"LOOKS LIKE A MONSTER SQUID," Rufus Leach said pointing at the mass of cables extending from the rear of the tunnel-boring machine. He and Gunter Heidrickson, the lean blonde-haired Project Engineer, were inside one of the large farm buildings, walking along the edge of a twenty-foot gash in the earth that created the necessary grade for the TBM to begin churning into the soil.

"Yes, it does," Gunter responded in perfect English as he observed the other technicians making final preparations to start up the LOVAT 165. "My men and I have no idea where we are," he said with a chuckle. "We flew in from Germany on a private jet, got inside a paneled van and were driven here. We haven't been off this farm since we arrived; could be in Texas for all we know."

"That's right," Rufus added. "We have to keep this place a secret for now. Don't want anyone to know there's a Civil War treasure buried here. Can't let the word out till we dig it up and have our experts verify what's in that box. If it's what we think it is then it will be worth all the trouble and expense."

Rufus stood back admiring the giant machine. His eyes wandered down its side and he noticed metal legs with large round footpads protruding every twenty feet. "Is this how it propels itself?"

"Every three minutes the tail is hydraulically pulled forward and the legs re-extend out to the walls of the tunnel where they exert a forward pressure. The process is repeated, undulating toward the front, essentially pulling the entire machine forward a few inches with each contraction. But the front legs have a different purpose. They are continuously planted to maintain pressure on the cutting discs."

Rufus pointed to a large box that was eight feet tall, nine feet wide and twenty feet long. "Will your men be okay in there?"

"It's like a submarine," Gunter said, "self-contained, because we will be working in an underground aquifer. They will eat, sleep and work in there for the next six days until your Civil War treasure is recovered and they return to the surface. Myself and the other technicians will constantly monitor everything from our work stations up here," and he pointed to the far end of the building.

"Is that the recovery vessel?" Rufus asked, pointing to another long metal box behind the operations center.

"Another marvel of German engineering," Gunter said proudly. "That's the drill and cut machine that will retrieve your treasure. Once the Ground Penetrating Radar locates it, the machine will cut past the exact location until this section of the TBM is centered beneath the package.

"The top will slide open and down like a garage door revealing an eighteen foot long platform. There is a six-foot drilling and cutting arm folded across that will rise up vertically and begin drilling into the limestone.

"Now, here's the real genius," he continued. "As it drills six feet up the platform rises with it, and regardless of how the box is positioned in the bottom of the old well, vertical or angled, the cutting arm can be controlled to cut very slowly along the outside length, turn and cut across the head and then repeat the process on the other side. When it is finished the treasure will slip gently onto the platform. At that point, it will be lowered down inside this section and the top will slide back over it and the LOVAT will return to the surface."

Gunter observed the admiring smile on Rufus' face. "You're welcome to ride along for the first hundred feet or so. After that we enter the aquifer and there will be no way for you to exit."

"No, thanks," Rufus responded with a laugh. "I'm good here on the surface," and remembered that he would have to go down to the target area before drilling began to turn off the four seismic sensors. "Let me know when you're ready, Mr. Heidrickson, and we'll go ahead and start the dig."

"But, the other gentleman, doesn't he have to be here?"

"He was called away on other business. I'll give him a call and let him know the dig is about to begin."

The City of Light

Sacre Coeur, Paris

"WHY THE LONG FACES, boys?" Annalisa Bertolla asked. She was a tall slender Virginian with long brown hair that partly concealed an oval face with hazel green eyes. She reached up with her left hand to pull loose hair behind an ear. "That's not how you looked when I left to get the wine. And so serious," she added with a questioning smile, as she walked around them with two small shopping bags in her arms.

Robert whispered to Jake. "We'll finish talking about this later at the café?"

"Okay, " Jake whispered back as Annalisa snuggled in between them. "Hey, you've been gone for quite a while. I was starting to get worried."

"Didn't look like it to me. You and Robert were so engrossed in your conversation you hardly knew I was away."

"That's not true," Jake said as he put an arm around the shoulder of his fiancé. "It's just that we are… " he paused, searching for the right words.

"In a foreign city," Robert chimed in, "and we have to be careful."

"But this is Paris," she whispered back. "We're okay here, aren't we, Jake?"

"As long as we don't do anything to draw attention to ourselves."

"Okay" she said, throwing her arms out around both men pulling them in for a hug. She let go and reached for one of the bags at her feet speaking with a playful flair in her voice. "I have three half bottles from the Cote du Rhone, a *Cha'teauneuf du Pape* for Robert, *Hermitage* for Jake and a fruity white *Pouilly-Fuisse* for me."

She reached down inside the other bag and pulled out several small items. "For our freshly baked bread we have cheese, a tasty Camembert and a little something fresh from the goat," she teased with a gleam in her eye.

Robert and Jake smiled at her performance then Jake pulled her over and softly kissed her crimson lips. She leaned into Jake's shoulder and they gazed out on the mesmerizing lights of Paris, and for a moment Robert felt as if the lovers had forgotten he was there.

Jake finally reached around for Annalisa's small backpack. He retrieved a pronged style cork remover from a zippered compartment and wobbled it down the insides of each bottle. He twisted the corks out and handed Robert and Annalisa their half bottles of wine.

"Tell me, again," Robert asked in a teasing voice, "how you and Jake became... " He paused with a little grin on his face, "such good friends."

"You know," Annalisa said. "I told you about how my father and Jake worked together at the CIA back in the seventies."

"He was my mentor," Jake added in a respectful tone. "We worked a lot of ops together including Operation Eagle Claw in 1980. Desert One was the rally point on Iranian soil for the mission to rescue the American Embassy hostages in Tehran."

He took a short breath, held it a moment then let it slip away. "Her father was killed when our helicopter crashed into the side of a C-130 Hercules. I was wounded, burned pretty badly when the fuel tanks of the prop aircraft blew up. I spent the rest of that year recuperating from surgeries in a Washington, D.C. hospital."

"After the loss of my father," Annalisa continued, "my mother and I decided to take care of Jake like he was a member of our own family. All those nights sitting with him in the burn unit, reading to him and listening to his stories of growing up with you and his other friends in North Carolina; I was just a young teenage girl and I guess I transferred the lost affection for my father to Jake.

"And ten years later," she added with a frown, "Jake rescued me from an impulsive marriage. He was a good-looking airline pilot who taught advanced instrumentation classes at a local community college. Within a few months I learned about his reputation as a flying hunk of love meat. He continued to bed flight attendants whenever he could. Finally, I confronted him and he beat me up, broke my nose and blackened both eyes.

"When I got out of the emergency room I made a phone call to the one man I knew I could trust, and the next day my ex-husband was found beside a highway beaten very badly, the apparent victim of a carjacking and robbery. I visited him once in the hospital just to let him know the marriage was over. Either that, or the next time he was found along a roadway, what was left of him would be taken to a morgue. He got the message." She looked over at Jake.

"After that Jake financed my advanced jet aircraft training, and when I completed all the certifications he offered me a job. He wanted me to fly him around in a gorgeous new Gulf Star to meetings all over the country."

Jake squeezed her hand as she continued the story. "At first I didn't realize Jake was the Operations Director for the New Democratic Right and that he was organizing a secret national organization. I would just fly him from state to state and wait for him in a lot of nice hotels.

"Later as our conversations lingered and became more intimate, I found my old affection for him growing into something much stronger." She looked at Jake and held his eyes in hers. "I'll never forget the night we were sitting at a table in the Oak Room of the Plaza Hotel and I finally summoned up the courage to put my hand over yours and whisper that I loved you, and that I was in love with you. Do you remember?"

"How could I forget, Annalisa? I was so nervous my hands were shaking. For all the survival training I'd been through I just wasn't prepared to let you know how I felt. I've been in love with you since those days in the hospital, but didn't know how to... "

"That's a great story," Robert said with a warm smile. He held his bottle up and the three of them clinked together, sipped wine and enjoyed the view from the staircase of Sacre Coeur. Their conversation turned to the old days of the NDR and that magical moment in Havana when the entire group reassembled at La Floridita, one of Hemingway's favorite watering holes.

"Oh, my God, Robert, you should have seen the look on your face when you saw Jake standing at the bar. Annalisa squealed with delight. "It was a classic moment!"

"Well, I thought I was gonna get my ass kicked, or worse," he responded as he tore off a piece of bread and spread it generously with goat cheese. Then he turned up his small bottle and sipped sparingly.

"No way I could ever do that," Jake added sincerely. "Next to Annalisa, you're more important to me than anyone in the world, like a brother, Robert."

Robert gazed past Annalisa who was sitting between them. "And you're my best friend, Jake, just like a brother."

"And I love you both," Annalisa chimed in as three bottles clinked together again.

"Well," Robert added, "at least he didn't feed me to the gators like he did those two boys down in Georgia."

"Jake!" Annalisa gasped. "You said that was an accident."

Jake glanced around. No one was paying any attention to the three Americans. "Those men were traitors," he whispered, "and they sort of fell out of their boat in the middle of a bunch of alligators. I just didn't do much to help them."

Robert chuckled recalling the story he had heard about a concussion grenade tossed in beside the small aluminum boat, ensuring it would capsize. "He did what he had to do, Annalisa, to make sure those men didn't expose anyone in the Georgia cell." Then he looked at his old friend, "Isn't that right?"

Jake glared at him with a *You shouldn't have told her that* look on his face. Annalisa leaned in to Jake. "I know that you would never hurt anyone that didn't deserve it, like that Russian mobster who was killed in your place to make people believe Dante had finally died."

Jake looked down at his feet. He rarely discussed, much less bragged about, any of the activities he had engaged in as the nefarious character Dante. "There were some things that didn't go as planned," he confessed.

Annalisa reached up and stroked his face. "Like pushing a 357 Magnum under the chin of that Chicago Tribune sports writer. It was a horrible mess, Jake, but I understood later, after you explained how the old football player committed suicide by attacking Dante in front of the Tribune's editorial staff."

Jake smiled at her. "I'm not the only tough guy here. You've had your moments, too." He looked over at Robert as if to suggest the pretty woman sitting between them had a more formidable character than her feminine charms might suggest.

"I know you fly airplanes," Robert said, "but what else do you do for the NDR?"

Annalisa stared softly into Jake's blue eyes. "I've done a few things that I'm not proud of, but only to help Jake get out of some tight situations. He knows that violence is not my nature. It takes a lot for me to go there." She turned up her bottle and swallowed twice, effectively ending the discussion of her past and the notorious violence of Dante, Jake's former persona.

Annalisa hugged Jake's arm then turned back to Robert. "What would we have done if you had not come back from Lebanon?"

Robert sighed, still shaken by his experience with Hezbollah. "Yeah, that was a tough ordeal, but…" and he let the words linger in the air.

"When do you leave for Iraq?" Jake asked.

"Iraq," Annalisa repeated. "Who's going to Iraq?"

"I got what I needed from Hezbollah," Robert said. "They're sending word to a Shiite cleric in Baghdad that I'm coming and that he needs to hear what I have to say."

"Iraq," Annalisa repeated. "Did you know about this, Jake?"

"Just heard a few minutes ago, and to be honest I'm a little concerned."

"Concerned," she repeated. "After what he's been through I'm scared to death." Annalisa took Robert's hands in hers intertwining their fingers. "You don't have to go."

"Perhaps not," he responded wistfully. "But you know what they say about good men who sit by and do nothing. So, if not me, then who? Someone has to try and make peace before the nuclear option is put into play." He looked over at his old friend. "You understand, don't you, Jake?"

"I understand you, Robert, that you believe this is the right thing to do. But I agree with Annalisa. I don't have a good feeling about this trip. Hezbollah was scary enough, but at least we could deal with them through the Syrians. Where you're going there are so many radical fringe groups, there may be no one to negotiate with."

"You may be right," Robert answered, looking sadly at his two friends. "But if anything happens, at least you will know the NDR has done its best through me."

The three Americans were looking out over the city when Jake's satellite phone began chirping inside Annalisa's backpack. He looked at them with a *Sorry, but I have to take this* look on his face. "This is Jake." He listened for a moment then said, "Okay, I'll be back tomorrow afternoon. Go ahead and start the dig."

The Faro Tunnel

Faro, NC

THE GULF STAR 550 flew in to New Bern, NC, the next after-noon. Rufus was waiting at the small airport, and after a quick dinner Annalisa left to fly back to Paris.

"That tunnel boring machine is an incredible piece of equip-ment!" Rufus exclaimed as he and Jake drove the four-lane highway toward Goldsboro, then another twelve miles northeast on the back roads to Faro. "Three technicians got inside that thing and within a few hours it disappeared into the earth like a mole on steroids."

Jake smiled at his NDR colleague. No matter the difficulty or danger nothing could diminish the fascination Rufus held for engineering projects. Two hours later they pulled onto a marl driveway off Big Daddy's Road just south of Faro. "Rufus, you didn't forget about those seismic sensors?"

"Hell, no, got all four of 'em turned off just before they cranked up the TBM. When I got back to the out buildings I stood on the edge of that trench looking down inside the door of the cabin where the technicians would be working. It was all cramped up in there, Jake, and they had some of those emergency air packs, like firemen use, hanging right next to the back door."

"Did it make you want to ride along with them, Rufus?"

"No way, too claustrophobic, but you should have heard it when those big engines rumbled to life. Gunter yelled out over the intercom, 'Engage the blades,' and you could feel a tremendous pressure on the entire length of the TBM as the hydraulic legs extended and the cutting blades began chewing into the soil.

"I'm telling you, Jake, everything felt loud and powerful as that large flex pipe extending from the back of the machine began filling with water and you could hear the rumble of slurry as it bounced along inside."

Ten minutes later Rufus and Jake were standing inside the warehouse speaking with Gunter Heidrickson. Two other technicians were working at a console near the back and they waved pleasantly at their employers. For all the majesty of their powerful machine, this was just another in a long series of underground contracts in yet another foreign country.

The Germans were only here to do a job then move on to the next contract. Though they were curious it didn't matter to them whether or not the Americans recovered the Civil War treasure they claimed was buried 180 feet below the surface. Either way Gunter and the technicians of WECO Engineering in Bremen Germany would be paid.

Early on the morning of the fourth day the surface technicians received a video call from the supervisor inside the TBM. The metal container had been successfully retrieved and they were returning to the surface. Jake glanced at Rufus, gave him a thumbs-up signal, and the two of them walked quietly out of the building. "Better get our scientists ready, Rufus. It's show time."

Two days later the TBM crawled out of the earth, its hydraulic legs pulling the huge machine forward inches at a time in a line parallel to the entrance tunnel. It took another three hours from the moment the disc cutting blades emerged until the huge tail was clear of the chasm. It was a slow and tedious process but finally the undulating monster was at rest. Three technicians emerged from the operations box in remarkably good spirits wanting nothing more than a cold beer and a shower.

While the Germans were celebrating inside the farmhouse the Russian scientist put on his protective gear. With a small Geiger counter in hand, Vladimir stood next to the lead lined box containing the Mark 41 warhead carefully measuring for any radiation. If there were a signature indicating the metal skin had ruptured, the box would remain closed, taken off its track and moved inside the underground bunker.

The air was thick and tense as the cover was slowly dragged open. A slightly corroded twelve-foot long, four-foot diameter stainless steel and nickel-plated tube lay inside the box. *No wonder they called it a Bassoon,* Petrov thought to himself as he lowered the Geiger counter inside the box. The front of the tube was crushed inward two feet from penetrating into the earth, but other than heavy denting it appeared to be in remarkably good condition. There was only a slight radioactive signature, little more than when technicians inserted nuclear fuel inside the three stages of the containment vessel.

Vladimir turned toward a small office in a corner of the building and gave a thumbs-up signal to Rufus and Jake. Then he rubbed his left arm indicating protective clothing would be required while moving the bomb to the lab inside the bunker.

Jake and Rufus put on yellow protective suits with helmets and walked out to assist the Russian. Rufus drove a small tractor with a long lift arm beside the TBM to the location of the warhead while Jake and the Russian crawled inside the lead lined box and fastened hooks to metal rings at each end of the bomb.

Rufus pulled a lever back and the warhead began to gently lift from the box. He toggled another lever and it moved slowly over a small flat bed trailer where its bulk could rest while being transported inside the bunker. Within an hour it was secure, where only the scientists, and Jake and Rufus could view it.

A few minutes later Jake walked with Rufus toward the house where the Germans were celebrating the success of their mission. They were drinking from several cases of Carlsberg beer and lathering globs of brown mustard on thick slices of bread stacked with bratwurst, provolone and liver sausage. The NDR leader reached out and pulled the engineer to a stop. "How many containment vessels do we have, Rufus?"

"Four. Vlad finished them after the test, but we'll need more cordite charges."

"I'll call Sergeant Oder. He says it's not a problem to get them from misfires on the artillery range at Fort Bragg. He should have them here by tomorrow afternoon."

"Sounds good," Rufus said. "Well, I'd better get old Vlad back in the shop. With all that fissionable material in there, he should be able to make three or four weapons."

"Good," Jake responded. "I need to get back to Paris, some unfinished business."

"That's fine, Jake, I can take care of things on this end."

Both were smiling as they walked back toward the farmhouse. The first stage of Peaceful Eagle, retrieving the old nuclear warhead from its one hundred eighty-foot grave, had been a success.

Hijack the Eagle

Paris, France

"WHY CAN'T I COME, Jake?"

"He said it was personal, something he wanted to discuss with me."

"But he can trust me, you know that?"

"I know, but Robert's about to leave for Iraq where we may not be able to help him, and honestly, I think this is about his daughter, you know, in case…" Jake cleared his throat.

Annalisa sat down on the king-sized bed. "You don't think something is going to happen to him?"

Jake stepped over, sat down and slipped an arm around her shoulder. "I don't know. Anything can happen out there, but it's Robert's decision to go. And right now he wants to talk to me, privately. You understand, don't you?"

"Yes, but… "

"No buts, Annalisa. You have to stop having those negative thoughts. Nothing is going to happen to Robert."

"Okay," she conceded with a half smile. She leaned in and kissed him gently. "Go then, and tell Robert that I'll be thinking of him. No matter where he is, I'll be thinking positive thoughts for him."

Jake left the rental house in Monmartre for the short walk down to the Rue du Chevalier de la Barre. He arrived at a corner eatery, the Café du Blanc that had an unencumbered view of the staircase leading up to Sacre Coeur. He found Robert at an outside table with a large bottle of Grand Marnier and two small glasses placed on a red and white-checkered tablecloth. As Jake sat down Robert poured two full cordials.

"What's on your mind, is it Libby?"

Robert smiled at the mention of his daughter's name. "No, not this time. Over the past few years I've transferred just about everything I own into her name. Libby, Early and the grandkids are well taken care of." He took a long drink from the tiny glass, savoring the orange flavored liqueur as it burst inside his nostrils. "Ahhh," he whispered in satisfaction. "I really enjoy this stuff."

Jake took a sip. "So, if it's not Libby, then what? Do you have concerns about going to Baghdad that you'd like to talk about?"

"No, it's not about going to Iraq. It's something else. Back at that house I had a chance to really talk with the professor, and when you think you're about to die, you share a lot of personal stuff. I even told him about Peaceful Eagle."

Jake leaned forward. "Robert, you realize that could jeopardize things, put all of us in danger."

"I knew it was risky but you have to understand, after a few days in that cellar, we really began to trust each other. And the truth is it was Yusef who finally convinced the Hezbollah commander that I had to speak with an influential Shiite cleric, one who had contacts with the Mullahs in Tehran."

"So, that's how you got them to set up the meeting in Baghdad?"

"Yes, and there were other things he shared that have opened my eyes to an even greater potential for Peaceful Eagle." Robert reached for his glass, turned it up and swallowed half a cordial of the liqueur.

"There was a moment when my teacher said that he wished all sponsors of terrorism in the region could be forced to sit down together and work out a framework for a lasting peace, that above all else, peace is what the people of the Middle East truly want.

Then Yusef laughed out loud and said he wasn't sure that would ever happen."

"A greater potential for Peaceful Eagle," Jake repeated and smiled at his old friend, the way he did when they were young boys playing sandlot baseball in North Carolina. It was always Robert who made sure everyone got to play, even the heavy-set boy with bright red hair whose mother worked nights in a diner; the same one that winced every time he went up to bat, closed his eyes, took a big swing and struck out every time. But Robert was still encouraging like a little league coach and sent him out to play right field where the ball was seldom hit.

"You're a good person," Jake said with a comforting smile. "Sometimes I regret getting you involved with the NDR."

Robert closed his eyes and recalled a tragic memory. "Guess it was like you said, after my wife and son died in that car crash… I needed something to snap me back to reality, get me back in the game. And I believe Dare would want me to do something useful with my life." He looked up hopefully at his childhood friend, "Don't you?"

Invoking the name of Virginia Dare Faircloth brought back memories of a kind, loving woman with flowing blond hair, deep blue eyes and a heart-warming smile that revealed her good nature. It was an image that always softened Jake's heart and he smiled sympathetically as he reached out and touched his old friend on the shoulder. "Okay, I'm listening. What's on your mind?"

Robert poured another glass of liqueur and leaned forward. "I think I've come up with an incredible plan for a peace ultimatum in the Middle East, a test of nuclear brinksmanship that cannot be denied."

Jake stared curiously at his old friend as he lifted a glass to his lips and drew deeply. "I'm intrigued, Robert. Sounds like you've been doing some serious thinking."

"I have, and this is what I've come up with. I want to hijack the eagle and expand the target list from one city to three."

Jake swallowed hard, coughing on liqueur that seemed to have gone down his windpipe and it took a few seconds to recover. "Robert, what are you saying?" He couldn't finish the sentence for coughing. Finally his throat cleared, "I'm not sure the prince would want us tinkering with the King's plan."

"That's just it, Jake. It won't be the King's plan anymore. It will be ours, sort of an Alpha-Omega strategy."

Jake stared incredulously. "What the hell does that mean?"

"Alpha, a new beginning, or Omega, the end of everything for three major cities in the Middle East."

"Three," Jake repeated. "But it still sounds like Peaceful Eagle."

"It is Peaceful Eagle, but with an expanded target list and much broader goals. Three jets and three nuclear weapons flying over three major cities in the Middle East."

Jake looked around to see if anyone might be listening. They were sitting four tables away from the nearest customers. Even passersby engrossed in their own banter were walking too fast to hear their conversation.

"Divide twenty-four by four," Robert said quickly, "and you have six megatons. That's nearly twice the size of the warhead on one of our Intercontinental Ballistic Missiles and more than enough to destroy any city in the world. That is," and a slight smile crossed his face, "if they should force us to implement the Omega option which we would never do."

"No blowing up three cities?"

"No, but we play it as if we would. What if we put three jets above three cities and gave each country the opportunity to concede to a very reasonable set of demands or face having their cities destroyed."

"Concede to what?" Jake asked intently. "Besides, the Mullahs in Iran are pretty hard core. They won't believe we will actually detonate a nuclear weapon til we do it."

"So, we'll detonate a weapon," Robert replied, "just like in Peaceful Eagle, drop one in a desert area of Saudi Arabia to prove to everyone that our threat is real."

"Wait," Jake said waving his hand in front of his face. "Three targets. What are they, and more importantly, why?"

The Targets

Café du Blanc, Paris

"TEHRAN, MECCA AND JERUSALEM," Robert answered with a grin on his face.

"Tehran like in Peaceful Eagle, Mecca because it's the center of the Islamic world, and Jerusalem the center of the Christian and Jewish faiths."

"Holy shit! Are you out of your mind?" Jake glanced around to see if anyone might be watching. "I understand why the Saudis want to target Tehran because of their nuclear weapons program, but why Jerusalem?"

"Because in a unique way Israel is also a sponsor of terrorism in the Middle East."

"Whoa, Robert, are you really saying Israel is a terrorist nation?"

"Inside Israel there are ultra orthodox groups terrorizing the Palestinians in the occupied territories and very few people in America understand this."

"Robert, every Christian, Jew, and Muslim in the world considers Jerusalem to be a holy city? I mean there are people in America that would rather see New York City destroyed than Jerusalem. Do you understand what I'm saying?"

"That's what I'm counting on," Robert said calmly. "And granted, terrorism in Israel pales in comparison to what the Wahabbists have done through their splinter organizations and what the Mullahs in Iran are supporting in Lebanon and Iraq. But the Israeli extremists are also guilty. Let me explain."

"Okay, I'm listening, but this better be good." Jake refilled their glasses.

Robert stared into the golden liqueur, his eyes growing narrow and his expression grim. "It's hard to comprehend that the Middle Eastern foreign policy of the most powerful nation in history is being held hostage to the ultra orthodox ideology of a relatively small number of Messianic Zionists. But America's unwavering support of Israel has created such an irony.

"It may be rooted in the belief that Israel is a democracy like our own, forged out of the mythical wilderness of Palestine into a shining example of what a free and independent nation can become. But, Jake, I've discovered that Israel has a cultural malignancy every bit as intolerant as the Wahhabists of Saudi Arabia, potentially as militant as al-Queda and as fanatical as the Nazis in Germany."

"Really, Jewish Nazis," Jake said with a mocking smile.

Robert leaned forward. "Conservative orthodox parties have always been a part of Jewish life, but the Messianic Zionists have a vision of a third and final rebuilding of the temple to prepare the way for the return of the Messiah. It's a relatively new form of chauvinism among the ultra nationalists. They are using religious bigotry and divine rationalization to demonize the Palestinians in the occupied areas, take their land, and further their vision of an expanded Jewish theocratic state."

"It began after the Six Day War in 1967, the third in a series of victories by the Israelis over the Arab nations of Egypt, Jordan and Syria. Those victories confirmed to the extremists that the 1800 year-old Diaspora, the dispersion of the Jews, was over and that Israel had finally returned to favor under Yahweh. They believe that as long as they follow a strict interpretation of the Mishnah teachings in the Talmud that God will finally allow Israel to fulfill its biblical destiny, a return to the greatness of the Kingdom of David, or the Hasmonean Dynasty of the Maccabeans."

"Sounds like somebody's been doing their homework," Jake said with a smile.

"I know you don't have much time to read, Jake, but books like *The Unmaking of Israel* and *The History of Jewish Terrorism in Israel* would give you a better picture of where this aggressive new ultra orthodox chauvinism may be taking the Israelis."

Jake sat back in his chair considering what Robert was telling him. "Okay, you said this ultra orthodox movement began after the Six Day War. Tell me more, but just the big picture, okay."

"Jake, it's difficult to explain without some detail, that there are ultra orthodox groups inside Israel and through their radical actions are beginning to undermine western support for the state of Israel."

"All right, Robert, some details but not too much."

Robert leaned back in his chair, his eyes diverted to a young couple walking by on the sidewalk. "In the early 70s, an ultra-nationalist rabbi by the name of Meir Kahane emigrated from New York to Israel and he lit the fire under the modern Messianic Zionist Movement. He got things organized and his radical message began spreading to all the conservative synagogues in Israel. That's when radicalized extremist groups like Gush Emunim began emerging and offering their support to any political party that would back their cause for expanding Israel.

"They were officially banned as a political organization, but the Kahane or Kach movement continued to grow especially among the *yeshivish*, or new emigrants. With growth comes votes, and with votes comes political power, and that's how the radical groups began to influence the social and political agenda of Israel.

"Shimon Peres, Minister of Immigration in the early 70s, needed land for the new immigrants and he persuaded Yitzhak Rabin, the Prime Minister, to allow new settlements in the occupied territory of Samaria. Those settlements fit perfectly with the Messianic vision for a new Israel and the ultra orthodox encouraged their members to volunteer and move to the new hilltop compounds."

"So, that was the beginning of the settlement movement in Israel?"

"Just the beginning, Jake. In the late 1970s, Prime Minister Menachem Begin quietly instituted the Israeli policy of retaining the territories captured by Israel in the previous wars."

"Begin," Jake said with an appreciative nod of his head. "Now that guy was one hell of a terrorist?"

"Really?"

"Hell, yeah! Right after World War II, during the campaign to expel the British from Palestine, he practically wrote the blueprint for modern terrorism. He left Haganah, the main-stream organization, to help create Irgun, a radical group that embraced violence to remove the British and create a new Jewish homeland.

"In 1946, Irgun initiated the first terrorist mass murder in modern history when they blew up the King David Hotel in down-town Jerusalem. They killed 91 people and injured another 45 including innocent women and children. And the world press just glossed over the atrocity making it clear there was no safe place for the British while they tried to fulfill their Mandate in Palestine."

"Well, you know what they say, Jake, one man's terrorist is another man's freedom fighter."

"Yeah, and an eye for an eye creates a lot of blind people. Anyway, terrorists all over the world learned from Irgun how to use violence to achieve their political goals. The author of *The Handbook for Urban Guerilla War* credited Begin for creating mod-ern urban warfare tactics. So, it's no wonder that with his philoso-phy, extremist groups were tolerated and their message allowed to seed and grow within orthodox synagogues."

"Well, now the chickens have come home to roost," Robert added, "just like in all those radical Islamist madrassas throughout the Middle East. Extremist ideologies have a way of evolving into movements, like al-Queda in Afghanistan and the ultra nationalists in Israel."

Jake leaned forward. "But wasn't it the Arab coalitions that initiated the conflicts you mentioned and doesn't the winner enjoy the spoils of war? Besides, the Israelis have tried negotiating captured lands for peace with the Palestinians, but it was Fatah, and now Hamas that say they won't stop fighting until the Israelis have been pushed into the sea?

"Israel did return the Sinai Peninsula to Egypt and that has secured a degree of peace with the Egyptians. So, if Yasser Arafat and the Palestinian Liberation Organization had been a little more truthful and reliable after signing the Olo Peace Accords in 1993, especially after he and Rabin shook hands... "

"I know, Jake, but bless his heart, it turned out Arafat was even more of a terrorist than Begin with his own agenda of self-preservation within the Palestinian Authority."

Jake laughed. "Bless his heart... you still sound like a southern boy."

Robert shook his head in frustration. "So, now on one side we have the Jewish Home Party with all the right wing Zionist groups under its wing and on the other Hamas, Fatah and Hezbollah, and each with their own agenda."

"You know, Robert, I've heard some leaders in the Israeli army claim the real problem in the West Bank isn't the Palestinians, but the Jewish settlers. Whenever anyone from the Israeli Defense Force goes to talk with them fights always break out. And whenever the IDF destroys an illegal settlement the settlers take revenge on the local Palestinians."

"It's the vigilante groups, Jake. Have you heard of Defending Shield and Terror Against Terror? They're responsible for a lot of attacks and vandalism against the Palestinian farmers in the occupied territories. At the settlement of Bat Ayin someone shot and killed a Palestinian farmer working in his own olive grove. They said he was working too close to their compound. And when the IDF came to investigate, a rock-throwing fist-fight broke out because they feared being thrown out by their government."

Jake sat back thoughtfully. "So, you're saying that through our support of Israel, we appear to be endorsing these radical ultra orthodox groups." He shook his head gently. "I don't think the average American has a clue about our foreign policy with Israel and what we may actually be supporting."

Robert sipped the last of the liqueur in his glass then held it up for Jake to refill. "It was a shock to me, too. I can certainly understand why Israelis are pissed off at the Palestinians, because of all the death and destruction from suicide bombings and rocket attacks. But I think both the Palestinians and the Israelis ought to be pissed off at their governments for screwing up so many opportunities to resolve this conflict in the past."

"Israel isn't going anywhere, Robert. You know that, and sadly, they may never have peace with the Arab world as long as they continue to build settlements in the occupied territories."

"Just seems to me, Jake, that the basis for the terrorism in Israel is the government policy of retaining Arab territories captured in previous wars and evicting Palestinians from their farms so the land can be resettled by Israelis."

There was a lingering moment of silence between the two men as they considered the decades of futility and conflict between the Israelis and Palestinians. "So you think someone's going to have to force the hand of the Israeli government?"

"It has to be forced, Jake. They can't do it on their own without losing support within their ruling coalition. They must be given the face-saving choice of rescuing Jerusalem or supporting the agenda of the ultra nationalist orthodox groups."

There was an 'aha' look in Jake's eyes but then his expression changed to one of concern. "You aren't really suggesting we detonate a nuclear weapon over Jerusalem?"

"Heavens, no!" Robert exclaimed. "But the Israeli government has to believe we have a nuclear weapon on board and that we will destroy their city. It's a deadly form of brinksmanship, pursuing a hazardous course of action right up to the edge of insanity."

"But we're not going to detonate anywhere?"

"Just the demonstration detonation in the Saudi desert to use as leverage for our demands, then we'll see what happens. And because our demands are reasonable I believe the Israelis, Iranians and even the Saudis will concede."

"Mecca, during the Hajj… that's pretty good, Robert. Should be three million Muslim pilgrims there from all over the world. Talk about leverage against the Saudis."

"Jake, you do know the Saudi Royal Family is financing the spread of Sunni Muslim communities throughout the world. They call it *The Project.*"

"Yeah, I've heard about it. They're using the liberal immigration policies of western nations and their massive wealth to buy influence, building mosques and creating Sunni Muslim centers where ever they can."

"What they're doing is perfectly legal, Jake. As long as they do it gradually and peacefully there is nothing in western law to stop them, at least not yet. Can you imagine the influence they must already have in America, buying politicians, donating to educational and medical institutions, even monuments to America's Gulf war heroes."

"Pretty slick if you ask me," Jake said as he sipped from his glass. "But what can you do? If someone wants to convert to Islam and become a Muslim then that's their right of religious freedom."

"It's a new kind of holy war, Jake, a peaceful take over of the West."

"Wow!" Jake said in admiration. "Anywhere in the world there's a Sunni presence, the Saudis are financing the construction of mosques. And all they have to do is keep it peaceful and legal, and one day... "

"It's happening through their international charities," Robert added. "The International Islamic Relief Organization, the World Assembly of Muslim Youth and the Charitable Foundation of al-Haramain. All of them channel money to Sunni based organizations around the world especially in Europe and America."

Robert stared down the sidewalk toward the steps that led up to the basilica. "Isn't that how Osama bin Laden got his start in Afghanistan?"

"Yeah," Jake replied. "He was sent over by the Muslim World League to coordinate their charitable programs, but what he mostly did was organize, finance and supply the Mujahedeen, Muslim resistance fighters. And that's how he learned to set-up al-Queda. It's like international dominoes, one bad thing leading to another."

"Okay," Jake said in agreement, "the Saudis are a viable target, but why Mecca?"

"Brinksmanship. The Saudis are keepers of the most holy sites in Islam. Once the Islamic world realizes Mecca is about to be destroyed, along with nearly three million pilgrims, then other Muslim nations will bring pressure on the Saudis to agree to terms."

"You really believe that, Robert?"

"I do. Islam is a very passionate religion. When stirred, Muslims are capable of incredible feats of courage and stamina and this time their energies will be directed toward the Saudis. Their choice is to reign in the Wahhabists, the primary source of all Sunni extremism throughout the world, or lose Mecca and millions of pilgrims."

Jake looked thoughtfully up the staircase toward Sacre Coeur. "So you want to hijack the King's plan and turn it into another kind of Peaceful Eagle. I think I understand the concept, Robert, but I'm not sure what the demands are for each country."

Robert grinned, reached for the bottle of liqueur and topped off their glasses. "You're gonna love this part, Jake."

The Demands

Paris

"WE HAVE TO KEEP the terms simple and viable. We cannot demand anything they can't accomplish or are unwilling to do in order to save their cities. For the Israelis there are four reasonable demands.

"One… immediately cease construction of all settlements in the occupied territories. Two… begin the process of negotiation to remove settlers from illegal settlements, because now we know these are mostly hard line extremists inside Israel. Three… agree to face-to-face peace negotiations with both Fatah and Hamas. The goal is a fair and viable two state solution, Jake, with secure borders that both the Israelis and Palestinians can agree upon.

"And four… the Israeli government must find a way to diminish the political influence of their radical elements or face the loss of military and financial support from the West, especially the United States." Robert fell back in his chair as if to signal he was ready for a response.

"Ambitious," Jake said, "I'm impressed. Now, how about the Saudis?"

Robert leaned forward. "One… the government, which really means the Royal Family, must crack down hard on the Wahabbits. Radical teachings that advocate Sunni terrorist groups initiate violence against non-believers can no longer be tolerated and clerics who do not respond must be removed."

"That may be harder for the Saudi government than you realize, Robert."

"Kings have done such things before, Jake. Remember when Phillip of France wanted to get rid of the Templar Knights in 1308? He initiated a secret plan to remove them, and in one night they were all arrested and charged with heresy based on their secret initiation practices.

"He burned several knights at the stake as a means of extracting confessions and used that as evidence to influence Pope Clement to withdraw their papal commission and dissolve the order. That was it for the Knights Templar in Europe and the Middle East."

Jake fell back in his seat laughing, then whispered, "So you want King Khalid to burn a few Wahhabitsts at the stake?"

"Whatever it takes, Jake, but you know those fanatical clerics will not go away as long as they can stir up trouble inside Saudi Arabia. So, yeah, he may have to cut the heads off a few snakes."

"Okay, I get it, Robert. What else for the Saudis?"

"Two... that they pursue a legal code of human rights for all Saudis, including women, similar to those that have been introduced by other progressive Muslim nations. Jake, Saudi women aren't even allowed to drive vehicles. Can you believe in this day and age such draconian measures are still in place?"

Jake laughed. "You know, that may be tougher than having them clamp down on the Wahhabists."

"I know, but the Saudi Royal family has extraordinary influence in the Sunni world. If they agree and set the example, it will not only spread through Saudi Arabia, but within all Muslim countries in the Middle East and beyond." Robert leaned back in his chair.

"That's it for the Saudis?"

"That's a lot for the Saudis, Jake, compared to where they're at now."

"Okay, what are the demands for the Iranians?"

"One... immediately end the program to enrich uranium into weapons grade material. In exchange the West will offer support for the development of facilities for peaceful applications of nuclear energy. Two... stop supplying Hezbollah and Hamas with military weapons and help convert these militant organizations into non-violent political parties. Then the West will agree to help fund the development of educational and institutional projects inside Gaza, the West Bank and Southern Lebanon.

"And three... Iran must use its influence to help diffuse tensions between the West and militant Shiites throughout the Muslim world. Western nations will then encourage their Sunni allies to reduce support for the militant Wahhabists in Saudi Arabia and Egypt and also the Taliban and their violent initiatives in Pakistan and Afghanistan. And by the way, that's already step one for the Saudis."

"Going for the whole ball of wax, aren't you?"

"Well, when you're about to go nuclear, Jake, you've raised the bar pretty high. So, the demands need to be equivalent to the threat, don't you think?"

Peanuts

Faro, NC

"DANGEROUS WORK," Vladimir Petrovski emphasized, as he stood beside a stainless steel table inside the underground bunker. He was discussing the delicate work of removing the nuclear material from the old three-stage warhead. "Anyone inside exposed to deadly radiation. I do this alone."

"How long will it take?" Rufus asked.

"Four or five hours, maybe more. I remove uranium and plutonium fuel to make sure is viable. If all is good, I re-assemble each stage inside new Secondary Containment Encasement and call you when work is done."

Rufus stepped up to the Russian. "I'm especially interested in the reassembly technique, the placement of the fuel and high explosive inside the SCE."

"Yessss," Vladimir said, slurring the word. "Exact tolerance critical or get poof instead of bang."

Rufus didn't smile at the joke and Vlad hurried along. "So, yes, the video. I give proper audio instruction as I proceed like on autopsy tape," and he smiled as if he thought that, too, should be humorous.

Rufus only nodded his head and curled his lips in a near smile. "That will be helpful," then he left the bunker.

The old scientist donned a protective suit and a lead-lined apron that extended from neck to boots. Then he placed a bell-helmet over his head and put on thick gloves as he began the delicate task of removing the uranium and plutonium from a fifty year-old containment vessel.

The twelve-foot long bomb was lying on its side secured on sturdy stainless steel tables placed end to end inside the bunker. Vladimir used a hand-held power wrench to remove the old bolts that held what remained of the fluted tail section. The parachute and surrounding tail fins had broken lose in 1961, as it penetrated the earth, but as far as he could tell, no water or dirt had penetrated the titanium bottom plate.

As he continued working Petrovski's broken English transformed into a near perfect discourse on the attributes of the Mark-41. "It was an American prototype nuclear weapon, meaning it was never officially test fired. It is an extension of the typical two-stage fission-fusion boosted weapons of the period, but in order to increase the yield, a third plutonium booster was added to increase the output to 24 megatons.

"Each stage is itself like a small nuclear reactor, but instead of applying the energy to boil water to create steam to drive electric generating turbines, this power is used to create a very powerful blast with a highly destructive nuclear wind."

Vladimir didn't know that a live feed of the video was being monitored inside the warehouse office or that his scientific ramblings were not appreciated by the man observing him. "Son of a bitch," Rufus whispered under his breath. "It's not a performance, Vlad. We don't need the history of nuclear weapons. Just do the job."

Rufus listened to the dry commentary for over an hour until Vladimir began removing the three internal stages of the thermonuclear weapon. The one-foot wide by two-foot long peanut-shaped packages were laid out on tables behind the scientist. "Here we have the three stages of the Mark 41," he said calmly and pointed at the first metallic skinned tube.

"High explosives are electronically fired in the American Swan style primary. They are shaped to compress a Plutonium-239 hollow-point core into super criticality, beginning a Tritium and Deuterium fusion-boosted implosion that will emit high energy X-rays along the peanut-shaped channels into the secondary."

He pointed at another elongated peanut. "Here an external polystyrene foam is instantaneously heated into a fiery plasma generator which compresses a U-235 sparkplug, further compressing the Lithium-6 Deuteride fuel into tritium and generating neutrons for a sustained fusion reaction in the secondary. Sufficiently heated and compressed, the Lithium-6 Deuteride fuel begins a fusion reaction that generates fission in the U-235 pusher and U-238 casing.

Rufus rolled his eyes and shook his head briskly trying to stay focused on the monotonous video. "Move it, Petrov," he whispered, "hurry it up."

Vladimir paused and reached up with gloved hands to rub his sweating neck. "Very warm inside this thing," he said then leaned back to stretch before continuing. "In conventional nuclear weapons of the period these two segments, in sequence, would yield ten to fifteen megatons depending on the amount of fuel in the secondary. But in the Mark-41, a third experimental fission stage was added," and he pointed at the last metallic skinned peanut-shaped vessel on the table.

"The tremendous heat from the secondary would be channeled around this tertiary stage to compress an additional plutonium core and its external uranium fuel into fission yielding, in sequence with the other two stages, another 10 megatons. A very powerful weapon indeed and this is typical of the thermonuclear weapons carried by U.S. Strategic Air Command bombers during the 1960s."

Even while Petrovski continued with the lecture Rufus was thinking about the three stages of the Mark-41, *each one a nuclear weapon itself*, and that's when he saw the Russian scientist add something to each stage.

"Here we have the boron tamper that will increase the compression rate and yield of each stage... " But Rufus was sure there were no tampers when Petrovski took the stages apart. *Son of a bitch*, he thought to himself, *he added those things, but why?*

He listened intently as Vladimir continued and noticed an inflection in the old man's voice as he explained how to reassemble the three stages. *Is that a sign of deception?*

Agitated Rufus rose from his chair concerned the Russian was up to mischief. *Better have Khan check that out when he gets here this evening.* He paced nervously inside the office concerned that the scientist might be trying to undermine Peaceful Eagle.

Just after 1600 hours Petrovski called to explain that all the nuclear fuel had been inspected, reassembled and placed inside the three peanut-shaped cylinders, and that it was safe for Rufus to return to the bunker.

"What the hell's he doing? Doesn't Vlad know that you don't mess with Jake Eastwood? I mean he's Dante for Christ's sake and he kills people for shit like this."

Maybe he's got a case of last minute conscience, Rufus thought. *No, he wouldn't give up a million dollar payday and a green card for that.* He stared at the monitor watching the activity in the bunker.

Could he be working for someone else, some agency we don't know about? Then he shook his head. *No, or we would have heard through our contacts at INTERPOL or the CIA. I'll just give him his vodka and send him back to the apartment. If he's playing games Khan will know, and then I'll call Jake.*

Rufus pulled the videocassette from the recorder and walked back to the rambling farmhouse. The Germans were in the kitchen finishing another case of Carlsburg. "Have a beer," Gunter shouted from across the room, "plenty more in the refrigerator."

The technicians were in high spirits having received $5,000 cash bonus payments for their work on the farm. They were discussing among themselves whether to return home immediately or extend their stay in America and enjoy themselves at a famous South Carolina resort all of them had heard about. Their unexpected surplus could be well spent in the bars, restaurants and strip joints of Myrtle Beach.

Rufus drank a beer with Gunter and his crew then went to a rear bedroom where he dialed an encrypted phone number. "Oh shit, Jake's not gonna like this."

Robert's Plan

Paris

JAKE TAPPED HIS FINGERS on the tablecloth then retrieved the bottle of Grand Marnier and poured the last of it into their glasses. "So, after detonating a nuclear weapon in the Saudi desert you want to play a game of nuclear brinksmanship over three major cities in the Middle East, putting millions of people's lives at risk?" He put the empty bottle down and smiled to himself.

"I agree with you in principle, Robert, that if it were to work it would be a significant contribution to peace in the Middle East, but I can also think of several reasons why it may not."

Robert interrupted. "Jake, if you really believe that Peaceful Eagle has a chance to succeed in Iran then you have to consider that my version has at least a small chance to succeed with Israel and Saudi Arabia. But I've said enough. It's your turn to talk. I'm willing to listen."

"Good, now let's start with the three weapons. Actually, it's not the weapons, it's getting our hands on three jet aircraft. Right now with the prince's help, we have access to one Strike Eagle, but three, Robert, I just don't know."

"Jake, I've been giving this a lot of thought and what I figured out is that where there's one Saudi F-15, there are many more. I've already checked out the military side of the Abdul Aziz Airport in Jeddah and they have three squadrons stationed there.

So, if you're going to take one, then why not three? I don't know how to do it but you're the kind of man that can figure it out."

Robert reached over with his right hand and shook Jake's disbelieving knee. "I've already worked out the timing for the three jets to arrive over their targets at the very same time. It wasn't that hard even for a civilian like me."

"But getting a Saudi F-15 into Israeli airspace without being detected, that will be hard to do, Robert. They have those Gulf Stream jets fitted with Phalcon Airborne Early Warning radar systems that can sweep the skies for 200 miles. And if they detect a Saudi aircraft entering their airspace they would more than likely light it up with a missile, shoot it down and ask questions later."

"I know, Jake, but all AWAC systems have weaknesses, especially down looking radar that tries to track aircraft low on the deck, and especially over water."

"You've been reading up on these things?"

"Yes, I have, Jake, and I'm sure the new guy in North Carolina, the one that flew F-15s in the first Gulf War, I bet he knows some evasion tricks that can help a jet get into Israeli airspace and over Jerusalem before they can target it."

Jake studied his old friend for a moment before asking the next question. "Okay, Robert, what if we make four bombs, get them to Jeddah, steal three F-15 jets, drop one bomb in the Saudi desert and get the others over their targets, then what?"

Robert grinned and leaned back. "That's when the game of nuclear brinksmanship begins and tell me, Jake, what nation in the world would let one of its most important cities be destroyed rather than at least verbally agree to the terms we demand?"

"That's another thing, Robert. What if they do agree, then what? And when we reach the targets we will only have a couple hours of fuel left. So, how do we play the game in three places at the same time?"

"You're gonna love this, Jake, satellite phones."

Jake looked curiously at his old friend. "You mean the jets will have satellite phones in the cockpit," and he nodded as he considered the idea. "Okay, keep going."

"As each jet approaches its target city, the pilots will call a pre-determined number where they will be put on a conference call. So, all three will be in direct communication with each other and will know exactly what is happening over each target."

"Damn, Robert, that's pretty good. You have put a lot of thought into this."

"It gets better, not only will the three pilots be in touch with ground control over their targets and with each other by satellite phone, but the number they call will simultaneously be connected to major media outlets throughout the world. This is how you seriously leverage brinksmanship," Robert added excitedly.

"The entire world will be listening to everything you say to the leaders of Iran, Saudi Arabia and Israel. Your satellite phone will be monitored live by the BBC, Al Jazeera and CNN. People all over the world will hear you, Jake, when you make your demands and when they hear that they are reasonable, they will hold world leaders accountable to the agreement."

Jake fell back in his seat. "Audacious, Robert, that's a brilliant twist and there's nothing like the audacity of an incredibly ambitious idea. Technically, we may be able to do this, but what if…"

The smiles vanished from their faces as each man considered the possibility that one or more of the target nations might not believe they have a nuclear weapon on board and refused to concede. "It's a possibility, Jake, and that's why we're going to have an American intelligence agency helping us."

"You gotta be kidding, Robert!"

"You and Rufus are going to make sure that the CIA and FBI know that a top secret nuclear bomb has been removed from the ground. They'll begin a high priority investigation and will verify to NATO and the United Nations that nuclear grade uranium and plutonium have been stolen from America, and may be on its way to the Middle East.

"Get it, Jake, now we have an intelligence agency and a nuclear explosion to verify that we have viable nuclear weapons on board the jets."

"But, Robert, what if… you know what I'm asking?"

"It could happen with the King's plan, Jake. What if Tehran didn't believe there was a nuclear weapon or refused to concede to Khalid's terms, then he would be faced with the same alternative. It's like you said before, what government in the world wouldn't at least verbally agree to save one of its largest cities?

"And it may be worth the entire effort to have them do that publicly in front of the whole world."

"All right," Jake said, and reached over to pat his old friend reassuringly on the leg. "Now, let's assume everyone agrees, then what?"

"Your last demand is to land and refuel your aircraft, because by then you will be low on fuel."

"But will they allow us to land with a nuclear warhead on board?"

"Really, Jake, what choice do they have? The weapon could go off at 2,000 feet with an optimum explosion radius or possibly on the tarmac of an airport. It's not a good choice for them, but it's better than having it go off in the air.

"You also tell them that since they have agreed to the terms and you believe they will follow through, that after you refuel you will fly to a location where the nuclear weapons can be safely disposed of, but any last second attempt to keep the jet on the ground will result in a detonation."

Jake nodded his head as if in agreement. "Let's see, in Tehran that will be the Imam Khomeini International Airport just north of the city. King Khalid International is on the north side of Riyadh, and for Jerusalem it will be the David Ben Gurion Airport west of the city."

He thought a moment longer. "Okay, let's be optimistic, Robert. Say we have given them our demands and the whole world has heard them concede live on major media networks. So we land refuel then take off again. Now, where do we go?"

Robert leaned forward. "Who can we give the bombs to that will make sure they are defused and never fall into the hands of any terrorist nation?"

"England, France, the United States?"

"But who has the closest airport?"

"I bet you've already checked it out?"

"The Ali Al Salem Air Base in Kuwait, a joint U.S. and Kuwaiti installation. It's just east of a mid-point that is equidistant from all three targets."

"And who are you considering for our three pilots?"

"You and Annalisa, and the new guy, Duke Disisto, an experienced F-15 pilot."

Jake gave him a skeptical look. "Don't count on Annalisa for this, Robert. Even if she agreed, I'm not sure I want her to do it." He paused in thought. "So, what happens when the jets land in Kuwait?"

"U.S. personnel will take possession of the warheads and the Kuwaitis will see that the F-15s are returned to the Saudis. Everyone wins, Jake," he said with a satisfied expression on his face.

"What happens to the pilots?"

"Surrender to the Kuwaitis. After a few days Nalum Taylor can arrange to have everyone flown to an independent nation for a well earned vacation."

"What about Khan, our Pakistani scientist? He's going with us to Jeddah."

"As soon as the F-15s taxi out of their hangar, he takes the first plane from Jeddah to where ever he needs to go."

"And you, Robert, where will you be?"

"Back in Paris or maybe Baghdad. As the only known representative of the NDR, I'll be making the circuit from Jerusalem to Tehran to Riyadh, speaking with anyone who will listen explaining that following up with the concessions is the best course of action for everyone."

Jake stared down the street toward the steps leading up to the basilica of Sacre Coeur. Even at this late hour there were tourists still roaming up and down the staircase, taking advantage of the fabled view of the lights of Paris. "I can see you've put a lot of thought into this, Robert. As long as everything goes exactly as planned it could work, but you know what Robert Burns said about the 'best laid plans of mice and men'?"

"I know," Robert said cautiously. "Even the best of plans can get fouled up, and usually from something no one anticipated."

"You understand, Robert, that even if everything works any one of the three countries may refuse to follow through with their concessions, especially Iran. I mean, once the nuclear threat is gone… "

"But the entire world will have heard them agree, Jake. The whole world will have seen a vision for a lasting peace in the Middle East, without Iran or any other nation having to go nuclear."

Jake smiled at the man he had known since childhood, lifted his glass with the remainder of the fine liqueur and gave a toast. "Here's to my good friend, Robert Faircloth. Perhaps one day when this is over, you might receive recognition."

Robert smiled in appreciation. "Then my plan will be put into play?"

Jake leaned back in his chair and looked reflectively up the hill toward Sacre Coeur. "It's ironic, Robert. I read something the other day about this being the most peaceful time in the history of the world, that as humans have become better educated murder, rape and all other types of violence have all decreased, and less people are dying in wars."

"Sounds counter-intuitive," Robert responded, "with all the violence you read about in the papers and see on television."

"I agree, but according to the article, as people have become smarter they are choosing to think for themselves rather than rely on political and religious dogma. Democracies are increasing, autocracies are decreasing and wars are much less deadly than they used to be. And yet," Jake continued, " since the end of the Cold War, the United States has been at war, of one kind or another, for 14 of the last 21 years."

"Peacekeeper for the world."

"Nope, that's the United Nations job," Jake retorted, "but America's defense budget is larger than nearly all other countries in the world combined."

"Really!" Robert exclaimed.

"It's true," Jake said as he looked down inside his empty cordial. "And just think, in a single instant a nuclear detonation over a population center could dramatically change all those historical statistics on death and destruction."

"But you will consider my plan, Jake?"

"I promise, Robert, I'll give it serious thought," then his satellite phone began chirping. "Gotta take this," he said. "It's from Rufus back at the farm."

"You need to get back here, Jake. Old Vlad is up to something. He may be trying to sabotage the project."

"What's he up to?"

"Not sure, but Khan thinks he's out of line with some of the procedures, like he's making the bombs but also making sure they won't detonate properly."

"Good thing we have Khan on board. I'll fly back tonight, Rufus," then he disconnected and looked grimly at Robert. "Gotta take another plane ride," and both men began walking back to the rented house on a hillside in Monmartre.

A Very Dirty Bomb

Faro, NC

WHEN JAKE RETURNED FROM Paris he was picked up and briefed by Rufus, then driven back to the farm. Later that afternoon the NDR Operations Director sat alone in the kitchen of the farmhouse reviewing the video of Vladimir's work on the bomb. He was considering what to do with the Russian so that he could still retain the effective service of Khan, the nuclear scientist from Pakistan.

At seven that evening a black mini van with tinted windows drove up to the farmhouse. "Right on time," Rufus said.

"Let's get Khan inside and go over the video," Jake responded. "Let him tell us whether or not Vlad knows what he's doing."

Khan sat in a chair in front of a large monitor sipping espresso and munching on barbeque flavored Frito chips. As he watched Petrovski begin to re-assemble the first stage he jerked straight up. "There, you see that? What is he doing?" he exclaimed in an agitated voice.

Jake's eyes flashed toward Rufus then back at Kahn. "Is that not the proper way to reassemble the primary?"

"Well, maybe," he responded, "if you want to make a huge dirty bomb, but not if you want a sustained nuclear reaction."

"Explain," Jake said tersely.

Khan leaned forward in his chair. "The boron tamper he put in there, it is detrimental to fission. It will absorb neutrons and the reaction will fizzle. No fission, no deuterium fusing with tritium, no thermonuclear explosion," he announced sharply. "Instead, the bomb will be torn apart and the blast energy only be equal to the high explosive used for initial detonation. It will at best be a very dirty bomb."

There was a moment of tense silence in the room until Rufus spoke. "Good thing we have Khan." He saw the anger in Jake's distant eyes and could tell the NDR leader was planning something special for Vladimir Petrovski.

A calm expression quickly returned to Jake's face and he asked the Pakistani, "Do you know how to reconstruct the Mark-41 to its original conditions?"

"Yes, I do," Khan responded quickly. "Any experienced nuclear weapons scientist should know how to do this. So what does he think he is doing? Doesn't he know I check his work every day?"

There was no response from either Jake or Rufus and for a moment silence filled the room. "He doesn't know?" Khan asked. "Oh, I thought he knew." Then he slipped back in his chair and resumed munching on Fritos.

Jake rose from his seat and walked toward a window. He seemed to be thinking deeply and without turning around addressed the Pakistani scientist. "How long will it take to open the sealed containment vessels and re-examine them?"

"Three, maybe four hours."

"And you will make a good quality video of the entire process?"

"Yes, if you wish."

Rufus jumped in. "Is there supposed to be a boron tamper in each stage?"

"Heavens, no," the Pakistani responded. "It is a safety device placed between the U-235 pusher and the U-238 casing during transport or for long term storage. It must be removed for effective critical mass to occur. The way he has it placed few neutrons will be released, certainly not enough to create a sustained reaction."

"It will not increase compression and yield."

"Certainly not. It will have the opposite effect."

"All right, Dr. Khan," Jake said calmly. "Let's leave the tampers in place for now and make sure we have precise assembly instructions."

"No problem," he responded in his thick Pakistani accented English. "We want the Saudis to be happy with their new weapon," he said in a matter of fact tone.

Jake flashed a concerned look at Rufus as he recalled what they had told the Pakistani to ensure his cooperation. "Our client must be satisfied, Khan, or they will not pay us." Then he glanced back at Rufus not sure if this were the right time to reveal the entire plan to the Pakistani.

"Dr. Khan, you know there are several new peanut shaped containment vessels in our lab, in addition to the ones removed from the M-41?"

"Yes, for back-up you said."

"Not exactly," Jake responded. He pulled a chair from the table and sat directly in front of the nuclear scientist. "Instead of one huge bomb, the Saudis want four smaller weapons. Do you understand? They want four small bombs."

Khan's eyes widened in shock. "For what? Only one is needed for deterrent, but four," and his eyes turned thoughtfully downward. "Besides, you cannot get four 6-megaton bombs out of this weapon. Perhaps three megatons each, but not six."

Jake glanced at Rufus as if the civil engineer should verify what the nuclear scientist was saying. "And why is that, Khan?"

"The three stages of the Mark-41 are designed to work together in a compound fashion each compressing the other to maximize yield. If the fissile material is separated there will be no compounding, reducing the yield to only the nuclear fuel in each stage."

Jake stared a moment longer at the scientist. "Three megatons," he repeated as he turned toward Rufus. "What do you think, shouldn't that be enough?"

"Damn right, Jake. Most American ICBMs have 3-megaton warheads, so I'd say this would be right in the ballpark."

"But why, Mr. Jake?" Khan asked. "Why do the Saudis want so many weapons?"

Jake looked over at Rufus to make sure that he was listening. "The Saudis have no nuclear program and no centrifuges to enrich uranium, at least none that any government in the world knows of. So, they want to detonate one of the bombs in an isolated desert area as a means of revealing that Saudi Arabia is a nuclear nation."

"Ah," Khan responded, "and that will be the deterrent," he said with a questioning tone. "But what of the other bombs?"

"The Saudi nuclear arsenal," Jake responded. "Two will be made available to the United Nation's International Atomic Energy Agency for inspection. Their secure position will be made known, and in case the Israelis, Iranians, or even the Americans destroy it, the Saudis will always be suspected of having another."

"Yes," the Pakistani said. "And in that case they will have another with which to deter the Iranians."

Jake leaned back in his chair with a satisfied expression on his face realizing the Pakistani scientist was accepting the new plan, or at least the version of it Jake wanted him to understand.

"So, you want me to prepare four smaller nuclear bombs instead of one large one. I get it," and he sat in his chair considering the task before him. "You know, it is good that we are working with a three stage weapon that utilized solid fuel lithium deuteride, rather than the liquid deuterium cylinders of the 1950s," he said thoughtfully.

"How's that?" Rufus asked.

"Much easier to handle," he replied, "but not so much the liquid cylinders; very high risk for leakage there." Then he nodded his head toward Jake, "Very good plan, yes. May I go to work now?"

As the Pakistani scientist left the house and walked toward the underground bunker, Rufus sat in his chair and glared at Jake. "What the hell's going on? I never heard this part of the plan."

"I know, Rufus. The plan is being modified from one target to possibly three."

"Holy shit!" Rufus yelped. "That's great," he exclaimed with a wide-eyed grin. "Really, we're gonna take out three targets in the Middle East?"

"One is definitely part of the plan, maybe two, and possibly three. It all depends on how successful Robert Faircloth is with his peace initiative. If by some small miracle he were to succeed, the bombs will be disarmed and probably destroyed."

"And if he doesn't?"

"Then," Jake said firmly, "Peaceful Eagle will fly by the end of this year." He paused a moment longer staring at his trusted associate. "You cannot mention this to anyone, not even inside the NDR. Do you understand?"

"Jake, you can trust me with anything. You know that."

Early the next morning Khan walked back inside the farmhouse and proudly reported, "You now have four thermonuclear weapons each with an estimated 3-megaton yield." He returned to his apartment with plenty of espresso and a large bag of his favorite barbeque flavored Frito chips.

Bad Ruski

Faro, NC

THE NEXT MORNING VLADIMIR arrived early ready to finish the job. He worked feverishly inside a one by four meter lead box that had been specially constructed by Duke Disisto in his shop on the Pamlico River. It was an exact replica of the keel for the Lightning Power Boat the Prince had ordered. The lead box was designed to hold all four bombs and shield the radioactive signature of the material being transported through the port at Morehead City.

Though surprised to discover four cylinders instead of the original three Vlad was anxious and in a hurry. He decided not to question Rufus or Jake as they carefully wrapped three-inch foam around the boron-tampered weapons. As they gently placed each one deep inside the foam filled box Jake was thinking about his final test for Petrovski, to make sure deception was his motive rather than safety concerns.

Another twelve-inch layer of foam was pressed over the containment vessels and with Jake and Rufus sitting on the lead cover, Vladimir used a small torch to seal the latches into place. "There," he shouted. "Finished! I am finished, yes?"

"Yes, you are," Rufus replied with a wink and a grin. He reached into his shirt pocket and pulled out a cashier's check, dangling it in his hand as he asked Vlad the test question. "Now explain to me again how the boron tampers will increase the rate of compression and the yield of each stage of the bomb."

Vlad's eyes widened as he stared back at Rufus like a deer caught in a spotlight. "Ugh," he stuttered conjuring his response. "You, see, it is very technical how a tamper can increase compression and how that in turn will increase yield. It would take some time to explain."

"Go ahead," Rufus said. "I've got all day."

Petrovski cleared his throat while his eyes flitted from side to side. He was not aware that Jake had slipped behind him and he barely felt the syringe sink into his neck and empty its contents.

"What the… " were the only words from the scientist's mouth as the drug flooded his brain and rendered him unconscious. He would not die, at least not until Khan could witness the fate of a man who had betrayed the NDR.

* * *

At seven o'clock that evening the black mini van drove up to the house as an eighteen-wheeler was pulling away from the farm. Inside the long trailer was a lead box, filled with enough nuclear weaponry to destroy any county in North Carolina. The truck was on its way to Duke Disisto's shop on the Pamlico River.

Khan was greeted warmly on the front steps by Rufus then taken inside. He was shocked at what he saw. The Russian scientist was sitting on a small wooden chair. A black cloth bag covered his head and his arms and legs were duct taped securely to the chair. At the sound of Khan's entrance, the Russian's head began twisting back and forth and a muffled groan was heard from under the bag.

Khan was horrified to see that IV lines had been inserted into each of Vladimir's arms and on the sides of the chair hung two large plastic bags. One was filled with three gallons of saline liquid. The other was empty. On the table in front of Jake was a vacuum pump connected to the IV lines.

Khan turned to start for the door but was caught by Rufus. "Whoa, hold on there, that's not for you. It's for that lying skunk in the chair, the one who tried to cheat us. Now have a seat over there next to Jake."

As Khan warily sat down Rufus walked around the table and pulled the black bag from Vlad's head. His eyes were bulging from their sockets and several swaths of grey duct tape were firmly in place over his mouth. He was petrified to see the lines inserted into his arms.

Jake turned to Khan. "You understand," he said calmly, "that Vlad tried to deceive us, and for this he must pay." Jake calmly reached forward and pressed the rocker switch on the pump. It hummed to life and the clear liquid in the bag on the left side of the chair ran up the line and into the Russian's right arm.

Vladimir squirmed and wrestled against his restraints, realizing he was being embalmed with saline. As the pressure of the solution began coursing through his veins, a thick red fluid drained into the bag on the right side of the chair. The Russian groaned, shook his head violently and let out a muffled scream.

Khan sat straight up in his chair, the horror reflected in his widened eyes as Jake continued. "Look at me, Kahn, look at me."

The Pakistani scientist turned slowly. "I did everything you asked. Everything," he repeated. "You have your bombs. Please, let me go. You can keep the money."

Jake spoke softly. "Look at this man who tried to cheat us. Look at what is happening to him." But Kahn could not look at his face, only at the floor and the bag that was pooling with blood.

"I want to ask you a few simple questions, and if you answer them correctly you will be paid." Jake stared a moment longer. "Are you ready to answer my questions?"

Kahn nodded his head trying not to hear the groans of the Russian at the end of the table. "Yes!" he squealed, "what questions?"

"Do we have four operational 3-megaton nuclear weapons?"

"Yes," he replied. "Yes, yes," he repeated. "You have four incredibly powerful thermonuclear bombs."

Jake then looked over at Rufus. "Would you mind giving us a moment? I have something very personal I need to discuss with Dr. Kahn."

Rufus was surprised. "Something you don't want me to hear, Jake?"

"Sorry, Rufus, but this is straight from Nalum Taylor."

To mention the NDR leader's name brought immediate deference. "Sure, Jake, I understand. I'll just step out in the yard."

Rufus went outside and immediately walked to a place where he could look back through the front window. He saw Jake lean in and begin asking questions. The Pakistani nodded his head. More questions followed by an explanation for each, and then he saw a look of enlightenment in the scientist's eyes.

Whatever Jake is telling Khan must really be good, Rufus thought to himself. After several more questions and answers Jake stood up and walked to the door. "Come on back in, Rufus."

Just like that, Rufus thought. *That didn't take long.*

"Kahn has agreed to accept the Russian's payment in addition to his own for ensuring that we have what we need, four operational nuclear weapons."

"Two million dollars," Rufus yelped. "You're gonna pay him two million bucks?"

"That's right."

"Damn, I should have studied nuclear engineering."

Jake looked back at the Pakistani who was stealing glances at the ashen-faced Russian. "He made a poor choice, Kahn, but you've made the right one.

"Here," he said extending his hand, "two cashiers checks, each for a million dollars made out to the bearer." He handed them to the dumbstruck scientist who only moments before believed he would die.

Jake turned to Rufus. "Dr. Khan has agreed to accompany me to Jeddah, Saudi Arabia, as a member of the Lightning team," and he smiled, "to make sure the Prince's new boat performs properly."

"Jake, you must have a big ol' horseshoe up your ass, 'cause everything seems to work out just the way you plan it. Man, we gotta get you to Vegas. With your luck we could make a killin' at the tables."

"Sorry, Rufus, I don't gamble. I only bet on sure things. And having Khan with me in Jeddah will make this a sure thing. But for now he'll stay with me at Duke's home on the Pamlico River."

"Great idea," Rufus added. "But what about the Russian?"

"No problem," Jake said as the vacuum pump continued to hum and suck the life out of the scientist. " He asked me the other day about going down inside the tunnel for a look. Well, he's going down to the aquifer level, but he won't be coming back."

."Oh," Rufus sighed, agreeing it was a good means of disposing of the body.

Kahn was ushered to the van while Jake made plans with Rufus to backfill the tunnel and remove any evidence that did not suggest a large farming operation was underway at the old Davies farm. Then Jake bid farewell to Rufus and left the farm, never to return.

The Lightning Boat

Beaufort County, NC

JAKE AND KHAN arrived late that evening at Duke DiSisto's shop on the Pamlico. The entire upper deck of Abdullah bin-Ghazi's new Speed Master was hanging in rigging above the concrete floor. Two 450 Mercruiser engines and a lead keel were all that was left inside the massive fiberglass hull sitting on the bed of the trailer. As Jake and the Pakistani scientist walked along a metal seam wall, Duke removed a protective mask and gauze cover from his face and stepped over to greet them.

"Hazardous stuff. You don't want to breathe any fiberglass into your lungs. Let's go in the corner office where we can talk." He led them through a door into a glass-paneled space that held two desks and several side chairs. "Have a seat, fellas."

Jake introduced Dr. Khan as the nuclear expert that would accompany them to Saudi Arabia. "How ya doin, Khan?" Duke said as he extended a hand to the new team member. Jake then inquired on the progress with the boat.

"Got started as soon as you called, but the deck was tough. They glue and screw those babies down pretty tight. She's up in the air now, so we have access to the hull."

Jake gave him a tired smile. "You're doing a great job here, Duke. Wish I could be more help, but not until I get some rest…"

"No problem. In another hour I'll be ready to switch the keel weights."

"Can you put the deck back on without anyone noticing it's been off?"

"Jake," he said with a gritty smile, "this is what I do, man. I pull parts off these decks all the time and I do my own fiberglass repair. Usually I tell them at the plant what I've done so they can inspect and make sure it's right for their customer," and then he grinned. "But not this time."

"How long till everything is done?" Jake asked.

"Should have the deck back on and the electronics in place by morning. But it will take twenty-four hours for the glue to set, and the fumes are pretty intense. We'll have to let it cure out back."

"Anything I can do?"

"Get some sleep, Jake, and you, too, Kahn. This thing should be ready for a quality assurance inspection in a couple of days. I'll ask the guys at the plant if I can make the test-run. I do that sometimes. After that they'll wrap it in plastic and crate it for shipment."

"And your time away from the shop, Duke; you have that cleared so they won't be surprised and start asking questions?"

"Thirty days, Jake, and longer if I need it. While I'm with you in Saudi Arabia they'll handle the electronics installation inside the plant. But they like for me to do it here because I do it cheaper and it clears their floor space for more hull and deck injection molds. Those things are huge," he said shaking his head.

Duke noticed Khan nervously clutching a pack of Turkish cigarettes. "Sorry, no smoking in the house but there's plenty of room outside on the deck."

"Yes," he replied meekly. "Can we please go, Jake? I need to smoke."

Jake smiled. "It's been a couple of hours since his last one. Guess I better get him to the house."

"Sure thing," Duke responded. "There are two bedrooms on the left that share a bath. Towels are in the cabinet below and help yourself to any stuff you find in there."

He stood beside the NDR leader. "Soon as I get things put back together I'll come to the house and we'll have some of the Prince's favorite liquor." He glanced at Khan. "Sorry, but some of my Muslim buddies enjoy good bourbon."

"That's okay," and Khan grinned at his host. "You know what they say about being in Rome," and he put his hand over his mouth to cover a mischievous smile.

Jake and Kahn walked back to the van and took a short ride down to Heron Point. The doors to Duke's home were seldom locked. They walked up the six-foot wide staircase, into the house, and headed for the bedrooms on the left side. A few minutes later as Jake brushed his teeth in the soft glare of a night-light, he noticed bags under the eyes of the aging man in the mirror.

What does a beautiful woman like Annalisa Bertolla see in a tired old man like me? A foamy ring of toothpaste spread around his lips as he continued brushing his teeth. He rinsed his mouth then looked up at his reflection to find another face beside his, the Russian scientist killed earlier that day. More dead faces spread out across the mirror, foggy images from his past as an agent for the New Democratic Right.

It wasn't the first time he had seen the ghostly apparitions. *Nor would it be the last,* he thought as he used a towel to wipe them from the mirror. *And how many more will there be if a nuclear weapon detonates above one of the cities in Robert's new plan?*

As he crawled into bed and his head settled on the pillow Jake's last thoughts were of a pretty brunette, and his best friend, Robert Faircloth, who had undertaken a thankless mission in the Middle East.

* * *

Two days later Duke idled the 48-foot Lightning boat half a mile out into the Pamlico then turned east and slowly pushed the dual throttles forward. The engines rumbled and roared as the long hull lifted and began slicing through the river. By the time the Speed Master screamed by Heron Point it was fully planed.

"Look at that beautiful boat!" Kahn yelped excitedly from a wooden deck chair at the end of the pier in front of Duke's home. He and Jake had been waiting there for the test run of the Prince's new boat. The quality assurance check of the electronic and mechanical systems had been completed, and because Duke owned a Speed Master, the plant Production Manager agreed that he could perform the water test. Duke put it through a dozen or more turns on the river, several stops and accelerations, and finally a top end check at redline RPMs for the twin 450 HP Mercruisers.

The Lightning sales manager had tried to convince his royal customer that four of the new 300 HP Mercury outboards would be more suitable, but the Prince said he wanted the same engines as in the other two Lightning boats he owned. "For ease of maintenance," he said, as he wrote a check for the entire $1.4 million purchase price.

Jake and Khan listened to the roar of the engines as the Lightning Boat passed by. "Nice lines," Jake said, admiring the elongated craft with its navy blue hull and glistening white upper deck. The boat skipped effortlessly above the water while running back up river toward 'Little' Washington and Jake realized the Speed Master, with nuclear weapons hidden below, was now ready for shipment to Saudi Arabia.

The Fall of Knight

Sadr City, Iraq

FOUR MEMBERS OF IRAQ'S Multi National Division in Baghdad had been hired to escort Robert Faircloth to a mosque in Thawra within the Sadr City District of the sprawling city. After his ordeal in Beirut the NDR insisted that he use a security team wherever he traveled inside Iraq.

A small white sedan stopped in front of the Royal Hussein Hotel near the Green Zone in the downtown area. Once a favorite of foreign travelers, it was now the headquarters of the international press and had often been a target of Special Groups, the Shiite militias operating under the Madhi Army of Mullah Muqtada al Sadr.

Three off-duty Iraqi soldiers in civilian clothes, with AK-47 rifles slung menacingly over their shoulders, exited the building in front of the American, scanned the street then led him to a car driven by another soldier.

As soon as Robert was in the back seat of the small sedan a beat-up green Volvo pulled in front of them. An arm extended from the driver's window and began waving indicating they should follow. "Is that our guide?" Robert asked his driver.

"Yes," the driver said flatly as he sped away from the hotel.

They drove north for ten minutes toward Al A'Zamiyah, then east toward what was formerly know as Revolution City when it was first constructed in 1959. Robert had been told that Saddam

Hussein later named the sprawling northeastern suburb after himself. In 2004, after Saddam was ousted the huge Shiite slum area became known as Sadr City, named for their Shiite spiritual leader.

As they drove through crowded dusty streets inside the slum, Robert was aware that even though the air conditioner was blowing forcefully in the front of the vehicle, very little cool air was reaching the backseat. Beads of sweat formed on his brow as he looked out the windows and noticed wary eyes peeking from windows and rooftops as if wondering who was being escorted through the Shiite enclave.

Instead of turning into the mosque in Thawra the old green Volvo continued along a main thoroughfare. The white sedan slowed cautiously and came to a stop by the side of the road while the four security men discussed the situation. The Volvo stopped, backed up and then a burly man in a long white robe and black head cover got out and walked toward Robert's car.

The security men held their weapons up, and over the noise of heavy breathing in his ears he heard the safety switches clicking off. It was a classic set-up for an Improvised Explosive Device roadside attack that had killed and maimed so many American soldiers, but the Shiite man seemed to be in no hurry.

He leaned down to the back window and spoke in English. "Mr. Faircloth, you are a fortunate man. We checked your story of being held captive by our friends in Lebanon and what you said is true. One of our most important leaders in Iraq, Mullah Ali Abdul Abayani, wishes to hear what you have to say. He feels that since you have once again put yourself in a dangerous position, you must have an important message."

The four security men looked at each other amazed that one of the most important Shiite leaders in Iraq would agree to see the American they were guarding. "And that is why we did not stop at the Thawra mosque," the driver of the white car said. "Our leader is in Jameelah, on the eastern edge of Sadr City where it is safer for him. So, we must continue another few miles." He shook his head as if they were all in agreement. "Please, follow me."

Ten minutes later the green car stopped in front of a small mud brick building with guards milling around outside. The driver got out and talked to the men at the front of the house, then disappeared behind a wooden door.

It was becoming unbearably hot inside the vehicle that had a barely functioning air conditioner. "Can we please get out?" Robert asked.

"Not unless they invite us to," the leader of the security team said. "We are on their turf and we will follow their rules. Please understand, Mr. Faircloth."

Robert wiped the sweat from his face and added nervously. "Of course, you're right. It's just that... "

Before he finished the sentence the driver of the Volvo walked out the front door and over to their car. "Mr. Faircloth, only you may enter the house. The rest of you must stay here with your vehicle, outside if you like, but next to the car. Do you understand?"

Each member of the security team nodded in agreement as Robert slowly exited the car. The guide pointed with his right arm to indicate the American should go into the house. Robert recalled that only weeks before in South Beirut another Shiite had led him into a building, and just after entering his arms were tied together and a beating followed. He took an apprehensive breath and considered what might be accomplished if he were successful. *There would be no need for nuclear weapons*, he thought as he willed himself through the doorway.

There was a small table with several chairs in a very clean and spacious room. He realized he was alone with a small man wearing a dark turban, a grey shirt with white collar, covered by a long black robe. His wire-rimmed glasses, gray-splotched beard and pleasant smile gave him a professorial appearance. Robert could not help but smile back in surprise at how genuinely pleasant the man looked.

"Ah, Mr. Faircloth, how good of you to come all this way."

The greeting was a stark contrast to the circumstances outside in the streets of Sadr City and in the rest of Baghdad. "It is very kind of you, Mullah Abayani, to see me."

"Please, sit, my friend," and he pointed to one of the chairs at the table with a white cloth and bowl of fruit in the center. "May I offer you our traditional Anise tea with cinnamon and honey? It is good for the digestion."

"You are very gracious, Mullah Abayani, thank you."

The Shiite cleric sat down across from Robert, poured two cups of tea, passed one to his guest then spread his arms in a welcoming gesture. "I am sorry that our friends in Beirut did not treat you well."

Robert paused in recollection, his eyes diverting down to the table. "But my time in the basement of that house with the professor was invaluable. He is a gifted teacher."

The Mullah smiled as he sipped his tea. "Yes, the same day you were released he was returned to his family." He set his cup down and waved his right hand in the air. "So, tell me, my friend. Why have you come so far and taken such dangerous passage?"

Robert could think of no other way to begin than with a frank declaration. "It is about the spread of nuclear weapons in the Middle East and what will happen if the Iranian government continues to enrich uranium."

For the next ten minutes, Robert revealed that if Iran were to become a nuclear power that another nation in the Middle East would obtain nuclear weapons by other means to counter the Persian threat. And worse, that a plan was already under way for a first strike capability against Tehran.

The Mullah shook his head gravely from side to side. "I must believe you, Robert Faircloth. Why else would you risk your life if not to bring such a warning? This is an alarming development. You say another Islamic nation would use nuclear weapons against the Iranians, which country," he asked with a disbelieving look in his eyes.

Robert looked at the Mullah with the saddest expression he could muster. "The Sunnis of Saudi Arabia are gravely concerned the Shiites of Iran will obtain nuclear weapons and use them to leverage their agenda throughout the Middle East."

There was genuine alarm in the eyes of the Mullah. "You know of such a plan?"

"It is called Peaceful Eagle and involves detonating a powerful thermonuclear bomb to encourage the Iranian government to give up its nuclear weapons program."

The Mullah stood, a fatal mistake, and walked behind his chair hands gripping the top edges. He stared at Robert. "You will be staying in Baghdad a few more days?"

"Yes, at the old Hussein Hotel near the Green Zone."

"Wait there while I go to Tehran and discuss this with Muqtada al Sadr. If the Iranians are to be informed, he is the one to tell them."

Robert could barely contain the emotions welling up inside his chest. He felt as if he were choking on the dusty air filling his lungs. "There is still time to stop Peaceful Eagle," he whispered hopefully.

"I agree," the Mullah said thoughtfully. "We must keep these insane weapons out of the hands of fanatical Islamists. If the radical Sunnis ever get hold of nuclear bombs… He paused, his own voice filling with emotion. He looked toward the sound of voices screaming outside the door.

The Shiite guards were yelling, warning of a vehicle speeding in their direction. Several volleys of AK-47 fire erupted, then the whoosh of an RPG firing from a launcher. The round exploded nearby, but the roar of the car's engine was coming closer. One of the guards burst inside the room yelling something to the cleric.

Mullah Abayani looked starkly at Robert pointing at the rear of the house as if telling him to run to the back door. But before he could utter a sound the world exploded around them. The suicide bomber had found his target.

Robert was hurled headlong to the floor as mud bricks flew like shrapnel above his head. He saw the body of the cleric fly against a wall then disintegrate into mangled flesh as bricks and wooden splinters tore into his body.

The noise from the blast was deafening. Robert's ears were ringing and he tried to scream words, but his mouth only quivered in uncontrollable utterances. He could hear nothing, feeling only pressure squeezing him into the floor as the house ripped apart. Moments later while lying on his back, he saw Shiite militiamen running through the wreckage till they found the body of Mullah Ali Abdul Abayani. They wailed and screamed, then ran back toward what had been the front of the house with guns blazing.

Robert watched in soundless slow motion as red streaks ripped into what was left of the back wall of the house and realized that he was still alive. Whoever attacked the house must be coming toward him. The room filled with strange men, heads wrapped in black and white shumags, shouting and pointing at the shattered body of the Mullah.

It seemed to Robert as if they were pleased the Shiite cleric was dead. Then they turned their attention to the rubble covered American lying on the floor. He felt several prods in his chest with the barrel of an AK-47 and they realized he was still alive.

Robert could hear nothing beyond the ringing in his ears. His sight was reasonably good and he stared passively as a morphine needle was punched into his left arm. He was picked up by his arms and legs, carried to a vehicle and stuffed into the trunk. That was when he spied the face of one of his own security team members grinning beside the others.

Tears pooled in Robert's eyes. *They used me to find Mullah Abayani.* As the trunk lid slammed violently above him, he realized the warning he carried would never be delivered to the Mullahs of Iran. He was now in the hands of fanatical Sunni extremists, a group known as the Allah Akbar Brigade.

Solar Star

Morehead City, NC

EARLY MORNING FOG DRIFTED ABOVE the roadway as an eighteen-wheeler pulled away from the Lightning Power Boat factory. On the rear deck was a forty-eight foot luxury model Speed Master securely strapped in a wooden shipping cradle. It was covered from bow to stern in sheets of white plastic then wrapped again from starboard to port in another layer of the same material. In the cradle it could be lifted aboard and stored below deck on any modern cargo ship.

"There she goes, Jake. We gonna follow her all the way to Morehead?"

Jake looked at his driver. "Yeah, Duke, but let's stay a respectable distance back. For the next two hours they remained a quarter-mile behind the low boy carrying the prince's new boat.

The Solar Star, a Panamanian registered freighter, lay moored against the sea wall of the port in Morehead City, NC. It had taken on fertilizer and feed from the phosphate plant in Aurora and other agricultural products from the eastern part of the state. Some of the cargo was bound for the Southern French port of Marseille where freight would be dropped and more taken on. The ship would then cross the Mediterranean and traverse the Suez Canal bound for Jeddah, the largest port on the Red Sea coast of Saudi Arabia.

The captain of the ship waited anxiously for a truck hauling a special order. If the boat were delivered on time in Jeddah, he and his mostly Malaysian crew were to receive a sizeable bonus. They knew it was a special delivery for a Prince of the House of Saud.

"Captain!" shouted the radio operator from the wheelhouse. "Look, they're crossing the bridge from Radio Island; should be here in a few minutes."

The captain checked his watch and calculated that his heavily laden vessel must be underway within three hours to take advantage of the high tide and slip the bar through Beaufort Inlet. He pulled his binoculars up and found the eighteen-wheeler on the down slope of the bridge. "Hurry, boys," he whispered to himself, knowing that customs would have to weigh and inspect the cargo. *But it's a Lightning Boat*, he thought. *They ship them out of here all the time.*

According to port protocol the truck was weighed, before and after its cargo was hauled aboard the freighter, then a pilot came on board to guide them safely through the inlet. As the 'Solar Star' pulled into the shipping channel, a white Toyota Tundra truck drove away from a tall chain link fence surrounding the docks.

"I almost feel like celebrating," Jake said, breathing a heavy sigh and realizing that half of the incredible plan had been implemented.

"Yeah, big relief," Duke exclaimed. "How 'bout we go to one of those seafood restaurants in Morehead and have some shrimp and oysters?"

"Too public," Jake responded. "We need a place with a lower profile."

Duke thought for a moment, then remembered a small out of the way oyster bar on the back roads that fried up some of the best oysters in the state. "Got it," he said with a grin, "if you boys don't mind waiting about half an hour."

He looked over at Jake then back at Khan who shrugged his shoulders. "I'm just along for the ride," he said with his usual smile.

After crossing the Neuse River on the Minnesott Beach Ferry they drove into the small community of Arapahoe, NC. "There it is, " Duke said with a grin, "Gary's Seafood. " He looked back at Kahn, "You ever had raw oysters?"

"I enjoy oysters," Dr. Kahn replied. "And I'm hungry, so please, let's go inside."

"You got any money, Kahn?" Duke teased.

"I have lots of money, but thanks to Mr. Jake it is safely deposited in my account in Karachi."

Jake pulled several one hundred dollar bills from his pocket. "Here you go, Duke, will this do?" The three men laughed together as they went inside for lightly fried shrimp and oysters, fries and coleslaw, all washed down with glasses of sweet iced tea.

They were sitting at a corner table enjoying a last round when Duke's cell phone rang. He looked at the number. "Who the hell is this?"

"DiSisto," he answered. He paused then looked over at Jake. "Yeah, he's sitting right here. No, we're at a restaurant on the back roads and his satellite phone is in the truck. Sure, I'll tell him," then Duke gave Jake a serious look. "That was Nalum Taylor. He wants you to call him back on the secure phone as soon as you can."

Jake's head jerked up and a serious look appeared in his eyes. "Something's up," he responded. "I'll be right back." He hurried through a screen door that banged behind him as he ran out to the truck.

Kahn was sipping the last of his tea when he noticed the headlights of the truck blink twice. "We must go," he whispered."

Duke glanced at the check. He waved at the waitress, laid a one hundred dollar bill on the table that included a generous tip, and the two men hurried outside.

"Is it the boat? Has something happened to the freighter?" Duke asked.

Jake stared through the windshield. "No, but we have to leave for Paris."

"Paris," Khan said gleefully. "I have never been there. Nope," he repeated to himself. "I have never been to Paris."

"One of our primary operatives, Robert Faircloth, left Paris for Baghdad last week. He's been captured by a Sunni terrorist group."

Jake sat quietly in the front seat staring out the window and the stillness was getting to Duke. "This Robert Faircloth, was his going to Baghdad part of the plan?"

"Yeah, a big part," Jake said. "Robert is the one person this entire operation hinges on. If he succeeds in his mission there would be no need for Peaceful Eagle, but if anything happens to him there may be no way to stop..." He paused, fearing he may have said too much about the King's plan for a nuclear detonation.

He turned to Duke and Khan. "Annalisa Bertola, another of our associates, is flying a Gulf Stream in from France. It's a big G550 model, plenty of amenities, including sleeping couches. She'll pick us up at the New Bern airport at 0800 tomorrow morning. So, gentlemen, pack your bags and passports. We're leaving for Paris."

The Bird is Out of the Cage

Faro, NC

"SHERIFF, THIS IS VERNON WHALEY."

"Whaley, I said my name's Vernon Whaley. Don't you remember me? I'm the farmer that had a pig pickin' for you over to the Shrine Hall in Pikeville a couple years back when you was runnin' for re-election.

"Yeah, that's me. Now listen, Sheriff, there's something strange going on over here in Faro down to the Old Davies Farm.

"Yes, sir," he said emphatically, "that's the farm I'm talking about. At first I didn't think much about it, all the blasting they was doing and all that heavy equipment they was bringing in. But I got to thinking, ain't no kind of farmin' needs that much digging and earth moving, no, sir. I mean how many farm ponds do they need? You know what I mean, Sheriff?

"Yeah, well, this morning me and the boys were at the store in Faro having a cup of Joe and Jabe Hardee came in and told a whale of a story. Said he was down to Nahunta Creek the other day settin' out bush hooks trying to catch some catfish, and all of a sudden the ground started shaking under his feet.

"Said he didn't know what to think at first, but he turned around and that whole field with all those little white pipes sticking out of the ground was just a shaking and vibrating. He said the catfish even started jumping out of the creek right up on the bank, along with some bream and blue gill. But he was too dang scared to get any and ran like hell for his truck near the bridge on Big Daddy's Road."

There was quiet on the other end of the phone line and then Vernon began nodding his head. "Yeah, Sheriff, me and Jabe can meet you down to the bridge in an hour. And I'm telling you something strange is going on at the old Davies farm."

A small convoy of jeeps and military trucks from Seymour Johnson Air Force Base drove slowly across Nahunta Creek Bridge. They pulled off on the shoulder of Big Daddy's Road beside the field where on a cold January night in 1961, a nuclear warhead buried itself 180 feet in the ground. A company of Military Police poured from several 'deuce and a half' trucks and took up positions to secure the perimeter.

"Sheriff Walker, I'm Colonel Geitner from Seymour Johnson." He looked over his shoulder. "And this is Lisa Tucker, a civilian staff geologist from the base. You called and said there may have been some disturbance in our field."

The Sheriff nodded his head a little perturbed at the Colonel for presuming that private property in his county was somehow owned by the Air Force. "Nice to meet you, folks," and he nodded his head toward the two farmers. "This is Vernon Whaley and Jabe Hardee. Jabe here's the one who felt the ground shaking a few days ago. And Vernon's the one who is suspicious of the blasting and heavy equipment being used just up that hill beyond those trees."

As Vernon and Jabe repeated their stories an Air Force Tech Sergeant recorded every word on a digital voice recorder that would later be transcribed at the base. While the stories were being told the geologist stepped away from the group and walked through the brush toward a corner of the field where a red-topped seismograph was planted. She flipped the solar head up, stared a moment then yelled. "Colonel, you better come over here!"

"Who in the hell turned this thing off?" the officer asked. "And why?"

"Better call the men in the corners," she added. "Ask them to turn up the heads and see if the other seismographs are in the 'Off' position."

"Sgt. Foster," the Colonel barked. "Make the call and relay that request."

"Yes, sir," the enlisted man replied. "Right away, sir," and the Sergeant turned away to make the calls on a handheld radio. It only took a few moments and he turned around. "Affirmative, Sir. The other three devices are in the 'Off' position."

"No wonder we didn't register a signature," the geologist said. "Whoever turned these off must have forgotten to come back and flip them back on."

Everyone stared up the hill toward the trees that hid the farmhouse and outbuildings on the Davies farm then Vernon spoke the obvious. "Reckon somebody's digging underground around here?"

The Colonel glanced down at his watch then over at the Sergeant. "Get Captain Randall over here. Looks like we're going to make a full scale assault on that farm."

Before the Tech Sergeant could turn around another voice was heard. "Hold on there, Colonel, before you take that hill."

Everyone's eyes turned to the two men walking toward them. "Who the hell are you?" Colonel Geitner asked indignantly.

Both men reached inside coat pockets and presented their credentials. "I'm Agent Noah Weller with the CIA and this is Agent Doug Jackson with the FBI. We're assigned to the National Counter Terrorism Center in Washington and this may be a matter of national security. While I appreciate your enthusiasm for carrying out your duties, Sir, this investigation is now under our jurisdiction."

The Colonel glanced over at the Wayne County Sheriff as if to ask who had called in the NCTC. Sheriff Walker looked him in the eye. "They're on my call list, Colonel. Protocol. I think you understand military protocol."

"But this is an Air Force matter, Agent Weller," the Colonel responded, not wanting to let an opportunity for recognition pass him by. "That's our bomb out there."

"And if it's no longer there, then it's our bomb. Do you understand?"

Geitner realized that he and his MPs were outranked by the NCTC and that if he cared about his nomination for a brigadier's star he'd better be part of a solution and not the problem. "So," he said with a resigned expression, "how can the Air Force help two agents from the National Counter Terrorism Center?"

Three helicopters circled above the outbuildings on the old Davies farm while a column of military vehicles approached along the crush and run driveway leading up to the farmhouse. As the 'deuce and a halfs' rolled to a stop the company of MPs took up a security perimeter around the buildings. No one would be allowed in or out without the permission of Colonel Geitner. The Sheriff and his deputies looked inside the house but it was bare. They headed for the small sheet metal building between the two huge outbuildings and ran inside but it, too, was empty.

"Damn," Agent Weller said to his partner. "They must have seen us down by the bridge and cleared out of here."

"Yeah," Jackson responded. "Why don't we get our forensics team in here and go over this place, see what they can find?"

"I've already made the call, Doug. They're on the way. Should be here in a couple of hours." He turned toward the military commander. "Colonel Geitner, could you have those birds search the roadways leading away from here? If they spot any vehicles that look like they are trying to make a hasty exit, notify the Sheriff's office and the North Carolina Highway Patrol and have them pull the vehicles. They need to inspect them and make positive identification of the occupants, and if necessary detain any persons of interest until Agent Jackson has a chance to talk with them."

Geitner nodded his head then walked over to Captain Randall. Within minutes all three helicopters were following roadways leading away from the farm. It was a long shot, but Agent Weller was handling the case like the national security issue he believed it had become.

"Looks like a lot of soil has been turned up inside these buildings," Jackson whispered to Agent Weller.

"From one end to the other but only thirty feet or so wide," Weller added, and then both men looked at each other with the same insight.

"Just wide enough for one of those new tunnel machines," Jackson added with a gleam of understanding in his eyes.

Agent Weller stood in the middle of the building. He walked along the line of disturbed soil with an amazed expression on his face. He turned toward Doug Jackson and shouted, "This line points directly at Nahunta Creek Bridge!"

Both men now understood what had caused the earth to move under the feet of Jabe Hardee, the farmer who had been fishing beside the bridge. It was the vibrating signature of a tunnel-boring machine making its way toward a nuclear warhead that had been buried in the ground for fifty years.

"Think they got it, Doug? Think they successfully retrieved the warhead?"

Agent Jackson stood quietly for a moment before he answered. "There's a front loader and a bucket excavator in the back of these buildings. Let's open the sliding doors and get that equipment in here. We'll start digging over there near the end of the building. If there's a tunnel, then it led out that way, and I'll bet they only filled it in just enough to cover their tracks."

Weller ran outside shouting for the Colonel, asking if any of the MPs had experience operating heavy equipment. Several men stepped forward and as they began moving the excavator and front loader into position, the CIA agent explained to the Colonel that he was declaring this a Top Secret, highly classified operation and that every one of his men must be ordered and sworn to secrecy. The last thing he wanted was for word to slip out to the press and the public that an American nuclear warhead may have gotten into the hands of terrorists.

It didn't take long to dig twenty feet down and expose a yawning four-meter cavern. Weller, Jackson and the Colonel dropped into the mouth of the tunnel with flashlights in hand and walked fifty feet inside. They found the remains of a shriveled white-haired corpse leaning against a limestone wall. The face was ashen, mouth gaped open and eyes staring as if screaming for help, while a black beetle ran over his upper lip and inside a nasal cavity. Beside the body was a plastic bag filled with thick black liquid.

Agent Weller leaned down on one knee and noticed the bluish remains of a tattoo on the inside of the man's left forearm. "Looks like some kind of number like the Germans used on prisoners in World War II."

"Think he was a war camp survivor?" Weller asked.

"Can't tell," Jackson said, "but I don't believe he was supposed to end up here."

Weller carefully wrote down the numbers of the tattoo and he turned to the other two men. "Think they got the warhead?"

"If they did they had to have some specialized help," said Geitner. "You don't just dig up a nuclear bomb, especially one that could be leaking radiation."

"Yeah, they had to have help," and then it occurred to Weller. "There's only one or two manufacturers in the world that make tunnel boring machines. Let's find out if any of them sent a machine to the United States in the past month. Must have been recent or else this body would have been in a much further state of decomposition."

"I never would have believed it," the Colonel exclaimed as the three men walked back to the tunnel entrance. "I mean, according to the Top Secret report I read on the B-52 bomber crash, the Air Force with all its resources couldn't dig up the warhead. And now somebody has come in here with newer technology and taken it out of the ground right under our noses."

"Yeah, it appears so, Colonel. Now, I have some phone calls to make," Weller said. "You, too, Doug. And remember, this thing is absolutely Top Secret until we have a better handle on what's going on. If the press gets their hands on this they could panic the entire nation, maybe even the world into some kind of hyper ventilated knee-jerk reaction and we definitely don't want that to happen." He looked both men carefully in the eye, "Agreed?"

"Absolutely," they responded as they climbed up out of the hole in the ground.

Agent Jackson went back to his car and made a phone call to the NCTC to file his report. Then he pulled out a small recently acquired cell phone, for which minutes were purchased on a card, and made an untraceable call to a number in Berryville, Virginia.

"Veramar," a voice answered.

"The bird is out of the cage," Doug Jackson said calmly.

"Very good," the voice replied and both phones clicked off.

Within minutes the phone rang in a rented house in the Monmartre District of Paris. "Yes," a man's voice answered.

"The bird is out of the cage."

"Very well, then. I'll let them know."

The Last Time I Saw Robert

Paris, France

NALUM TAYLOR, THE AGING patriarch of the New Democratic Right, had flown to Paris after receiving word about Robert Faircloth. He was sipping tea in a cafe below Sacre Coeur with his NDR associates, Jake, Annalisa, Duke and Abdul Khan. They were staring at each other with blank faces as buses drove by their sidewalk table, stopping at a nearby corner to discharge sightseers who were anxious to ascend the white marble staircase leading up to the basilica.

It had been two days since they learned of Robert's fate in Iraq and the mood at Nalum's table was tense and somber. "How could they do that to a human being?" Annalisa whispered through clenched teeth, the taste of tears salting her lips.

Jake's face was hard set, the steely look of revenge in his eyes. "The last time I saw Robert was here at the Café du Blanc." His head slipped down. "We sent them our best Knight, offered them an olive branch, but they've chosen swords. It seems the fanatics always have to learn the hard way and take so many innocents with them."

The video image of Robert Faircloth on his knees pleading for his life was fresh in the minds of the NDR members gathered at the table. To their credit Al Jazeera had refused to broadcast the inflammatory recording of yet another beheading, but instead furnished the tape to the International Red Cross. As Robert whispered despairingly to his captors the words Peaceful Eagle and Alpha-Omega had fallen on deaf ears, but resonated like a raging fire in Jake's heart.

Nalum had learned from a source in Baghdad that the Allah Akbar Brigade was but one of many desperate gangs in the city that tried to mask their illegal activities in a cloak of Islamic legitimacy. Normally they wanted only ransom for their kidnap victims, but in Robert's case they had become inflamed with their own hate rhetoric and could no longer contain an irrational passion for shedding blood.

"He was speaking to us," Nalum said, his lower lip quivering slightly. "He was telling us to move forward with Peaceful Eagle."

"Alpha-Omega," Jake whispered to himself, believing the words were a message for him to implement Robert's plan.

At the moment of death Robert was staring up at a screaming man standing in front of him. His lips barely moved as the first blow fell on the back of his neck. It was a crude effort, mortally wounding but not killing him. Removing a man's head with a saber required more strength and skill than his captors realized.

Robert fell onto a dirt floor as the second blow glanced off the back of his skull and skimmed down his neck. Then another hacking blow fell, and several more, until one of the masked gunmen reached down and pulled Robert's head away from his body. He stood for a moment in front of the camera holding a bloody skull while screaming something about Allah being great.

Jake Eastwood, the Sword of the NDR, had never been so enraged. All he could see in his mind's eye was a fiery mushroom cloud enveloping everyone and everything in the city of Baghdad. But Robert had warned of the possibility and cautioned Jake to contain his passion for revenge. No matter what happened Robert believed his version of Peaceful Eagle was the best option for peace in the Middle East.

Neither Duke Disisto nor Abdul Khan knew how to respond to the atrocity. They continued to sip cups of espresso as Annalisa nervously wiped her eyes and every one of them looked to Nalum to ask what should happen next. With an air of aged wisdom Nalum drew his long thin frame up in his chair and nodded toward Jake.

"Robert gave the last full measure in hope that Peaceful Eagle could be avoided. But you see what has happened and you know what must be done. I am very sorry for the loss of one of our most respected associates, our best Knight as you said, Jake, but I am never the less convinced that we must continue with our plan. So, please move forward as expeditiously as possible."

Nalum Taylor folded his napkin and nodded to his guests. "Time for this old man to consider the benefits of a short walk and a nap." Though he continued to use his NDR code name within the organization, the former Vice-President of the United States no longer wore a disguise to conceal his identity.

He didn't think it necessary and after Peaceful Eagle, it would no longer matter. Once there was a nuclear explosion in the Middle East there would be no means to conceal the planning and strategists from the scrutiny of world intelligence communities. All would eventually be discovered along with the participants, and he was resigned to the outcome. "But you should know," Nalum added. "The bird is now out of the cage."

"How close?" Jake asked.

"Our FBI contact will try to guide the investigation. They will soon discover the Lightning Boat factory and arrive at Duke's shop on the Pamlico River. Once they realize how the enriched uranium was shipped, they will go to the port at Morehead and identify and follow the voyage of the Solar Star. Eventually, they will arrive at the warehouse in Jeddah where tomorrow you will await the arrival of our weapon."

Weapon, Khan thought to himself. He looked sharply at Jake. *Doesn't he know there are now four weapons?* But after what had happened to the Russian scientist back at the farm, he knew better than to question Jake and turned his attention back to Nalum.

"Doug Jackson will try to ensure the American and Saudi intelligence services arrive at the warehouse within a few hours of the weapon's departure from the airport in Jeddah. Once in the air there is little they can do to stop Peaceful Eagle because they will not know the destination. But based on what they find, they will learn that an operational nuclear weapon is on board a Saudi F-15 Strike Eagle and that intelligence will be communicated to the rest of the world, particularly the nations of the Middle East.

Nalum paused a moment and studied his four younger protégées. "For the present Doug advises that we expedite our initiatives. The Solar Star left Marseilles a week ago. Tomorrow it will arrive in Jeddah so each of you must make yourselves ready.

"You are the Lightning team. Now go and recover the Prince's new boat and do not forget that Robert has already made the ultimate sacrifice."

Nalum's personal assistant was sitting nearby. As soon as the venerable NDR leader rose from the table the young man was at his side. Everyone got up to bid Nalum goodbye and he waved his hand. "You young people stay here as long as you like. Under the circumstances enjoy yourselves in this beautiful old city as much as you can, as I once did."

Jake sat quietly at the table watching Nalum as he was escorted across the street making sure he was far enough away before speaking. "The plan has changed," he announced dramatically staring at each team member before continuing.

Annalisa's mouth fell open. "What are you saying, Jake? You can't change Nalum's plan." She looked quickly at Duke and Khan. "And speaking like this in front of people new to the organization," she added.

Jake's face softened as it usually did in discussions with Annalisa. "I know," he said, "but I have good reason." Then all of them leaned forward as Jake explained.

"While Robert was held captive in Lebanon there was another man locked in the cellar with him, a Shiite professor from American university, and together they came up with something new for Peaceful Eagle. As it exists Peaceful Eagle benefits the Sunnis of Saudi Arabia and their plan to colonize Europe and America."

"But it will also benefit the West by influencing the Iranians to give up their nuclear weapons program."

"That's true, Annalisa. Even so, Robert and his teacher came up with a new strategy, a plan with much greater potential for peace in the Middle East."

Duke leaned forward in his seat. "What are we gonna do, Jake?"

The NDR leader looked at each of them as he announced, "We're going to hijack Peaceful Eagle and turn it into Robert's plan."

"Robert's plan," Annalisa repeated with tears gathering in her eyes.

Duke leaned forward. "To tell you the truth, Jake, my loyalty is more to you than Nalum Taylor or anyone else in the NDR. So, if you say the plan is changing then I'm still with you all the way."

For the first time in two days a smile crept over Jake's face. "Thanks, Duke. Robert called it the Alpha-Omega option and Khan, you're a big part of this."

Abdul Khan was both surprised and pleased to hear that he was a vital member of the team. "What is this new plan?" he asked cautiously.

"Three bombs, three targets, and if Robert's plan works, only the Saudi bomb in the desert will be detonated." Jake leaned forward in an aggressive posture and began explaining the details of the new operation.

Kahn was skeptical of one critical part of the plan. "Let me see if I understand this. Duke will fly over Makkah while you fly to Tehran and Annalisa will fly to Jerusalem. Then you will announce Robert's demands for each nation to save their cities. And to prove that you have nuclear weapons on board, a Saudi pilot will fly into the desert and detonate just like in the previous plan?"

"That's right, Khan." Jake knew he was still deceiving the Pakistani scientist, but realized he needed his skills and expertise to complete the refinements to Robert's plan. "The Saudi jet will have a viable nuclear weapon on board. The others will be decoys."

"To scare the Israelis, Iranians and Saudis into agreeing to a peaceful outcome," he shouted with enthusiasm. "I get it now, I understand, Jake." Then he smiled to himself. "Yes, I can help you with this."

Annalisa saw a familiar look in Jake's eyes. He seemed to glance down and to the left, a look of deception that she had seen before when he was manipulating other people. There was more to this plan than had been revealed, she was sure, but was also aware of Jake's passion for compartmentalization. He only told people what they needed to know, when they needed to know it.

The Regency

Myrtle Beach, SC

AT FOUR O'CLOCK ON Friday morning a team of NCTC agents, including Noah Weller and Doug Jackson, rode an elevator to the fifth floor of a new luxury hotel overlooking the Atlantic Ocean. It was built near the former downtown pavilion area of old Myrtle Beach that had once roared with roller coasters, bumper cars, and endless carnival games.

Three agents quietly positioned themselves outside each of the doors to the five rooms where the German technicians were tucked in for the night with some of the highest priced topless dancers in Myrtle Beach. At the same time key cards were inserted into locks, doors slammed open and bright lights and gun barrels turned on the occupants.

It was organized chaos, utterly confusing to the Germans, but oddly familiar to the women. The men stood naked beside their beds arms raised above their heads, the women, too, and it was an amusing sight. A condom dangled from the penis of Gunter Heidrickson, the TBM group manager; full of the joy he had shared with a woman whose bosom looked as if volleyballs had been sewn under the skin of her chest.

"Put your clothes on, Mr. Heidrickson," Agent Weller said. "You and your men will be coming with us."

"But we have done nothing wrong. This woman is my friend. She has been staying with me for a week. I don't understand."

"It's not about the woman," Doug Jackson added. "It's about the tunnel."

There was a moment of recognition in Gunter's eyes. "Yes, the tunnel. But they had permits, all the proper permits."

"Good," Weller answered. "Now get dressed and come with us."

There were several meeting rooms on the ground floor and each technician was taken to a private interrogation center. Most of them knew little about the contract with WECO Engineering that sent a tunnel-boring machine to America. Only Gunter, the team leader, knew more than the others.

"It was just another job," he shouted. "The TBM was sent by freighter to a port in Morehead City. We were told that we were going to Charlotte, to dig tunnels for a new subway system that was being designed. A private jet picked us up in Bremen, but when it landed we were not in Charlotte. I'm not sure where we were.

"We were put into a paneled van and driven to an old farm. Nobody told us where it was. By the time we arrived the LOVAT 165 had been transported there. The man in charge, a Mr. Rufus, then explained what was really going on… "

"Rufus who?" Agent Weller asked.

"I don't know. I never heard his last name, but he explained everything about the need for secrecy. You see we were not really going to dig subway tunnels, but recover a lost Civil War treasure."

Weller and Jackson looked at each other with grim smiles on their faces. "And this treasure, what was it supposed to be?"

"I don't know much about your American history, but they said it was part of a payroll that had been captured near the end of the Civil War at a place called Bentonville. And that plans for a counter attack by a Confederate general against the Union army were put in a large container, along with the payroll, and buried at the bottom of a well.

"Mr. Rufus also said that instead of attacking, the general surrendered to Sherman and that the men who had buried the chest decided to keep it there, in case the Confederacy might need it later. But in the late 1860s, he said an earthquake struck this area and caused the well to collapse. And a fault opened under ground, creating a huge aquifer where once there was only a small pocket of well water."

"And you believed that?"

"Well," Gunter said, shrugging his shoulders, "it did not matter. WECO was being paid and these men were paying us a cash bonus to do this job. The other man, Mr. Jake, he was called, offered each of us a five thousand dollar bonus if we hurried and successfully retrieved the treasure."

"And this Jake, he paid you the bonus money?"

"Yes, five thousand dollars in one hundred dollar bills. And rather than hurry home," and he paused as if slightly embarrassed, " we decided to spend our money here at this marvelous beach resort."

"Okay, Gunter," Agent Weller said with a sigh, "I want you to tell me everything there is to know about Mr. Rufus and Mr. Jake. What did they look like... height, weight, hair color, skin tone, visible scars, and anything else you can remember."

"What about the Russian and the Pakistani, do you want to know about them?"

Weller spun his head around toward Jackson then looked back at the German with a serious expression. "Yeah, the Pakistani, tell us everything you can remember about him, too."

"Yes, of course," Gunter said agreeably. "If these men have taken something that was not theirs, then I want to help you. There were two scientists," he continued, "one a Russian and the other a Pakistani. And also, there was an underground lab that was constructed for them to do their secret work.

"The lab," Weller said calmly trying to contain his excitement. "Where is it?"

"Behind the large buildings where we bored the tunnel. There is a wide ramp that goes down twenty feet below the surface and a heavy door that leads into the bunker. If they moved much dirt around and filled in the staircase, you might not be able to see that it was there."

* * *

Catherine McVey, a nuclear weapons specialist from Livermore Labs in California, was dispatched by fighter jet to Seymour Johnson Air Force Base outside Goldsboro, NC. She was sent to evaluate whether or not enriched uranium had been recovered from the B-52 bomber crash site. By the time Agents Weller and Jackson finished their interrogation of the Germans at the hotel in Myrtle Beach and taken a helicopter back to the farm outside Faro, the Livermore specialist would be there.

Agent Weller was staring out the helicopter window. "This shit would be exciting if it weren't so dangerous, Doug. I mean, what do you think American terrorists are planning to do with a big load of weapons grade uranium?"

"Who said they're terrorists?" Jackson responded. "They could be businessmen who want to sell the stuff on the world market. But then," he said with a thoughtful expression, "if they're selling to terrorists I guess that makes them terrorists, too."

"And they should be treated as such," Weller added with disgust.

Doug Jackson turned away and looked out the window beside his seat, smiling privately about something he could never share with the other agent.

A Matter of National Security

Faro, NC

THE UNDERGROUND BUNKER AT the farm in Faro had been located and the ramp dug out by a group of Air Force Military Police. Cathy McVey, a tall graying brunette with a doctorate in Nuclear Physics, led the way down the staircase. She wore protective clothing with a Scott Air Pac mask over her head and carried a Geiger counter in her gloved right hand. Agents Weller and Jackson, also in protective gear, pulled open the heavy door to the bunker. As soon as Dr. McVey stepped inside the counter began to register a slight buzz.

"Higher than you would normally expect," she said with a muffled voice through her breathing device, "but nothing of concern."

The bright fluorescent lights in the ceiling revealed a sparse utilitarian lab. There were several long stainless steel tables in the center of the room and cabinets lining one wall and a set of deep stainless sinks on the other. As they moved around inside the lab her Geiger counter would occasionally spike to higher levels but would then retreat. Agent Weller stepped over to a large cabinet with a heavy lead-lined door and pulled it open. "What about this?" he asked.

As Dr. McVey turned toward him the needle on the Geiger counter pegged all the way to the right and began to register an irritating high-pitched buzz. "Bingo," she yelled through her mask. "You just located the shell of a 1960s era secondary encasement vessel for a thermonuclear weapon."

She stepped beside the agent and handed him the Geiger while she used a flashlight to examine the 'SCE.' She stood and surveyed the lab, "Yeah, whoever they're using sure knew what they were doing. This looks like the set up we used to find in some of the old Soviet Bloc nuclear labs."

Weller looked over at Jackson and nodded his head. "Vladimir Petrovski," he said, sounding as if he were speaking through an underwater aquatic microphone.

"Petrovski," she responded with surprise. "Good one. He's a legend among nuclear weapons scientists."

"How's that?" Weller said.

"Ever heard of Tzar Bomba?" she asked.

Weller and Jackson shook their heads as she continued. "Back in the early 1960s, the Soviets couldn't keep up with the advances in American nuclear technology nor our production of nuclear weapons. So in 1961, Kruschev ordered his scientists to build the biggest nuclear bomb ever developed and they did.

"Petrovski was one of the project managers for Tsar Bomba," she added with a nod of respect. "The Russians claimed it was a 100 megaton weapon but our scientists later determined it had a yield of 57 megatons," and she laughed behind her mask.

"When it was detonated, the Bomba created a sixty mile wide fireball and generated 500 mile per hour winds over 200 miles from ground zero. One of their scientists later confessed that the fuel burned for over five minutes, twice as long as they predicted. And for a moment they wondered if they had lit the hydrogen in the atmosphere on fire creating an uncontrollable fusion reaction that might never stop.

"But we had our own slip-up out in the Pacific in 1956," she added. "One of our test weapons was designed to yield a thirty-megaton explosion, but it unexpectedly yielded forty-eight. We got the same scare the Russians had with Tzar Bomba. And right after that both sides agreed to stop expanding yields for nuclear weapons."

She looked through the plexi-glass lens of her air pac into the eyes of the two men. "Guess all this talk of megatons just blows right by you," she said. "Let me give you an example of what I'm talking about.

"The Hiroshima and Nagasaki bombs were in the 15 to 20 kiloton range. That's 15-20 thousand tons of dynamite, just babies compared to what you're dealing with here. When you move from a fission reaction to a thermonuclear fusion explosion you get into the megaton range, or a million tons of dynamite. So, if you divide 20 kilotons into 24 megatons you get 1.2 million. That's how much greater the yield is for this version of a Mark 41 as compared to the yields of Fat Man and Little Boy."

She could see the wheels turning in their heads, both men considering the enormous calculation and potential for destruction, and decided to change the subject. "I heard Petrovski retired somewhere in Odessa. Guess he was doing well until the new regime cut retiree pensions in half. That's when I heard he went out as a freelancer. So is he working for your bad guys?"

"He was," Jackson added. "But he must have screwed up. We found his body inside the tunnel."

"You sure it was him?" she asked with a concerned expression on her face.

"Got a positive 'ID' an hour ago from the tattoo on his left arm. Did you know he was captured by the Germans in World War II and held in a nasty POW camp? It was the kind of place where guards would shoot Russian prisoners for even speaking."

"No, I didn't know." She shrugged her shoulders, closed the heavy cabinet doors and the radiation levels dropped considerably. As they climbed up the ramp from the underground lab Dr. McVey pulled the Air Pac from her head and turned toward Weller.

"Okay, it's verified. Your bad boys have the goods. And based on an old Mark 41 design, they probably have around one hundred forty kilos of nuclear fuel. Have you any idea where they may have taken it or what they want to do with it?"

"We're working on it," Jackson said. "You got any thoughts on the subject?"

"Well, unless they were trying to kill themselves and irradiate a whole lot of other people, look for something fairly large and lead lined that can absorb radiation."

"How big?"

Dr. McVey pulled down the zipper on her protective clothing and began stepping out of the yellow protective suit. "Any vehicle that could carry a good-sized lead container away from this location should be considered."

She gave Weller the protective clothing. "Well, good luck with this, Gentlemen," then added. "It's critically important that you find out what happened to that weapons grade materiel. Needless to say, this is a matter of national security."

Code Name Cobra

Falls Church, VA

AGENTS WELLER AND JACKSON stood before a gathering of senior administrators and intelligence analysts inside the National Counter Terrorism Center somewhere near McLean, Virginia. Every resource of the NCTC had now been diverted to a top-secret operation given the code name Cobra.

"This is what we know so far," Weller said. He used a live screen mouse to pinpoint the areas he was discussing on an 8x12 foot screen with a live satellite feed of Eastern North Carolina.

"Here is the small community of Faro, NC, about twelve miles northeast of Goldsboro. Right in this area is where the B-52 bomber went down in 1961, and here's the location of the old Davies farm where the tunnel started." The cursor moved further down the screen. "And this is where the 24 megaton nuclear warhead went into the ground nearly fifty years ago.

"That's 24 megatons, people. Or put another way, that's 24 million tons of dynamite," he said, emphasizing the urgency of the situation. "We don't know who these people are but we do know this. They have successfully retrieved the Secondary Containment Vessel. And they also hired one of the old Soviet Union's top nuclear weapons specialists to help them and possibly another nuclear scientist from Pakistan.

"We know this because we found the Russian's body in the tunnel they dug. It seems they managed to have a four-meter tunnel-boring machine brought in from Germany to the United States to a port in Morehead City, NC, then transported to a farm just up the hill from where the bomb went into the ground without anyone from Homeland Security noticing what was going on.

"And, folks, we now have the potential for one of the greatest disasters in human history to occur, because I don't think they plan to use that weapons grade uranium to fuel a nuclear reactor." He paused a moment and looked over his audience.

"Our greatest fear is that they have in their possession an operational 24 Megaton nuclear weapon or possibly a number of smaller warheads, because in Vladimir Petrovski they had just the right person to build the proper firing mechanisms for one or more weapons.

"I hope you can comprehend the urgency with which we speak. We must learn who these people are and what they are planning to do with 140 kilos of uranium and plutonium. We need to know how they managed to transport nuclear material away from the B-52 crash site without revealing a radioactive signature that would surely have been detected at an interstate inspection site.

"Is the uranium still in this country?" he asked the group rhetorically. "Is it being sent to another country? Has it already been taken there and if so, for what purpose?"

Hands began flying in the air from among the analysts. "How long since they acquired the enriched uranium? What method of transport is suspected? Where in America might they take it? And if the plan was to take it out of the country, how would they accomplish that especially considering the weight of a lead concealment vessel that would be needed to shield the nuclear signature?"

Doug Jackson smiled and nodded toward Weller. "Now that is a damn good question, Noah. Let's get to work on that."

The analysts were divided into two working groups, one for domestic terrorism and the other for international. "Doug, you work with the homeland group. I'll take the international side and all the agencies that will need to be notified."

Doug knew what he meant, once they had verifiable information that could be shared with INTERPOL and every anti-terrorism organization throughout the world. As he sat down at a round table with his team he thought to himself. *This is going well. I'll feed them just enough to keep the investigation moving forward and if they get too close before we're ready, I'll provide misinformation.*

"Okay," he said to the analyst who mentioned the lead container. "How big a container, how heavy, and how large a vehicle would be needed to transport it?"

"Depends," she responded. "Are we talking about just the nuclear material or completed nuclear weapons?"

"Let's go both ways," Doug answered, and he smiled at the young woman who eagerly tossed out ideas to her peers, the best and brightest minds in the intelligence field.

"Start with something that would be required to carry the 140 kilos."

"A large van like a UPS truck could do that," one of them responded. "Yeah, wouldn't take much," another analyst said. "A lead box about six feet long, three feet wide and two feet high would fit into the back of one of those."

"What if it is a completed 24 Megaton bomb?" Doug asked.

"With a firing mechanism?" they asked, looking nervously at each other. "A lot longer, maybe ten to twelve feet."

"Take a look at this," one of the analysts said as he clicked the send button on his laptop. He had accessed a search engine for nuclear weapons then scrolled through several sites with pictures and histories of the American nuclear weapons program. He found a black and white picture of a Mark 41 just like the Broken Arrow lost in 1961. Within seconds the image appeared on the huge screen in the room.

"That thing is huge," said one of his peers, looking at the twelve-foot long tubular bomb.

"Three and a half tons," he added while propping glasses up on his nose, "containing 138 kilos of weapons grade uranium and plutonium."

"What's the diameter of the bomb?" asked another analyst.

"Forty-two inches and the warhead has to be less than that to fit inside. So, with that diameter plus another ten feet for the three stage firing mechanisms, our lead box needs to be around twelve feet long, four feet wide and four feet tall."

All the analysts were nodding their heads in agreement when Doug spoke up. "Okay, I'm beginning to get a feel for what the lead box would look like, but how heavy would it be? And could a small transport vehicle carry it?"

One of the analysts tapped furiously on a scientific calculator then looked up at the team. "Well, the lead walls would need to be at least two inches thick to shield the radiation and with the dimensions you have mentioned, I would expect it to weigh around 3000 pounds."

"Can you get that inside a UPS truck?" another analyst asked.

"Probably not," Doug added. "You would need a bigger vehicle and some means of lifting a one and a half ton box onto, or inside, the vehicle."

"Okay, a large truck then," said one of the team members. "Maybe a big flatbed, or a low-boy, or one of those eighteen wheelers."

"Sounds good," Doug said encouragingly. "But even if you had the means to transport it from Faro, NC, where would you want take it, and why?" With that question he left his team poring over maps of Eastern North Carolina while he went to check in with Noah Weller and see how the other group was progressing.

Dhul-Hajj

Jeddah, Saudi Arabia

A BLACK CHEVY SUBURBAN drove carefully through the crowded streets of Jeddah toward one of the largest seaports in the world. Inside the SUV were four Americans, the Lightning Boat team, who had flown in to the 'Paris of Arabia' the day before. They were on their way to the harbor to observe the arrival of the Solar Star.

For several weeks forty thousand pilgrims a day had been arriving at the King Abdul Aziz International Airport north of Jeddah. The annual December Hajj to Makkah was underway. It was a massive logistical undertaking to process, transport and care for the millions of Muslim worshipers that were making their way to Makkah to complete the fifth of the Five Pillars of Islam.

Most of them would ride the new train from Jeddah to the Holy City while others would humbly walk the remaining thirty-eight miles. There they would circle the Ka'ba, the sacred shrine that held the venerated Hajar, the black stone of Muhammad. By the end of the first week over two million Muslims had arrived and surrounded the City of Makkah with their white desert tents.

Jake exited the Suburban and walked over to a rail by the water's edge. Duke and Khan joined him. "Right on time," Jake said. "In a few hours the Prince's new boat will be delivered to Warehouse 40 right over there," and he pointed to a private quay across the harbor.

A pretty brunette walked up behind the three men, a large white scarf wrapped over her head and around her shoulders. "So this is it," Annalisa whispered sadly, "where Peaceful Eagle meets Alpha Omega."

Jake turned, reached out his hand and pulled her in beside him. He looked down into hazel green eyes that had lost their joy since learning of Robert's death at the hands of Islamist fanatics. "We knew it might come to this," he whispered. "Now we have an opportunity to finish what Robert started."

"I know," she whispered and glanced toward Duke as if to ask a question.

"Yeah, I'm in, Annalisa. This needs to be done," then he shot a look at the Pakistani. "Right, Khan?"

The nuclear scientist took a deep breath, patted his chest with the palm of his right hand and let out a heavy sigh. "It is dangerous, yes, what we do. But, I agree, and we shall see who is wise enough to avoid destruction."

Jake looked proudly at the small man who had embraced Robert's plan. "As soon as the Prince's new boat is inside the warehouse and the shipping container is delivered with the tools and equipment, our work begins. We must hurry," he added. "Our contact in the NCTC is holding back the investigation, but he can only do it for so long."

Jake knew what had to be done and quickly. "We have to remove the top of the Prince's new Speed Master to gain access to the lead keel weight in the hull. Then we'll take the bombs out, insert the firing mechanisms and load them inside auxiliary fuel tanks for the F-15s. The next day we'll deliver them to the Royal Saudi Air Force Base adjacent to the airport. That's where the belly tanks will be attached to the jets.

"The 8th Wing of the 92nd Squadron of the RSAF has nine Boeing F-15 Strike Eagles purchased from the United States. They share a common runway with the commercial aircraft, but have their own secure facilities on the eastern side of the tarmac.

And with the high security badges obtained through the prince, our team should have no problem gaining access to the base."

"Will we have to fuel and set up the aircraft?" Duke asked.

"Fortunately not," Jake answered. "As part of the security arrangements for the Hajj, the Saudi's keep three F-15s in the air at all times. They fly a twenty-mile radius around Makkah at twenty-five thousand feet. No other aircraft are allowed to approach or enter the secured air space during the Hajj.

"Nice accommodations?" Duke said, changing the subject.

The Royal Villas of Le Meridien were in a part of the city known as 'New Jeddah' just across from the airport. The three-story villa offered privacy, three bedrooms in a luxurious environment, and secure garage parking on the ground floor. The team could come and go in their Suburban unseen by prying eyes.

"I love the room service," Khan said with a grin. "Twenty-four hours, anything we want." As special guests of Prince Abdullah bin Ghazi, money was of little concern to the Lightning boat team.

Arrows and Olive Branches

Jeddah, Saudi Arabia

ANNALISA WAS ALONE ON the rooftop of the villa, lying back in a deck recliner with her white cotton robe pulled open to enjoy the last rays of the afternoon sun. She was staring out toward a Red Sea sunset three miles away thinking about Robert Faircloth. Jake stood in the open doorway to their bedroom studying the long curves of her olive toned body that radiated sensual warmth.

Her brown hair glistened in the glow of the setting sun, a smile on her lips as her eyes slowly closed, the second glass of Merlot performing well. For the moment she was free of the sadness of Robert's loss. Jake walked out to join her, a wine glass in his hand, and he sat down on the edge of the recliner.

She reached up with her hand to stroke the hair on his chest, then broke the spell by asking, "Why did the Saudis name their operation Peaceful Eagle?"

Jake didn't want to answer or discuss anything, other than his smoldering need. He sighed to himself, realizing she was still in pain and wanted to talk, and took a sip from his glass. "The eagle is a powerful symbol of courage and strength. Many governments use it in one form or another."

"How does America use it?" she asked without opening her eyes.

"Have you ever looked on the back of a dollar bill?"

"Yeah, it's green, really green," she whispered.

"On the right side, there's the seal of the United States with an eagle inside. In one claw there's an olive branch that represents peace, and in the other a clutch of arrows that represent war. So, the eagle on the dollar suggests that while we desire peace we must always be ready for war."

"I never thought of that before," she said, and sat up to look out toward the Red Sea sunset. Jake noticed that her smile had slipped away.

"Ever heard of the War Eagle flag?" he asked.

She turned toward him and he could see that whatever she was thinking had brought the sadness back. "No."

"Whenever America is at war our military flies the War Eagle flag, and on that banner is an eagle that has dropped the olive branch of peace. It carries only arrows in both claws."

In spite of the effects of the wine her eyes began to brim with tears. "And Robert, he was our olive branch."

Jake felt the pain sting his own heart. He could barely speak. "Yes," he mumbled, "Robert was our olive branch. And he was sacrificed. So now, it's arrows."

Annalisa sat up in her chair, tears still in her eyes. "I understand, Jake. I understand what Robert was trying to do. He didn't succeed, so we have to make his plan work."

She smiled at him, remembering a young girl enamored of a handsome man her father brought home for dinner back in McLean, Virginia. He was kind and gentle, a patient man, reading her stories and poems, correcting her homework, even helping her with puzzles. It was many years later before she understood she was in love with him.

Annalisa leaned up and tenderly kissed Jake's lips, recalling the night in New York that she made her confession. She reached for his hand and rose from her chair. "Jake, I need you now, because I don't know how much longer we…"

She couldn't finish the sentence. She didn't have to. Jake understood. He rose from the chair, slipped an arm around her waist and held her close as they walked quietly into the bedroom.

The NCTC

McLean, VA

NOAH WELLER RUSHED INTO the room where Jackson and his team were working. Doug had called to say they had figured out where the fissile materiel was taken. "We examined every possible means of transporting a lead box with the dimensions required to carry one, or several warheads. A rental truck could have carried it, but then we asked ourselves where, and for what purpose? And that's when Mr. Harrison over there mentioned that with that size and shape it reminded him of the keel for an old sailboat he used to have."

"A keel," Agent Weller repeated excitedly. "A lead box used as a keel for a sailboat." Then he looked at Jackson with a pained expression on his face. "How big a sailboat?"

"Not very large," Doug added. "Something in the twenty-five foot range is all that's needed for the right sized keel."

"My God, Doug, they could sail a boat like that into any harbor in America and no one would ever know, because there's no way to check for radiation on every single small vessel entering harbors and marinas."

"It gets better," Doug added. "One of the analysts suggested that a sailboat might be too slow, because once the bad guys have their weapon they would want to get it to their target as fast as possible. So, if it were disguised as a keel in a boat and a sail boat is too slow, we started looking at power boats that could use the same size keel."

"Bingo," shouted one of the team members. "We found a boat manufacturer only two hours away from Faro that makes the fastest power boats in the world."

Agent Weller shouted, "Good work! What's the name of the company?"

"Lightning Power Boats," Doug added. "It's on the Pamlico River near Washington, NC."

"Well, we'd better get down there as soon as possible," Weller said.

"We will, but first we're going to have a little video conference with the Plant Manager for Lightning Boats," and Doug turned to one of the analysts in the back of the room. "Do we have Mr. Ellis on the line?"

"Yes, sir," she answered. "I've got him on video iChat through his gmail account. He's at the plant now and will use the camera on his laptop to give us a view of the keel for a Lightning Power Boat."

"Great," Doug said. "Can you switch that image up to the big screen?"

With just a few clicks on her computer a close-up image of a red headed man filled the huge screen at the front of the room. William Ellis, the plant manager, was holding a laptop computer in his arms staring at an imbedded camera on his iMac screen. Noah Weller watched as the manager's face seemed to weave and bob on the large screen of the NCTC.

"Mr. Ellis, can you see me and hear me?"

"I sure can. I can see you real good. Can you see me okay?"

"I can, Mr. Ellis, but I need to ask you to stand still while you're holding your computer. It's creating a shaky picture for us up here."

"Oh, sorry 'bout that." With a little effort he stood perfectly still and the image on the big screen stabilized.

"My name is Noah Weller. I work for the National Counter Terrorism Center in McLean, Virginia, and I was wondering if you might be able to give us some help with a case we're working on."

"I sure will try, Mr. Weller, anything I can do to help. When Ms. Phillips called me at the house and told me she needed me to get down to the plant and get online for a video conference call with the NCTC, well, damn, who wouldn't want to try and help if they could. Know what I mean?"

Noah Weller smiled to himself, still impressed that so many Americans were willing to drop whatever they were doing and offer to help their government whenever asked. "Mr. Ellis, could you use the camera on your laptop to show us what the keel for one of your Lightning Power Boats looks like?"

"Sure, got one right over here that we're getting ready to install in a Speed Master, one of our most expensive boats. But now the picture is going to be a bit shaky while I walk over to it. Just shipped one of these a few weeks ago to a prince in Saudi Arabia. These days they're about the only ones who can afford these things."

He wasn't able to see the shocked expressions on the faces of everyone in the room at the NCTC, as all of them realized in one collective moment that the Saudis might be trying to buy nuclear weapons on the black market. Weller looked back at the camera. "Did you just say that you shipped a boat with a lead keel like the one you're about to show us to a Saudi prince?"

"Yeah, we sure did. He paid cash up front. Best kind of deal for us."

Weller's head began to spin with possibilities. *A purchased nuclear weapon can be just as deadly as anything the Iranians might develop.* The tension in the room rose dramatically. "Do you remember the name of the prince who purchased the boat?"

"Sure, he's one of our best customers. This makes his third Lightning boat. He comes in for a personal visit each time and our marketing boys make a big deal out of it, booze, blondes and lots of entertainment. He sure likes blondes, know what I mean?"

"His name?" Weller asked again.

"Oh yeah, bin Ghazi, Prince Abdullah bin Ghazi. He's some kind of political big shot up in New York."

Everyone in the room recognized the name of the Saudi Ambassador to the United Nations. As they watched the image on the big screen they could almost feel each step as the Plant Manager bobbed to the right and back to the left till he stopped in front of a large object.

"This is one of our 2,800 pound stock keel weights. We order them fourteen feet long, four foot wide and four foot high then trim them down as needed to fit inside the hull of the model boat they will be used in."

Weller looked over at Jackson. "We're recording all this, aren't we?"

"You bet we are," Jackson answered.

Agent Weller turned back to the camera. "Mr. Ellis, is it possible to hollow out one of those keel weights?"

"Damn!" he exclaimed. "Now who would want to go to the trouble to do that? It would be a whole lot easier to take some slag pieces and weld them together and make a hollow box, rather than try... "

"What?" Agent Weller asked, interrupting the Plant Manager. "What did you just say about slag pieces and making a hollow lead box?"

"Yeah, look over here," and the camera swung in a long arc to a pile of lead sheets that had been cut away from the stock keel weights. "We have to cut and trim the stock keels and we just pile the slag over here. Sometimes we need a bit to add to a keel, but most often we just sell this as scrap to anyone who wants it. Come to think of it one of our subs bought a big pile just a few months back. Said he wanted to rebuild a keel for an old sailboat he was remodeling."

Agent Weller cleared his throat and tried to ask as noncha-
lantly as possible. "Think we might be able to talk to this person?"

"Yeah, sure. His name is Duke DiSisto. Owns a shop just down
the road from here. He does near 'bout all the electronics work
for our new boats. Yeah, Duke is a great guy," then he paused in
thought. "But come to think of it, he's on vacation. Told us he'd
be out of town for a few weeks, so I guess he might not be available."

Weller cleared his throat again, a nervous habit he resorted
to whenever he was excited about something. "Did he mention
where he might be going?"

"France, I think. Said he'd never been to Paris and always
wanted to go there."

Jackson leaned over and whispered to Weller. "We need to get
down there ASAP and scan the area for radiation levels, especially
that electronics shop."

Weller turned back to the camera. "Mr. Ellis, would you mind
if a team of our agents came down to your plant and looked
around a bit and maybe inside Mr. DiSisto's electronics shop?"

"No problem for us here at the plant, but I'm not sure who
might have a key to Duke's shop. I can try to get one tomorrow.
When do you boys want to come down?"

"We can be there in a two hours," Weller said anxiously.

The laptop spun around and settled on the face of William
Ellis. "Wow, you boys must be working on something big?"

"Could be, Mr. Ellis. So don't say a word about this to anyone
and we'll see you in a couple of hours."

Warehouse 40

Jeddah, Saudi Arabia

THE SPEED MASTER WAS unloaded from the freighter onto a six-wheeled boat trailer then delivered to a warehouse at the end of a concrete quay in the harbor of Jeddah. A red-walled shipping container with all the special tools and equipment required by the Lightning maintenance team had also been delivered. Inside the container were several crates of consumer goods, specially ordered by the prince, including cases of French wine and Crown Royal that were acquired in Marseille.

Before the deck could be raised Duke and Jake used hydraulic drills with large Phillips heads to remove dozens of four-inch stainless steel deck screws, then applied a special solvent to dissolve the glue between the deck and hull. The warehouse filled with fumes that leached through the carbon filters on the breathing masks the Americans were wearing, but the work continued.

After securing guy wires to both sides of the deck Duke pressed a green button on the hand-held control for an overhead crane. He and Jake watched as the forty-eight foot polycarbonate deck lifted slowly away from the hull and rose ten feet in the air. Duke stopped the lift and rotated the switch that would move it forward along a ceiling mounted rail. As the deck cleared the hull it was gently lowered onto cross rails on the floor then the crane was toggled back over the gaping hull of the Lightning Boat.

Jake climbed over the edge and down inside. He carefully examined the huge lead box and the five latches that had been sealed in place. He looked up at Duke and smiled behind his breathing mask. "All of the latches are securely sealed!" he shouted.

Duke began waving his hands in front of his face and motioned for Jake to come over and join him. "Before we can continue, Jake, we have to lift the doors at each end of the building just a few feet, to let a cross breeze carry these fumes out of here or else we're gonna pass out."

"How long do they have to be open?" Jake asked, conceding that it must be done.

"A couple of hours at least," Duke answered.

"Okay," Jake said. "Break time." They grabbed two folding metal chairs and went to the front of the hangar to sit by the door. With cold bottles of water from a small refrigerator on the floor they waited for Annalisa and Khan to arrive with a picnic lunch.

While a Red Sea breeze ventilated the building, Jake queried Duke on the details of flying a Saudi F-15 Strike Eagle. "If you've had experience flying any kind of jet," Duke said, "you can fly an F-15. Essentially all the elements for take-offs and landings are the same. Once the engines are warmed up you push the throttle forward and the jet begins to roll.

"The only complicated things about military jets are the weapons systems and radars. They take a lot of special training and experience to learn to operate, but taking off and flying in a straight line is pretty simple for an experienced jet pilot."

A black chauffeur-driven sedan pulled up to the high chain link fence surrounding the warehouse. After presenting identification to the guard Annalisa and Khan passed through the gate and their car drove up beside Jake and Duke.

"Oh, my God," Annalisa squealed as she stepped out of the car and approached the two men sitting by the hangar door. "It smells like…" Her voice trailed off as she held a hand over her nose.

"I know," Jake said apologetically. "It's the solvent, but if you think this is bad, you should have been in here before we lifted the doors to vent the place."

"You okay, Khan?" Duke asked.

The Pakistani scientist had also raised a hand to cover his nose. "Yes, but this smell will give me a headache unless I sit in one of those chairs by the door."

Annalisa stared at the long lead box on the concrete floor with a Geiger counter sitting on top. "You two work well together. You've gotten so much done."

"Duke's a great supervisor. I'm just doing what he tells me," and a rare smile crossed Jake's normally intense visage.

It was a working lunch, from a large platter filled with olives, pickles, sliced carrots and cucumbers. Jake and Annalisa focused on hummus, salad and Falafel wraps, while Duke and Khan paid attention to the lamb and chicken kabobs. And all of it was washed down with bottles of lime-flavored carbonated water.

By mid afternoon they were ready to pull the cover off the lead keel. The entire team donned protective clothing to shield them from any radiation that may have leaked inside. The seals were cut with a small blowtorch and after they cooled, Duke and Jake pushed the heavy two-inch thick lid off and let it slip down beside the box.

There was only a slight register on the Geiger counter as Khan pulled the insulation away from the components inside. While Jake stood and admired the four peanut-shaped nuclear weapons, the Pakistani looked up and asked, "When will the belly tanks arrive?"

"They're on the way. Annalisa just got off the phone with the Prince."

"And he agreed to send four?" Khan asked with some surprise.

"I explained that auxiliary tanks were very difficult to cut in half," Jake answered, "and that we needed several in case we made any mistakes. That seemed to satisfy him."

"Okay," Khan said, "let's get these out of here, set them on a palette and cover them with a tarp until the truck arrives. When Duke starts cross-cutting the fuel tanks I will begin assembly of the weapons."

Thirty minutes later the front garage door of the warehouse began to lift open. The four Lightning team members stood in front of the heavy blue tarp and listened as cables and motors groaned while raising the huge door. Even before it had lifted all the way a beeping twenty-foot cargo truck began backing slowly inside.

When the van stopped the driver got out and without so much as a glance at the deck and hull of the gutted boat he walked back outside. As the heavy door began to drop Jake saw the man get inside one of the Prince's shiny black cars and drive away. He looked over at Duke. "Time to cut up some fuel tanks."

"Yeah, open the back doors, Jake, and I'll crank up the fork lift."

Four brand new twelve foot long, one thousand gallon auxiliary fuel tanks were fastened to a wooden rack inside the truck, two on the bottom and two on top. They were separated by 4" x 6" wood blocks running the length of the tanks.

Duke retrieved a diamond tipped saw from the red shipping container. "Okay," he announced, "everyone put on hearing protection," and the shearing whine of the blade cutting through metal filled the warehouse.

At the other end Khan carefully inspected and assembled the firing mechanisms for the four nuclear weapons. "Jake," he shouted above the whine of the saw. "Come see." The NDR leader told the scientist he wanted to inspect each one of the warheads before they were inserted into the belly tanks.

Jake ran his hands over the compression charges attached at each end of the two-foot long peanut-shaped bombs, tugging gently on the wiring that would run up inside the aircraft to the cockpit. With a diameter of just over twelve inches, they would easily fit in the rucksacks still hanging inside the red shipping container.

After a careful examination, Jake looked at Khan. "Let's get the packs."

"The what?" Khan asked.

"Come with me," Jake said. The two men walked over to the container. Strapped to the interior walls were four oversized military backpacks with aluminum frames and one large parachute that appeared to be rigged and ready.

Khan understood that the three hundred pound warheads would fit inside the heavy-duty backpacks, but the parachute confused him. "What's that for?" he asked.

"I'll explain later, but first, let's get the warheads inside these rucksacks." As they carried the packs over to the table where Khan had been working Jake said, "Hard to believe the equivalent of three million tons of dynamite will fit inside one of these bags."

"Even more amazing," Khan added, "are the nuclear artillery shells with a yield equivalent to the Hiroshima bomb, but fortunately they have never been used."

As they placed the packs on the table Khan looked at Jake. "This is a good idea, putting the weapons inside the packs and hiding them inside belly tanks. Who would look for them in a stack of reserve fuel tanks?"

"One is to be fully armed, Khan, for the demonstration. Remember?"

"Oh, yes. It is a very simple thing to do. As you can see I have removed the boron tamper from this one that Petrovski installed." Jake watched carefully as Khan showed him exactly how to pull out the neutron absorbing material.

"See here, where I have connected two wires from the blasting caps to the cordite compression detonators at each end. And this wire will run up inside the cockpit of the aircraft to a hand held detonator. This way, the pilot will have full control over the weapon at all times. It cannot be detonated unless the pilot arms the weapon and fires it."

Jake understood little of the science involved, but was a quick study in weapons technology and detonations. "So, to partially arm the bomb, you removed the boron tamper and wired the blasting caps to a hand held device that will be in the cockpit."

"Yes," Kahn said confidently, holding up one of the hand-held devices. "When the Saudi pilot is ready to detonate all he has to do is squeeze the handle, pull this o-ring and remove the quarter inch cotter pin from the device. When he releases a green light will appear indicating it is ready. All that's left for him to do is squeeze the handle again. A red light will appear and then… well, nothing. The fission reaction will occur and he will evaporate inside the fusion fireball."

"Small change of plan here," Jake added, "and that's what the parachute is for. No since wasting a perfectly good Saudi pilot."

"I thought that was the plan?" the Pakistani asked with a surprised look.

"Duke's an electronic genius. He's come up with a timer to delay detonation. So, instead of exploding the weapon on board the pilot can jettison the fuel tank at altitude. The parachute will exit the end of the tank and let it descend slowly. The pilot will go to afterburner, clear the airspace, and just before the weapon hits the ground the timer will send the firing signal through and the weapon will explode."

"He can do that, make such a timer?"

"He already has Khan. So, along with the armed weapon we will also install the timer and parachute in the back section of the fuel tank."

"Very good," Khan responded with a satisfied smile. "Now the pilot will not have to be sacrificed. Yes, I approve of that."

"Okay then, I'll get the forklift and we'll use it to position the weapons so we can place them inside the rucksacks. Then we'll use the exterior straps on the packs to lift them for insertion inside the fuel tanks. Sound good?"

"Very good, Mr. Jake. I can do this." Khan placed a hand over his heart and closed his eyes. "I pray for this to work just as Mr. Robert has planned and that nothing will go wrong."

"So do I," Jake added in a comforting tone. He was trying not to betray his plan to arm the other three weapons then turned to the far end of the building. "Duke!" he shouted. "Can we get one of those fuel tanks?"

"Come and get it," Duke shouted back. "Three are done, I have one more to go," and a loud shearing whine rose above the level of everything else.

Two hours later after Annalisa and Khan left the warehouse to return to the villa, Duke connected the wires to the compression charges on each of the other three weapons partially arming all the warheads.

The next morning after the fuel tanks were attached to the jets he would connect handheld detonators inside the aircraft then wire automatic detonators to the aircraft's Threat Assessment Radars. If a missile were fired at one of the jets the TAR would detect it and detonate if the missile came within a thousand feet of the F-15.

"Guess if Khan knew you were going to arm all of these he might have done something stupid like disconnect a wire or two."

"Couldn't take that chance, Duke. He's a good man and I want him to make it home to his family in Pakistan."

"I don't get it, Jake, if we're not going to let the Saudi pilot fly one of the jets out in the desert and detonate, then how are we going to set off a demo explosion?"

"This is where it gets a little complicated," Jake said solemnly, "and where I must be able to count on you and your skills."

"I told you, Jake, I'm in this to the end. You can count on me for anything."

"Okay, this is how it will work. You and Annalisa will be carrying a 3-megaton nuclear weapon in your belly tanks, but I will be carrying two weapons."

Duke's eyes brightened, "And where will you carry the second one?"

"Back seat. We'll use the bomb lift in the hangar tomorrow morning to raise the rucksack and lower it carefully into the back seat of my jet. Then you'll wire it just like yours including to my Threat Assessment Radar."

"Guess it won't matter where the bomb is on the jet," Duke added thoughtfully. "If it goes off then it's over. So, you'll be dropping your belly tank somewhere over the desert for the demo detonation?" He smiled. "When do you want it to detonate?"

"Just before it hits the ground," Jake responded firmly. "That way there will be plenty of time for us to clear the area and for the world to learn that we have viable nuclear weapons on board."

"I'll set the timer for two minutes after you release."

"That should do it, Duke, and the drop site is on our way to the midpoint. It's the same mountain valley bin-Ghazi's pilot was going to use. No one lives there. Hardly anyone goes there. It's that remote."

After the two men made a last inspection of the weapons and loaded the four auxiliary fuel tanks into the van for transport the next morning, they returned to the villa for their last night in Saudi Arabia.

A Matter of International Security

Beaufort County, NC

"USE THE PRY BAR," Weller said to an agent trying to pick a lock on the side door of the electronics shop. There had been no enhanced radiation at the Lightning Boat factory and they learned from the plant manager that the Prince's new Speed Master was shipped on the Solar Star, a freighter bound for Marseilles and Jeddah.

The agent placed the split end of the metal bar into a section where the dead bolt locked into the door jam. He gave a heave and the metal jam ripped apart. The NCTC agents entered Duke's shop with a Geiger counter held in front as they walked along the walls. Near the back a radiation signature was detected and the instrument began to buzz. When they reached a locker in the corner it rose to a steady growl and the needle on the Geiger counter jumped to the right.

"Let's clear out of here," Weller yelled, "this area is hot." As they rushed out of the building he looked over at Jackson. "This is it. This is where they brought the uranium and plutonium."

"And it looks like DiSisto made a hollow keel that was somehow installed inside the prince's new Speed Master boat."

"Sweet Jesus!" Weller exclaimed. "It's on its way to Saudi Arabia."

"If it's not there already," Doug sighed. He looked intently into the eyes of Noah Weller. "And this is no longer just a matter of national security."

"What do you mean?"

"It's now a matter of international security."

The Wood Shed

Washington, D.C.

EVERYONE STOOD WHEN THE President entered the room beneath the West Wing of the White House. Created in 1961 by President John Kennedy, after the failed Bay of Pigs invasion of Cuba, it had proven its value in 1962 as a provider of real-time information during the Cuban Missile Crisis. Known as the 'Wood Shed' by top government officials whose performance had been rebuked there, the Situation Room was now staffed 24-7 by senior staff officers of the various agencies of the American intelligence community.

The Commander-in-Chief took his usual seat at the head of the table with the Directors of National Intelligence and the National Security Agency on his immediate left and right. "Gentlemen, please sit down," he said and began his opening comments. The heads of every intelligence gathering organization in the nation including each branch of military service was represented, along with a host of other intelligence officials sitting in chairs against the walls.

"I have been briefed on this latest, most incredible series of events that threaten a nuclear catastrophe in the Middle East. And I have asked each of you to come today to listen to the two men who have spearheaded the investigation from its inception. Afterwards I will solicit your thoughts and opinions on our best course of action in this matter." He turned toward the Director of the CIA. "John, do you have any opening comments?"

"No, Sir, Mr. President. I think it best to go to Mitchell Lane, Director of the National Counter Terrorism Center. His agents have been on point in this matter."

"All right, Mr. Lane, you have the table."

Before he began Lane surveyed the faces of the directors of the Central Intelligence Agency, National Security Agency, Drug Enforcement Agency, Defense Intelligence Agency, Federal Bureau of Investigation, the Vice-President, Secretaries of State and Defense, and the four star generals seated at the table.

"As many of you know from the Top Secret brief before you, this most recent event had its genesis in the 1961 crash of a B-52 bomber trying to make its way back to Seymour Johnson Air Force Base near Goldsboro, NC. The Broken Arrow, a Mark 41 thermonuclear warhead, was lost and never recovered.

"In the past week we have discovered that someone has managed to retrieve the warhead that has been buried 180 feet deep in an underground aquifer for the past fifty years. They somehow managed to bring into the United States a tunnel-boring machine that could successfully maneuver into and through the aquifer.

"While we do not yet know who these people are we do know this much. One, they have retrieved the warhead and the nuclear fuel that it contained, two, they hired two nuclear scientists, a Russian and a Pakistani, who we believe have created at least one very powerful nuclear weapon or perhaps several smaller ones, three, they were able to hide the signature of the enriched uranium inside the hollow lead keel of a large powerboat, four, that this vessel was shipped to a Saudi prince in Jeddah, Saudi Arabia, and it arrived there two days ago, and five, either the Saudi government, or operatives within Saudi Arabia, now have in their possession one or more very powerful nuclear weapons."

There was nothing in the NCTC director's comments that had not been included in the brief. What the group now wanted to hear was from the two agents conducting the investigation. The director realized that. "Gentlemen, I give you Senior Agent Noah

Weller of the CIA and Agent Doug Jackson of the FBI, both of whom have been assigned to work as liaisons with the National Counter Terrorism Center."

The room grew impossibly still as the two agents rose from their chairs against the wall and walked around to the far end of the table so they would be standing directly in front of the President. Noah Weller began. "Mr. President, there is some additional information included in your most recent update that we were not able to include with the brief everyone else received. I would like to go over that, if I may."

"Please do, Agent Weller," the President said. "I think it's important for all of us to understand everything there is to know about this situation."

"One very important additional fact we have gathered is that Prince Abdullah bin Ghazi, the Saudi Ambassador to the United Nations, is the man who purchased the Lightning Power boat that was recently shipped from a port in North Carolina to Jeddah, Saudi Arabia.

"Bin Ghazi is therefore a prime suspect in this case and can most likely identify and lead us to the other perpetrators. He is no doubt the man handling the money, financing an operation that is costing in the tens of millions of dollars."

"Excuse me for interrupting," the President said as he leaned forward, "but may I ask if we know the whereabouts of bin Ghazi?"

"Yes, Sir, Mr. President. We know that he has returned to Saudi Arabia and that he is either in the capital, Riyadh, or at his home in Jeddah. But he is technically beyond the diplomatic reach of the United States at this moment.

"Furthermore, we do not yet know his motives or intentions. Our first thought is that he is working within his government to create a nuclear capability for Saudi Arabia as a counterpoint to that being developed by Iran. Or, second, that he may be working independently as a rogue, perhaps to pressure his government to adopt reforms that other progressive Muslim monarchies in the Middle East have embraced. Or, third, that he is working with terrorists within Saudi Arabia to unseat the House of Saud and perhaps take over as monarch."

"But money would not be much of a motivator for a man such as bin-Ghazi?"

"No, Sir, Mr. President. Bin Ghazi is already quite wealthy."

"Excuse me, Mr. Weller." The Director of National Intelligence was addressing him. "Is there another possible motive for bin Ghazi being involved? We're not yet sure if King Khalid of Saudi Arabia has knowledge of this. So, if bin-Ghazi is acting alone, can you think of any other reason why he would want to obtain nuclear weapons?"

Noah Weller cleared his throat, a nervous habit when speaking in front of groups. "Sir, the last possibility I can think of seems beyond the pale."

"And what is that, Agent Weller?"

"That either bin Ghazi or possibly the King of Saudi Arabia has a plan to use these weapons for reasons that are not yet known to us."

There was a sobering silence in the room as each of the intelligence directors considered that nuclear weapons might be detonated in the Middle East. The President broke the silence. "Is there anything else you would like to share with us, Agent Weller?"

"No, Mr. President. That pretty much covers everything we know at this time."

"Okay then, how about you, Agent Jackson? Is there anything you wish to share before we have to make what appears to be some pretty tough decisions?"

"Yes, Mr. President, there is something else I believe needs to be considered."

"And what is that?"

"Now that we know nuclear weapons have been transported to Jeddah and could find their way into the hands of any number of groups, from their government to radical Wahhabists, this may be the proper time to alert the intelligence communities of the world so they may go on high alert as we search for these weapons."

"I agree," the President responded. "That is one of several courses we must consider. Also, I believe it will be helpful if you and Agent Weller take an immediate flight to Jeddah. Get there as quickly as possible and let the Saudi General Intelligence Directorate know the imminent threat they are facing. And while you're there," the President added, "help us determine whether this is a Saudi government initiative or the lone efforts of one Prince Abdullah bin Ghazi."

Al Sultanah

Jeddah, Saudi Arabia

A BURNISHED ORANGE BALL dipped into the Red Sea as a black Chevy Suburban pulled into an elevated parking area near the town of Al Sultanah, a small suburb of Jeddah next to Abdul Aziz International Airport. From that vantage point the team could observe the civilian and military buildings on each side of the runways. From behind their darkened windows, Jake and the other team members used ten power binoculars to observe a flight of gray F-15 Strike Eagles taxi out on the tarmac. The long pointed nose with box side intakes and Saudi insignia painted on the twin vertical stabilizers gave the aircraft a distinctive profile.

"Looks like the next group out," Jake said. "Every four hours during the Hajj a fully armed flight of three F-15s takes off to relieve the previous group flying a wheel around Makkah. And soon, we'll be taking our turn."

He looked over at the newest NDR member. "Duke, why don't you go over with Annalisa and Khan some of the information on F-15s you shared with me this morning."

"Sure," he said, looking at the two sitting in the middle seat. "F-15 Strike Eagles were initially single-seat tactical fighters, like the ones I used to fly in Iraq, and they were the first American aircraft that could accelerate while in a vertical climb. On take-off an F-15 can go from idle to after burner in four seconds and after a short run can nose straight up and accelerate out of sight."

"Wow," said Khan from the backseat, "like a rocket."

"That's right," Duke answered with a grin, "one hell of a ride. In 1988, as the mission for these aircraft expanded a two-seat model was added, a fighter-bomber with a front seat for the driver and a back seat for the Weapons System Officer. The Saudis bought several squadrons of both models from McDonnell-Douglas, but the major advantage for us using the two-seat model is that it has much greater range with its extra fuel capacity."

"How much fuel?" Annalisa asked while peering out a window toward the sleek jets with blue and yellow Royal Saudi Air Force tail codes painted on the tails.

"The F-15 E holds about 6,700 gallons. But the belly tanks on our aircraft will be empty, so better say 5,700 gallons or about 45,000 pounds of fuel."

Annalisa looked at Jake. "Will that be enough to get us to our targets?"

"Enough to reach our targets and wheel around for a couple of hours."

"An F-15 flies pretty much like any other military jet," Duke continued. "The Flight Control Stick is between your legs," and he paused. "I used to call mine 'ET' because the head had two silver control buttons that reminded me of the little guy that just wanted to go home." After a quick smile he continued. "There's a throttle on your left, nose wheel steering switch below the head, and brakes and rudders at your feet. There are a few other bells and whistles that you don't need to know much about... "

"Like what?" Annalisa asked.

"Well, like the Terrain Following Radar that you can monitor in the green Head Up Display."

"Terrain Following Radar," she repeated. "How low will we be flying?"

"We have to avoid ground radar systems," Jake explained. "And in case any AWACS are up and monitoring the area we fly through, the lower we are to the surface the harder it will be for them to distinguish us from ground clutter."

"He's right," Duke said. "The laser gyro and altimeter will continuously monitor the aircraft's position in relation to the ground and provide data for the central computer that will generate a digital moving map. So, we'll fly 100 feet above the ground or should I say desert," he added dryly. "That way we should be nearly invisible to radar."

"Can we do that?" Annalisa asked. "Can we fly an F-15 that low?"

"The Israelis did it," Jake answered, "during Operation Opera in 1981, when they destroyed the Iraqi nuclear reactor south of Baghdad."

"The bombs were carried on F-16s," Duke added, "but their escorts were F-15s, so yeah, we can fly that low to get under ground based radar systems."

"How fast will we be flying?" she asked.

Duke looked over his shoulder at Annalisa then back at Jake. "Haven't you told her anything about the flight?"

"Compartmentalization," Jake said. "Need to know and all that, and now is the time for her to know."

Duke looked back at Annalisa, "We'll fly below just below Mach 1, about 700 miles per hour. It may take a few minutes longer to get there, but there's always a compromise between speed and fuel consumption." He pointed toward one of the jets on the runway. "You see those F-15s, fully loaded with armament and wing and belly tanks? With that kind of profile creating air turbulence, it would be pretty hard to handle while breaking through the sound barrier. These jets perform best without exterior fuel tanks. So, when we reach the mid-point we can drop our wing tanks and..."

"Okay," Annalisa interrupted. "Now what's a 'mid-point'?"

Jake reached across the front seat and took her hand. "I've had to rely on Duke's experience flying F-15s to make the necessary adjustments for speed, payload, and fuel."

"I understand," she said, "but what's a 'mid-point'?"

"It's a location in the desert, 800 miles northeast of Jeddah, just below the Kuwaiti border that is equidistant from each of our targets. When we reach the mid-point, that's when we separate and fly to our destinations."

Her face darkened. "You mean our destinies."

"And you'll have the Dead Sea," Jake answered, "to help keep you hidden from any down looking radar systems."

"He's right," Duke added. "The Israelis use a Gulf Stream mounted Phalcon System, an Active Electronic Sound Array, two on each side, one in the nose and one under the tail with a down looking view to determine azimuth and elevation of objects. It only has one weakness, water, trying to get a bounce back from the surface. Something as small as a wave can confuse it."

"So, you'll fly with us to the mid-point then turn west on your course directly to Jerusalem," Jake explained. "When you reach Jordan and the Dead Sea you'll hit the deck hard."

"Like drag your ass in the water, girl," Duke added. "The spray kicked up by your thrusters will keep you hidden till you cross into the West Bank and lift up over the Judean Hills."

"That's when Israeli ground radar will get a good look at you," Jake said, "but at Mach. 9, by the time they see your blip on their screen you'll be over Jerusalem and making your mayday call to their air traffic controllers."

"Plus," Duke added, "they have a treaty with Jordan, and unless they're on alert they won't be expecting a breach of Israeli airspace from the west. Their new 'Iron Dome' missile defense batteries are deployed on the northern borders with Lebanon and Syria, and Gaza to the south."

"Okay, you boys have it all figured out," she said, "but how about clearance for take-off? Who will communicate with the tower?" she asked.

"Only the flight commander will speak with the controllers," Jake said.

"So, how's your Arabic?"

"Not very good, but this is an international airport with a shared runway and planes arriving from all over the world. Both towers communicate in English, as well as the Saudi pilots who were trained in the U.S. First, the military controller gives us clearance to leave the hangar then the civilian tower tells us when to move into take-off position. I'll give the command for Eagles one and two to takeoff and I'll be last to leave the ground."

"Well," Annalisa said dramatically, enjoying the irony of a woman flying a Saudi military aircraft. "Guess I'd better keep quiet then. They don't let women drive cars, you know, and would be absolutely horrified if they knew a female was flying one of their precious jets." Everyone laughed at her stab at the Saudi 'Men's Only' culture.

Khan leaned forward against the back of the seat. "Jake, what about the Saudi pilots and the flight crews in the hangar, what will happen to them?"

"I didn't tell you about them, Khan, because you won't be there, remember? Tomorrow morning you'll remain at the villa. After we leave for the warehouse you'll make sure all our communications equipment is working properly before you go to the airport. Then you will take a flight home to Pakistan."

"Oh," Khan replied with his usual smile. "I understand, compartmentalization. I only know what I need to know."

"That's right," Jake responded as Duke drove out of the parking area and turned back toward the hotel. It would be their last night together in Saudi Arabia.

Last of the Arabian Nights

Jeddah, Saudi Arabia

THE NDR TEAM MEMBERS sat in leather wrapped chairs around a cypress table in the kitchen. The mood was somber and reflective, because each of the pilots knew that if anything were to go wrong the next day this would be their very last evening.

Annalisa reached for Jake's hand without looking at him. It was not the possibility of dying that concerned her, but the possibility of living without Jake. *How could I live without him*, she asked herself lifting her eyes toward the aging warrior. She and Jake were not married, but both understood they were joined forever.

"Any last thoughts?" Jake asked the group.

Khan spoke first. "What is the thing one should do on their last night? I mean there is no certainty that I will be able to catch a flight out of Jeddah, or that any of us will live to see another day."

"A letter, Khan," Duke said. "I'm writing a letter to my mother. She lives on a sheep ranch in Ireland and I just want her to know that if this goes badly she gets all the money I received for the farm, and that…" He paused and everyone knew what he wanted to say. The last words to his mother would be *I love you*, but Duke wasn't the sort of man who could easily speak those words in front of others.

Jake addressed the Pakistani. "Khan, you're sure that after we're over our targets we can call back to a phone in this room and talk to each other?"

"Quite sure, Mr. Jake. It is a simple matter of a conference call. After the third one connects, this satellite phone is programmed to call the information desks of a dozen media outlets around the world. So, by way of a larger conference call they will be able to hear your conversations with Duke and Annalisa and your communications with the control towers at each of your targets. But," he added with a cautionary tone, "you must sound very convincing when they first get on the line or they might think you are a prank call and hang up."

"I don't believe that will be a problem. By the time I make the call here the adrenaline will be pumping wide open." Jake leaned in toward Khan. "I've relied on you to make sure we had viable nuclear weapons. But this is the part of Robert's plan where he is counting on you to make sure this becomes an international event, putting even more pressure on the Saudis, Iranians and Israelis to concede."

He leaned back and changed the tone of the conversation. "What are you going to do with all that money when you get home?"

"I don't know," Khan responded. "I've never had any money before. But if I survive what comes after this, I will think of you, all of you, and remember what we were trying to accomplish here. It will either be done and the world will be a safer place, or we will not succeed and it will become even more dangerous. One way or the other, tomorrow the world will change."

The team members nodded in agreement. Khan had summed up what each of them was feeling. No one spoke of Robert's death in Iraq, but his sacrifice was on the mind of everyone.

Annalisa rose from the table still holding Jake's hand. "If this is my last night then I want to spend it with you, alone," she added with conviction.

Jake looked up into her wistful green eyes. "I'll be right there. You go ahead. I've got to make one last call to Nalum."

She smiled, pausing to study the face of the man she loved. "Hurry," she said as she let go of his hand and waved good night to the other two men.

"A letter," Khan said as he rose from his chair. "That sounds like a good idea, Mr. Duke. I think I will compose some last words for my family, just in case, you know. They probably have not looked into my personal affairs and do not realize what has been deposited in my bank account. And I don't want my wife's greedy brother to get his hands on that money. He is such a lazy man who lives off of his family and friends."

He paused a moment longer to look at the two men still sitting at the table. "It is my great hope that Robert's plan will work just the way he wanted it to." He nodded affirmatively and went to his room.

When Kahn's door closed Jake looked across the table at Duke. "Thanks for helping me with this."

"My pleasure, Jake. I told you before that I support the cause."

"I mean today, at the warehouse."

"Oh, yeah, that; well, I mean if they do try to shoot us down then why shouldn't we detonate? It wasn't that bad, removing the boron tampers from the other two weapons and wiring the detonators. Kid stuff," he added with a boyish grin.

"And tomorrow morning you can wire the auto-detonate mechanisms into the Threat Assessment Radars?"

"That should be the last thing, Jake. If any missile gets within a thousand feet of one of our jets, then it will automatically detonate the weapon over the target."

Jake slipped back against the leather-wrapped slats of his chair. "It's getting a little confusing. I can hardly remember who I've told what."

"Well, Khan still believes its Peaceful Eagle, only a detonation in the Saudi desert. But what about Annalisa, what does she know?"

"She knows everything, Duke, except for the auto-detonate feature. If the Israelis try to shoot her down," and he took a long deep breath. "Well, then they deserve to lose Jerusalem."

"But they won't, Jake. In a crisis the Israelis have proven to be very practical. As we discussed before they are the least likely to shoot down a nuclear-armed aircraft. That's why it's better for Annalisa to fly there."

Duke studied the NDR leader for a moment longer. "You're the only one with a handheld detonator, Jake. You gonna stick to Robert's plan or do something creative?"

"I'm doing this for Robert, so I'll stay with his plan. But if the Israelis shoot Annalisa down then it's Omega for Tehran."

"What about me, Jake? If one of those Saudi pilots gets missile lock on me and fires the auto detonate feature will take over, and you know what that means?"

"Yeah, Makkah and four million people including all the pilgrims from one hundred sixty Islamic countries will turn into toast."

"That's right. So, if the Saudis take me down, what will you do?"

Jake stared solemnly toward the courageous young man. "I give you my word, Duke. If the Saudis take you down, then I will call Annalisa for some last words and follow you into eternity."

"That's what I wanted to hear," Duke said solemnly. "That's what I need to know. So, tomorrow morning I'm going to hardwire a detonation device into my cockpit and if the Iranians take you out, or if you go down after Annalisa, then I will detonate right behind you. Like I said before, I'm in this thing all the way and if I go down then you and I will both know that I did my best to accomplish the mission."

Jake reached out with his right hand and shook that of his teammate. "You're one tough son of a bitch, Duke, just like Rufus said. You're fearless, dedicated, and able to stick with the job until it's done."

Duke rose from his seat with a smile and headed toward his bedroom. "Get some rest, Jake. I'll see you at 0400."

Jake was sitting with his back to his bedroom door. He didn't notice that it was cracked slightly open, or that it was now quietly closing. Annalisa had been listening to their comments about automatic detonators.

Stay Tuned to CNN

Jeddah, Saudi Arabia

JAKE REACHED FOR HIS satellite phone. He dialed the number of a spacious French-villa in the upper Shenandoah Valley near Berryville, Virginia. Allowing for the ten-hour time difference, he thought Nalum should be having his morning coffee on the veranda of his home next to the tasting rooms of the family-owned winery at Veramar.

"A call for you, Sir, on your secure line," announced one of Nalum Taylor's personal assistants as he walked out on the patio with a portable phone.

Nalum glanced over his shoulder, "Who is it, Gordo?"

"It's Mr. Jake."

Nalum knew the time was at hand for the Peaceful Eagle mission to launch and he reached for the phone. "Jake, what time is it over there? Is every thing ready?"

"Time is not a problem anymore, Nalum. I just wanted you to know that everything is in place to begin tomorrow morning, Saudi time, at 0800."

"So, by noon it should be over?"

"If everything goes as planned, it will be over by then one way or another."

Nalum cleared his throat. "You'll be making history tomorrow, Jake. No one has tried to force the hand of a despotic state with a nuclear threat since Jack Kennedy. You and everyone on your team should be very proud of what you are about to accomplish."

There was a distracting pause in the conversation as Jake considered what he had to say next. But before he could continue Nalum interrupted. "Jake, is everything okay? You seem rather quiet." He let the question linger.

"I just want you to know, Nalum, that I know everything. I know who you really are, who you work for, and that the NDR is an extension of something bigger."

Nalum swallowed hard. "Jake, you know we've discussed this before. That whole thing about a New World Order is just a conspiracy theory that has no basis in fact. How can you say such a thing?"

"Robert discovered it, Nalum, and he shared it with me the last time we were in Paris." There was more silence on the line before Jake spoke again. "Your name was on the list, Nalum, just like Robert said it would be."

"But, Jake, that list is purely speculative. No one knows for sure..."

"It's okay, Nalum," he said in a resigned tone. "Even if I had known from the beginning I probably would have worked undercover as Dante. I still believe in what we did in America, but I want you to know this is my last mission for the NDR or whoever it is that we've been working for."

"Jake, after this mission you and Annalisa need to take some time off, a long vacation anywhere in the world. You know how I feel about you. You're like a son that I..."

"It's okay, Nalum. You don't have to worry. Tehran is still the target." As soon as he said 'the' target instead of 'a' target, he wondered at the significance between the two words, one singular and the other implying plural. It didn't matter, he knew he was deceiving Nalum into thinking the original Peaceful Eagle plan was being implemented and it was, but it had been expanded to three targets.

"Jake," Nalum whispered with some relief. "Why don't we talk about this when you get back? You are correct that the days of the NDR in America have passed. After the investigation that will be held into the detonation of a nuclear weapon in the Middle East, it will only be a matter of time before everything is discovered. All of us will have to assume new identities in other countries. So, yes, this is your last mission for the NDR. But our friendship will never end."

Jake smiled into his phone. "Thank you, Nalum. I agree, no matter how things turn out tomorrow, you and I will always be friends." He took a breath and sighed heavily into the phone. "I have to go now, need to get a few hours sleep before the mission starts."

"Oh, one more thing, Jake. Doug Jackson, our NCTC contact, and his partner are on their way to Jeddah. They're flying in military jets and should be there in the morning. So consider that as soon as they tell Saudi intelligence officials what is going on, they will start closing down all escape routes including the airport in Jeddah. You might want to get that F-15 airborne as soon as possible and get out of there."

"Thanks for the heads up, Nalum. What time will they arrive?"

"Doug said their flight time will be a little over four hours, so they should arrive just about the time your jet takes off."

"Okay, Nalum, I understand."

"So, once the Prince's pilot rolls out for take-off, make sure Khan gets on a flight to Pakistan. Then you and Annalisa and Duke hurry back to the warehouse and get that Lightning boat in the water. You can make it across the Red Sea to the port in Halaib, Sudan, in two hours. One of our planes will be waiting there to pick you up."

"Got it," Jake said, knowing they would not be carrying out that part of the original plan. There would be no effort by the NDR team to escape from Saudi Arabia by speedboat. "I've never been to the Sudan," Jake added.

"Well, it's not a place you want to go for a vacation, but money trumps politics there and that's why they're willing to help us."

"Okay," Jake said with a fake yawn in voice. "Stay tuned to CNN. There should be some very interesting news to report tomorrow morning." Jake said good-bye, hung up the phone and walked toward his bedroom.

As he opened the door he saw Annalisa sitting in a side chair, tears in her eyes, waiting for him. "Automatic detonators, Jake. What does that mean?"

It was not the conversation he wanted to have on what could be his last night with Annalisa Bertolla.

Flying on a Lightning Bolt

Langley Air Force Base, Virginia

NO EXPENSE WAS SPARED flying Noah Weller and Doug Jackson to Jeddah in the shortest time possible. With the approval of the Secretary of Defense and the Joint Chiefs, they were whisked from the White House on a jet helicopter down to Langley Air Force Base near Hampton, Virginia.

They were greeted by a one-star Air Force general holding tightly to his hat. "Follow me," he shouted above the rotor noise and guided them inside a massive secured hangar where two experimental F-35 jets were parked. They were not the Lockheed-Martin single-seat Joint Strike Fighter models scheduled for service later in the year, but the new Northrop Grumman F-35DX, a two-seat model designed as a fighter-bomber.

"Gentlemen, let me introduce you to your pilots. Agent Weller, this is Lt. Colonel Faron Mitchell, one of our most experienced test pilots." Then he turned toward Doug Jackson, "And this is Major Sharon McCoy, another of our highly skilled pilots. I've been told that both of you have ridden back seat in jets before so I assume you've been through the one-day school and know the protocols."

Weller and Jackson answered at the same time. "Yes, sir, we have."

"Okay, then let me explain what's about to happen. This will only be the third international flight for the new two-seat model. Even though it's capable of Mach 3 you will be cruising at Mach 2.5, and it's like flying on a lightning bolt," he added.

There will be one mid-air refueling, over Spain. Clearances are now being arranged for landing in Jeddah, Saudi Arabia. Once you have exited the aircraft our pilots will refuel and immediately take-off for their return flight. Do you understand?"

"What about personal effects, clothes, hygiene items, that sort of thing?" Weller asked the DOD official.

"No problem," he answered. "Representatives from our embassy in Riyadh will be on the ground in Jeddah to meet you. They will have, or can obtain, anything you need including clothing, personal items, etc."

"What about our brief cases?" and Weller looked down at the bag in his hand.

"There's very little room in the back seat of this aircraft. We can strap your case to your lap, if you like, so that you can have access during the flight, but it may be a bit uncomfortable."

"How long in the air?" Weller asked.

The DOD official looked over at the pilots and Major McCoy responded. "Roughly 8,125 nautical miles at just over nineteen hundred miles per hour, should put us there in 4 hours, 18 minutes."

Weller glanced over at Jackson who was smiling and both men wore the same expression. *I can't believe what we are about to do.*

"We're fueled and ready," Lt. Col. Mitchell said. " I suggest you make a trip to the Men's Room and take care of any last minute necessities," he added with a knowing expression. "Four hours in the air is still a long time."

"Yes, Sir," they replied, as they ran off toward a bathroom to put on specially designed pairs of moisture and odor absorbing underwear.

D Day

Jeddah, Saudi Arabia

THE BLACK SUV BACKED out of a parking garage attached to the villa at Le Meridien at 0400 on a Monday morning. In another hour the Muezzin would begin calling morning prayers from minarets around the city.

As planned Khan remained behind at the villa to make last minute checks on the technical equipment to ensure that all three jets would be able to communicate with media outlets around the world. "No problem," he said to Jake while Annalisa gave him a hug good-bye. "I will take care of everything. Call back here anytime after 0900 and the box over there will dial the numbers programmed into it."

"Kahn," she whispered. "Once you have everything setup, take the hotel limo to the airport and fly home to your family."

"Yes, thank you. I will do that. Once the bomb is detonated in the desert everything will change in the Middle East. So I must hurry home while I can." Khan watched from a doorway as the three pilots left for Warehouse 40. By the time he discovered the changes to Alpha-Omega he would be thirty-five thousand feet in the air on a commercial jet bound for Pakistan.

Duke drove slowly through the darkened streets of Jeddah to the waterfront docks. The tension that had been mounting as they prepared for the mission was no longer evident. The team was prepared and ready. When they arrived at the warehouse a guard stopped the vehicle just outside the entry gate. For a final time Duke showed the identification papers that had been furnished to the Lightning repair team by the Prince.

"You come early today," the guard said cheerfully in English. "Must be near the end of your work for Prince Abdullah bin Ghazi?"

"That's right," Duke responded. "If we work hard this morning we should be finished today."

"Okay," the guard said as he pressed a control button allowing a long wired gate to slide open.

The auxiliary fuel tanks with the nuclear weapons inside were already stacked and secured on wooden slats inside the van. All that was left was to check their gear, review the plan, then drive north to Abdul Aziz International Airport.

At 0430 Jake's satellite phone beeped. He lifted the oversized cell phone to his ear, "Eagle One." He listened for a moment then pressed a button to disconnect. "The Prince is sending his F-15 pilot, Captain Wahib, to drive us to the airport and handle the conversation with the security guards. He'll meet us at the guard shack outside."

"Same guy as the one that drove the van here?" Duke asked.

"Same man," Jake said as he pulled three taser pistols from a military style duffel bag. "Only he won't be flying today. So we'll have to take care of him at the same time we subdue the other pilots."

Duke took one of the taser guns and studied the firing mechanism. "I've seen these non-lethal weapons before, but never actually held one."

Jake stood beside him. "It's easy. Just turn the safety off, aim and pull the trigger. Two wired talons will fire out and stick in your target. Keep the trigger depressed and 50,000 volts will put your victim down. Let go of the trigger and the current stops. Pull it again and it fires another charge."

"Will these be used on the pilots?" Annalisa asked.

"Correct," Jake answered. "According to a diagram of the hangar there is a sleeping room at the back. We'll open the door and shock them in their sleep then tie them up. It will be painful at first, but they will live to fly again."

"So the pilots will be asleep when we get there?"

"Should be, Duke. During the hajj they have a six-squadron rotation. Three jets are in the air at all times with a four-hour tour above Makkah. An hour before they are due back, the next rotation is up and preparing for their shift."

"So, we should arrive at the hangar before our squad gets up for duty." Duke said.

"That's right. The next flight is due to take off at 0800. But just in case we need something a little stronger than a taser..." Jake bent down and reached inside the small military bag and pulled out three 9mm automatic pistols.

"I hope we don't need those," Annalisa said.

"We shouldn't, but better to have them than need them and not." Jake added, "I'll pass these out when we reach the hangar."

Jake returned the weapons to the bag then stood erect and looked each team member in the eye. "This is it," he said with a firm tone of voice as he prepared to give them final words of encouragement. "Time to initiate Robert's plan.

"We'll be flying Royal Saudi Air Force F-15 Strike Eagles near Mach One, one hundred feet above the desert floor. Our targets are three large metropolitan centers. Instead of fuel in the belly tank we'll be carrying forty-five kilos of enriched uranium and plutonium with a thermonuclear yield of three million tons of dynamite.

"If they try to shoot down any of our aircraft the Omega option will be put into play. This could be a one-way mission for some or all of us." Then he paused, feeling like a coach just before his team left for the field. "Any questions?"

Duke shook his head vigorously. "I'm with you all the way, Jake."

"Jake, I…" Annalisa's voice trailed off.

Jake's eyes locked onto a pair of green ovals staring back at him. "We're going to play Alpha as far as we can, Annalisa. And like Khan said, we hope that it will work just as Robert planned. But if not…" and his words trailed off.

She stared at him for a moment with a watery look in her eyes. "I'm okay, Jake, I'm okay. I have my concerns, but after what they did to Robert I'm not worried about me anymore, it's just the thought of losing you."

"I know," Jake said softly then he glanced back at Duke. "Unless you need to speak directly to me I'll do most of the talking. I will communicate our demands to each targeted government and they will have one hour to concede. If they do not then we threaten the Omega option."

"But what if they don't try to shoot us down, Jake, and they don't concede to our demands? What then?" Annalisa asked. "We're not going to detonate and kill all those innocent people?"

"No, we're not," Jake responded with assurance. "The only way we detonate is if they try to shoot us down. After the hour passes and if they don't concede, then we will have played our Alpha hand and have to try another option."

Duke and Annalisa listened eagerly as Jake continued. "One option is to request to land and refuel. That way we can fly back to our rendezvous base in Kuwait and surrender our weapons to the Americans and our jets to the Kuwaitis."

"But we'll be vulnerable on the ground," Duke said. "They could take us out with just about anything even a vehicle crashing into our landing gear."

"That's right, Duke, they could. But they will be told that if they do not let us land, refuel and take-off again that we will either detonate in the air above their cities or on the ground. And according to Robert, even if they don't concede to all our demands they should at least agree to let us refuel and take-off again."

"But, Jake, I have no way to detonate on the ground. What if the Israelis allow me to land then capture the aircraft and me?" Annalisa asked.

"Actually, that's another option, giving each of them a nuclear weapon. It's been rumored for years that the Israelis already have one or more nuclear bombs and the Iranians want to build a nuclear weapons program. And now the Saudis want to purchase nuclear weapons as a deterrent to the Iranians.

"So, after we play out Alpha and if it doesn't work, then one option is to land our aircraft and surrender them to the Israelis, Saudis and Iranians. Then everyone will know that each nation has at least one weapon. Sort of a nuclear detente, wouldn't you say?"

Duke burst out laughing. "Good one, Jake. I like that option. Give each of them a nuclear weapon and scare the hell out of everyone."

Even Annalisa smiled at the seemingly ridiculous notion of arming each country with a nuclear bomb. "Sort of like back home," she said, "the argument between those advocating for gun control and those who want everyone to have a gun."

"Yeah," Duke added, "and look what we have there. Gun manufacturers getting rich while the United States is the most dangerous nation in the world for its citizens to walk around on the streets. Not sure I like that part, Jake, but it seems inevitable, sooner or later these nations will acquire nuclear weapons one way or another."

"And then there is the Omega Option," Jake added with a serious expression. He looked directly at Annalisa. "If the Israelis were to shoot you down then I would have no qualms about detonating over Tehran. Then me and the Mullahs could discuss the details while we're roasting in hell."

"And if Jake detonates," Duke added with emphasis, "then Makkah is toast."

Annalisa reeled back realizing that if the Israelis fired a missile at her aircraft the automatic detonator would fire her nuclear weapon, melting Jerusalem in a nuclear fireball and killing over a million Jews, Muslims and Christians.

"Jake," she gasped. "I don't know if I can do this. I don't want to be responsible for…" and her voice trailed away as her hand rose to cover her mouth.

"It's okay, Annalisa. No one wants to detonate," he reassured her. "It's the last option to consider."

Her eyes were flitting back and forth as she realized the moment she feared had come. She thought of her life with Jake and of the man holding Robert's head screaming 'Allah Akbar.' Something clicked in her mind and her expression changed.

"Okay," she whispered, staring back at them. "I think I know how to do this. I can do this for Robert," she said with a conviction that reassured both Jake and Duke.

"All right," Duke added, playing Khan's role as the eternal optimist. "Enough of this negative talk. Omega will not be needed, I'm sure of it. What government would sacrifice one of its major cities when the opportunity for negotiation has been offered? It's just not realistic."

Annalisa smiled at Jake. "I agree. Unless something really stupid happens we should all be meeting for dinner in Kuwait."

"Very good," Jake said. "It's the U.S. Air base in Kuwait for cocktails and dinner," and everyone tried to laugh. Then he added, "I received word from Nalum last night that an American intelligence team is on its way to Jeddah to officially inform the Saudis of the nuclear threat. According to our contact they should be arriving just about the time we're taking off, so let's get moving."

The Hangar

Aziz International Airport

WITH THE HELP OF Captain Wahib the Lightning team easily cleared the security gate to the military side of the airport. He drove them down the tarmac to the last of five hangars facing the runway. "Wait here," Jake said to the Saudi pilot. "In a few minutes the hangar door will open, then back the van inside. Wahib nodded in understanding as the team left the van to enter the hangar by a side door.

The dim lights in the ceiling cast an eerie glow over three F-15 Strike Eagles parked inside. They were armed, fueled and ready for their 0800 rotation in the security flights around Makkah. It was still two hours before the five-man maintenance crew would arrive for final technical checks on the aircraft. It allowed enough time for Jake and Duke to subdue the pilots, remove the belly tanks from the F-15s and install their own auxiliary tanks.

They walked quietly to the sleeping room at the end of the hangar. The door was slightly open. Jake pushed it gently and stepped inside. There were six cots, but only two were occupied. "Where's the other pilot?" Duke whispered.

At that moment a toilet flushed in the bathroom. The third pilot walked out and flopped down on his bed, unaware of the presence of two men standing near the door.

Jake pointed in the direction of the man that had just come out of the bathroom. Duke signaled back that he understood, and he took a position at the foot of the folding bed.

Jake stood between the cots of the other two pilots, reached down and gripped their covers then pulled them back at the same time. He did not want to take a chance that the blankets might prevent the darts from making effective contact.

One of the men sat up and stared as Jake pulled the trigger on the tasers. Both darts shot into the man's chest and he immediately began convulsing on the bed. As Jake turned toward the other pilot he heard the thump of Duke's taser fire into the pilot who had returned from the bathroom. Jake fired the taser in his left hand. All three pilots convulsed for several seconds, then moaned in pain as they tried to comprehend their collective nightmare.

Jake pulled a handful of heavy-duty plastic cable ties from his pocket like the ones law enforcement officers used to subdue prisoners. He looped a tie around one of the pilot's wrists and pulled hard until it zip-locked securely in place. He pulled his arms up to the top of the bed and with another tie secured the pilots hands above his head to a metal bar.

He reached over to the other pilot and repeated the process. After their hands were secured he tied their ankles together with plastic ties, and used another to secure their feet to an iron bar at the end of the bed.

Duke stood and brushed his hands together like a cattle roper that had successfully lassoed a calf then dropped down from his horse and tied its legs together. But they weren't finished. Duke listened to the rip of duct tape as Jake pulled out several foot-long strips to wrap over the mouths of the pilots. Another rip and Jake handed him a length of grey tape for the man who had returned from the bathroom.

The pilots were becoming more alert as the effects of the electrical shock diminished. Duke listened to the muffled voices and shook his head from side to side. "Sorry, fellas, I don't understand Arabic," and slapped Jake on the shoulder as he headed for the door to go back out into the hangar.

Annalisa had also been busy, positioning electric V-berth hydraulic lifts under the belly tanks on each of the jets, then raising them up until they made contact. When Jake and Duke returned they removed the bolts securing the twelve-foot tanks to the aircraft allowing them to settle comfortably down in the cradle. As Annalisa lowered them below the aircraft the fuel line that went inside to the engines was exposed. Duke turned a small handle to the off position so that when disconnected, JP-4 would not back wash and pool below the jets.

"Excellent work, you two," Jake said.

As Duke and Annalisa continued with the other two planes Jake found the main control panel and opened one of the large hangar doors. Captain Wahib had been waiting patiently in the van. As the door began to lift he backed inside, and as soon as the front of the vehicle passed a yellow line painted on the floor Jake closed the huge door.

The Saudi pilot stepped out of the van and walked over to the jets. "Which one of these will I be flying?" As he turned around to look at Jake he saw a strange looking weapon in his hand. The talons stuck in his chest and 50,000 volts dropped his body to the floor.

Duke zip-locked his hands and legs together then dragged the quivering pilot down to the sleeping room where he would join the other men. A minute later he exited the room with a roll of duct tape in his hand. "Another one roped and branded," he said with a grin. Then he hopped on a small forklift and headed for the back of the van ready to lift a rucksack and three specially modified belly tanks, and lay them gently on the hangar floor where Jake would carefully inspect each one.

Within an hour the newly modified auxiliary tanks had been installed on Eagles Two and Three, the jets to be flown by Duke and Annalisa. Eagle One required more time because of the delicate connections between the hand-held detonator switch in the cockpit and the timer inside the fuel tank with the parachute. It took another thirty minutes for Duke to sync the Threat Assessment Radars to automatic detonators, and in Eagles One and Three made sure the wires to the hand-held joystick detonators were properly connected.

As Duke crawled down a single-pole ladder that folded neatly into the body of the aircraft his brow was beading with sweat. "Okay, we have three jets armed with nuclear weapons. Now what?"

"We wait," said Jake, "over there in that office. When the five-man tech crew arrives we subdue and tie them up, just like the pilots."

"What if they resist?" Annalisa asked.

"Don't think they will when they see three 9mm pistols pointing at them. Not many unarmed people will argue with that kind of force. I'll have them lay down on the floor while Duke and I gag and zip-tie them together. After that we open the hangar doors, climb aboard our jets and fire up the engines."

Cowboys and Eagles

Aziz International Airport
Jeddah, Saudi Arabia

THE FIVE-MEMBER TECH CREW was taken by surprise and offered no resistance to the Americans. "Keep your guns on them," Jake said as he escorted the men to the back of the hangar. Duke secured their hands and feet, covered their mouths with tape then dragged the Saudis into the pilots' sleeping room. "Let's get back to the aircraft. I want everything ready to depart the hangar by 0730," Jake told them.

Annalisa climbed the ladder to the cockpit followed by Jake and he assisted her with the safety straps as she settled into the pilot's seat. Duke climbed up the other side and went over the controls that he had described earlier. "Here's your throttle on the left, stick in the middle with nose wheel steering and brakes down below. You're an experienced pilot, Annalisa, so that's all you need to know to get this bird in the air.

"Here's your Terrain Following Radar. Once we drop down to a hundred feet, just flip this switch and tap in your heading to the mid point. This plane will practically fly itself, but don't take your eyes off the sky or your hand off the stick. You never know when you might need to avoid a big ole' bird or something."

He pointed to another control on the left side. "Once you leave the mid-point flip this on. It's your Threat Assessment Radar. In case they try to shoot you down at least you'll know ahead of time."

"How much time?" she asked nervously.

"Ten, maybe twenty seconds. Missiles are fast, depends on how far away they are but for a trained pilot a few seconds can be enough time for evasive maneuvers."

"But I'm not... "

"Neither is Jake," he added, as if that might be encouraging. "But they would be pretty stupid to shoot any of us down, now wouldn't they? I mean that would cause a detonation and they will know that. So I don't think you have anything to worry about."

"Your turn," Duke said to Jake as he backed down the ladder on the opposite side.

Jake looked into Annalisa's eyes and noticed they were moist even though she had promised herself that she wouldn't cry. Tears streaked down her cheeks as Jake whispered in her ear, parting words that Duke could not hear.

After a long embrace and lingering kiss Jake slipped back down the ladder.

His eyes were also moist, but he spoke in a firm voice. "Duke, go back up and show her how to crank up the Auxiliary Power Unit to get her engines started. " He turned away and marched to the ladder of his aircraft.

At 0715 all three APUs kicked in with high piercing whines. As they wound up to 500 rpms Duke flipped his engine start switch and heard it winding up. Annalisa was next and Jake could see hot gases escaping from the rear of Eagle Two. Then he fired his turbines and for the next three minutes the throttles were held slightly forward with the brakes firmly locked.

After the warm up period Duke waved to Annalisa, who then waved to Jake and the jet engines idled downward. Jake pulled the cup to his face and with his best Arabic-English accent spoke into the receiver. "Flight 49 requesting permission to leave the hangar?"

"Captain Wahib," the controller in the military tower responded. "What is wrong this morning? Do you have another cold?"

Jake coughed a little and answered, "Yes, a cold."

"Perhaps you should have the flight surgeon check that out to make sure you are qualified to fly."

"Will do when I return."

"Okay, Flight 49, you are cleared to depart the hangar and contact civilian air control. Good flying, Captain."

Jake looked over at Annalisa, saluted and gave a thumbs-up signal. She immediately forwarded the sign to Eagle Three. Duke engaged his nose wheel steering, pushed the throttle forward and the F-15 began rolling slowly out of the hangar. As soon as he cleared the yellow line on the floor Eagle Two began inching forward. Then Jake followed them out onto the tarmac.

They were lined up in a row going through another warm up procedure. All three pilots had the brakes punched hard as the engines revved higher and higher. Duke glanced over at Annalisa, and satisfied their engines were performing well gave her the thumbs up signal, which she communicated to Jake.

Showtime! Jake thought to himself as he pressed the transceiver at his neck. He looked down at the flight number on a card in his hand and spoke with his best Saudi tinged English "Flight 49 requesting permission to taxi runway five for take-off."

"You are early today, Captain Wahib," the traffic controller responded from the tower. He spoke perfect English. "Anxious to fly to Makkah again?"

"Time to go to work," Eagle One replied.

"Well then, Flight 49, taxi down to the end of runway five, but hold your position for an incoming flight on parallel ten."

Jake leaned forward in his seat hoping to catch a look from Duke but he had already powered up and was moving. Duke pulled his stick to the right, tapped the brake with his foot and the F-15 made a ninety-degree turn heading south to the end of the concrete. As soon as he straightened out Annalisa waved her hand at Jake then began rolling forward to make her turn onto the runway. As Jake throttled up and moved forward he smiled, *I wonder how many beautiful women know how to fly an F-15?*

The three jets taxied to the end of the runway when the tower called. "Hold your position on five, Flight 49. Two American aircraft are arriving in thirty seconds and, pilots, feast your eyes on these new X-35 experimental jets."

It had to be them, Jake thought to himself. Doug Jackson and Agent Weller from the NCTC were arriving in Jeddah just as the NDR team was taking off. *Good timing*, Jake was thinking when the tower broke in.

"Captain Wahib, do you see them?" the controller asked excitedly. "This is the new advanced stealth fighter jet that can take-off and land vertically. It is much more advanced than their F-18 Super Hornet and F-22 Raptor. Perhaps one day the Americans will sell these to our government and you will be flying one."

Jake had to smile at the enthusiasm of the controller who was obviously a fan of American aircraft. All he had to do was scan the internet for information on America's newest break through airframe, engine and weapons technologies. Jake replied to the controller, "Yes, one day."

It had been an incredible ride for the two NCTC agents, four hours, 18 minutes and 25 seconds. *Wow*, Jackson thought to himself as the wheels of the F-35 touched down. *Major McCoy sure knows her stuff. Better not play poker with her.*

The two jets rolled up to a small building on the military side of the runway where a black Mercedes was waiting for them. There were formal introductions, handshakes and exchanging of pleasantries, but the two agents only wanted to find the nearest bathroom.

"Flight 49, you may take off on runway five."

"Thank you," Jake replied back to the tower.

"Thank you," repeated one of the controllers to the others in the room. He leaned back in his chair. "I think Wahib has been spending too much time in America. He seems to have forgotten our traditional Arabic greetings," and laughed to himself.

"Eagle Three, cleared for take-off," Jake said.

Duke pushed the throttle forward and the jet began to move, then pulled the stick to the left and tapped the brake as it turned to line up with three kilometers of concrete that seemed to undulate in the early morning heat. He punched both brakes down hard and pushed the throttle forward. The engines screamed furiously, but Duke held the brakes until the needle moved above 5,000 rpms.

He pulled both feet off at the same time and the F-15 took off with a sizzling roar in a perfect straight line. Duke held the stick straight and glanced at the speed indicator on the panel. *What a rush*, Duke thought to himself as the needle climbed above 100 knots. Three seconds later he pulled the stick back slightly and felt the rear elevator tilt up. The nose began to lift and in the same moment he raised the ailerons. The concrete seemed to drop away from the aircraft as the tower cut in.

"Eagle Three, this is the tower. Climb to altitude five thousand and turn East Southeast at 98."

"Roger that, tower," Duke replied.

"Roger that, and copy that" one of the other controllers said with a laugh inside the tower. "What is it with these guys?"

Jake called to Annalisa. "Eagle Two, proceed to take-off."

She pushed the throttle forward slightly and pitched the stick to the left to line up with the runway. Then she punched her brakes and revved the engines.

Jake watched the smoke and burning gasses for several seconds and as quick as a leopard she streaked down the runway. As soon as the nose of her aircraft tilted up he pulled into position and began revving for take-off. As she lifted away from earth he released his brakes and followed her into the sky.

"Eagle One, this is the tower. Climb to five thousand and proceed on 98."

"Roger that," Jake replied, as his F-15 lifted into the cobalt blue sky.

"Another one!" screamed one of the controllers with delight. "All of them talk like American cowboy fighter pilots."

The tower phone began ringing. One of the controllers answered and listened to the man screaming at him in Arabic. "What's the matter, Ahmed? Who was that?"

"That was Colonel Hatani from General Intelligence. He says to lock down the airport. No planes are to leave. Those coming in may land, but none can take-off."

"Lock down the airport? What does that mean? This has never happened before."

"And why?" another controller asked. "What has happened?"

Ahmed stood in the middle of the room shaking his head. "The director said that American mercenaries have smuggled a nuclear bomb into our country and they are trying to hijack one of our planes to deliver the weapon, possibly to Makkah."

"Americans," one of them yelled, "with those cowboy voices..."

Ahmed grabbed a mike transmitter. "Flight 49, come in. Captain Wahib, this is the tower at Jeddah. You must return immediately. Do you understand? You must return to base immediately."

For a moment there was only silence as everyone listened for a reply. And then it came. "Sorry about that, tower. No can do. We've got a big job to take care of so it's 10-4, good buddy. Over and out."

"Here," one of the controllers said to the others. "I have them on my radar screen. They are flying at five thousand feet on a course for..."

"Where are they going?' one of the men screamed. "We must tell the colonel."

"I don't know," the radar technician said in amazement. "They have dropped off the screen."

The Quay

Jeddah, Saudi Arabia

THE HEAD OF SAUDI intelligence ran over to Agents Weller and Jackson. "I am sorry," Colonel Hatani said, "but for the moment we cannot locate Prince Abdullah bin Ghazi. We will find him soon enough, but in the meantime we have discovered a warehouse on the quay here in Jeddah where his new speedboat was delivered. Our agents have secured the perimeter."

"We'd better get over there and see what's happened to that boat," Weller said.

"Yeah, better find out if they removed the lead keel," Jackson added. "Do you have the Geiger counter we requested?"

"Yes, it is in my car. This way, Gentlemen." The Colonel led them to a black Mercedes parked on the tarmac, and with alarm sirens blaring a convoy of security vehicles rushed through the crowded streets of Jeddah on a southwest course to the waterfront docks.

"There," the Colonel said, pointing toward the end of a long concrete pier. "That is Warehouse 40 where the Prince had his new boat delivered."

As they pulled up to the guardhouse two large uniformed Saudi agents were holding the private security guard between them. "I don't know what they were doing in there," the guard told them. "They said they were fixing the Prince's new boat, adding things to make it run faster."

"How many of them were working on the boat?" Weller asked.

"Four, usually four, three men and a woman."

"A woman," Weller repeated, and he looked at Agent Jackson.

"They came early for two days. They worked all day long then left, but this morning they arrived very early, before daylight. One of the men said they would be finished today."

"Did they leave?"

"Yes, I think so. A van left the building just before morning prayers."

"Who was driving?" Weller asked.

"A Saudi man arrived as the van pulled up to the gate. The American that was driving moved over and the Saudi took over the driver's seat."

"Where were they going?"

"I don't know, I don't know," the frightened guard told them. "They just drove away and I have heard nothing from inside the warehouse since they left. I assume all of them were inside the van."

"Colonel Hatani," shouted one of his agents. "Come quickly, a message for you." The head of the GID turned and walked toward his car.

"What did you hear while they were working inside the warehouse?" Weller asked the guard.

"Noises, loud noises. A high pitched whine like a saw cutting metal."

Weller shot Jackson a look that seemed to confirm what they suspected, but before he could say anything Hatani walked up behind him. "Bad news, Gentlemen, very bad news. Three Saudi F-15s have been hijacked from the airport. Three," he repeated with emphasis. "If they have only one weapon why would they need three aircraft?"

Weller looked over at Jackson to see if he had any idea, but the look of shock on Jackson's face surprised him. "Doug, you okay?"

"I don't know," he stuttered in surprise. "I mean," then he paused. "You don't think they have," and he stopped again. *Damn!* He thought to himself. *Better call Nalum. Something's gone wrong with Peaceful Eagle.*

"More than one weapon?" Weller added, finishing Jackson's thought.

"Yeah, that's what I'm thinking," Doug said.

"Colonel," Weller said, "grab the Geiger counter and let's get inside that warehouse. We need to find out exactly what we're dealing with." The three men and a host of Saudi security agents rushed toward the side door of the warehouse.

"Holy shit!" Weller screamed. The top of the Lightning boat was resting on the floor in front of the hull and the lead keel was sitting beside it. Jackson held the Geiger counter out and it barely registered, but as they approached the keel it began to click.

The cover was on the floor beside the keel and all of them could see the hollowed lead box was empty.

"Big enough for more than one weapon?" Jackson asked.

"I don't know," the lead agent responded. "Wish we had Dr. McVey here now."

"What do I tell the King?" Colonel Hatani asked anxiously.

Weller paused for a moment as he considered the question. "Better tell him the same thing we're going to tell our president, that three Saudi F-15s have been hijacked with at least one, and possibly three, nuclear weapons on board."

"But where are they going?" the Colonel asked.

"We don't know," Weller said, "but those jets can only fly so far."

Doug interrupted. "I think we'd better start making some phone calls, Noah, so the president will have time to notify the world intelligence community."

"Yeah, because in a couple of hours those jets will arrive wherever they're going and somebody somewhere will probably appreciate the heads up."

Agents Weller and Jackson stood on opposite sides of the Mercedes speaking into their encrypted satellite phones. They were making numerous calls back to various levels of management at the NCTC. As Doug finished his first call he looked over his shoulder at Weller who was deep in conversation with Michael Lane, the Director.

From memory Doug dialed a number in Berryville. Virginia. The phone was handed to Nalum Taylor and Jackson gave him the shocking news.

"But Jake assured me Tehran was the target," Nalum said in surprise.

"It may be one target," Jackson said. "Got any ideas on the other two?"

"No," Nalum whispered into the phone. "None at all," he added while staring up at the eastern hills on the other side of the Shenandoah River.

A Flight of Eagles

The Mid-Point near Hafir al Batin, Saudi Arabia

THE F-15S FLEW A predetermined northeast course only a hundred feet above the desert floor. A steady gust of sand and dust rose up behind the small formation that would appear as wind-driven ground clutter on any radar-tracking screens.

As they approached the desert-mountains of the southern An Nafud, 180 miles east of Medina, a small bowl-shaped valley appeared in front of Eagle One. Duke and Annalisa were flying behind and to the side of Jake and saw his belly tank fall away. It waffled nose first through the air until a parachute deployed and it began to sway under a large white canopy. The pilots knew that if everything went as planned the remote valley would soon erupt in a fireball.

As the formation continued to the northeast two young boys herding goats beneath the peak of a mountain saw the jets swoop away. They watched the object fall from the first aircraft and the parachute deploy then continued to observe as it descended to the ground. They left the herd and ran toward an encampment where their grandfather was boiling water on a steel grate above a propane heater. The old man was listening to the boys when the valley exploded and their faces were frozen in wonder as they disappeared inside the fireball.

Forty-eight minutes later the F-15s arrived at the mid point, east of the town of Hafar al Batin, and they began flying a wide circle. "Eagle Three to One and Two," Duke said, breaking radio silence. "Time to reset target coordinates and turn on Threat Assessment Radars."

Annalisa flipped the TAR switch Duke had indicated earlier then watched a green radar display as it came to life on her instrument panel. "All clear, Eagle Three," she replied back then looked out to catch a glimpse of Jake's profile as he wheeled far to the left in front of her. She would soon break away to the northwest and fly toward An Nabk near the border with Jordan. From there it would be a straight shot to the Dead Sea, then rise above the Judean Hills of the West Bank and arrive seconds later over the Temple Mount of Old Jerusalem.

"Eagle Two to Eagle One," she said as sweetly as her trembling voice would allow. "My heart goes with you, Jake."

"And mine with you, Annalisa."

Duke listened patiently in case there were any other words between them. After a moment of silence he broke in. "Okay, Eagles, time to get down to business so that we can get this job done and meet for Happy Hour in Kuwait."

"Roger that," Jake replied.

"I'll have a nice smooth Merlot, Jake. What about you?"

"Anything you're having will be fine with me, Annalisa."

Duke laughed into his radio, "And I'm having the biggest martini the bartender at that Air Force Base in Kuwait can make."

Eagles One and Two heard his laughter over the radio then Duke cut back in. "Okay, time to punch in target coordinates."

Duke knew that in order to cover the same air miles as Jake and Annalisa that he would have to fly east with Eagle One to the edge of the Persian Gulf. When Jake turned north toward Tehran he would turn southwest for Makkah.

"It's 0914," Jake said over the radio. "We will break for targets in one minute." Each of the three pilots looked hard to the left to catch a last glimpse of the other two jets before breaking the circle.

"In 75 minutes," Jake continued, "at 1030 hours by my watch each of us should be over our targets. As soon as you arrive break radio silence and announce yourselves. Tell the controllers that will be monitoring your aircraft that you are on a peace mission and will be flying a circle above their city. Let them know you will call again in three minutes with further details."

"Jake," Duke broke in. "You and Annalisa are going to be targeted for sure as soon as you arrive, but don't let that buzz from the Threat Assessment Radar bother you. That's just to let you know they have missile lock on your aircraft. But if you hear a high-pitched beeping, that means they've fired and it's coming at you. And the closer the beeps are together, the closer the missile. Do you understand?"

"Copy that, Eagle Three," Jake responded.

"But it won't matter," Annalisa added. "If a missile gets near my aircraft it will automatically detonate."

"Correct, Eagle Two," Duke said confidently. "And they will know that so there's no reason for them to shoot any of us down, including me. I mean, Makkah may not have a missile defense system, but there will no doubt be several Saudi aircraft on my tail and one of them will probably have me locked up. But if they fire they lose Makkah, so I'm going to encourage them to not lock on. No need for an accident."

"Satellite phone test," Jake announced. Each of the pilots pulled out what appeared to be an oversized cell phone and attached a mini plug from the dual ear buds already inside their helmets. Jake pressed the 'On' feature and watched the display power up. In seconds he had acquired a satellite then pressed the button for Annalisa's programmed number.

"Jake, it works. Thank goodness," she answered.

Jake smiled at the sound of her voice. "Hang on while I put you on hold and add Duke to a conference call."

Seconds later Duke's voice came on the line. "I'm here, Jake. You on, Annalisa?"

"I'm here, Duke." Each of them was smiling at the novelty of satellite phones working from inside the cockpits of their F-15s.

"Just before we reach our targets I will call you," Jake said. "Once I have you on the line and you have announced your position over your target, I will make the call to Jeddah to connect us to media outlets around the world." He paused before announcing, "And Robert's Alpha-Omega plan will be in play."

It was difficult for Annalisa to comprehend. They had planned, discussed and practiced as much as they could, and even though they were on the way to their targets, she could not conceive the power of the weapon held beneath her aircraft.

"Okay, its show time," Jake announced, "0915 hours. Next time around, Eagle Two, break out of the wheel."

"Jake," a small voice said. "Take care, and I'll see you in Kuwait."

"Copy that, Annalisa," he responded. "I'll meet you for dinner in Kuwait." Seconds later he watched as she pulled away to the northwest.

He felt an urge to call her back, but recalled the image of a terrorist holding up the head of Robert Faircloth. It was all the motivation he needed to continue with the mission. "This one's for you, Robert," he whispered to himself.

The other two F-15s turned east skirting below Kuwaiti airspace toward the Persian Gulf. As they reached the coastal highway above Al Jubayl Jake broke in, "God speed, Eagle Three."

"Back at you, Eagle One. Say hello to the Ayatollah for me." Duke dipped his wings and broke away to the southwest. In less than an hour the spirit of Robert Faircloth would descend over the Middle East.

The Patriot

Jerusalem

"GREENBERG!" A VOICE SHOUTED from outside the Fire Control Center of the Patriot Missile Battery. The PAC-3 was one of the last American made units still stationed around Jerusalem. It had not yet been replaced by the newer 'SPYDER' as part of Israel's 'Iron Dome' missile defense system.

Samuel stood up and looked over the side of his vehicle. It was Lieutenant First Class, Gabriel Bernstein, calling from the ground. "Get your headset on. Col. Mahron just issued an alert. Initiate 'Standby' command and wait for further instructions." He looked up at the American expatriate who had emigrated from America to become an Israeli citizen. "And stop reading that shit, Greenberg. It's only going to mess up your head."

Technical Sergeant Samuel Greenberg served as the Tactical Control Assistant on the missile battery located on Beit Zait, a hilltop four miles west of the Old City in Jerusalem. "Look," the lieutenant said, "I know you didn't make it as an engineering student back in New York. And we appreciate that you've come over here and joined the IDF, but you know you're not supposed to read any of that ultra orthodox literature from the Jewish Home Party while you're on duty. So, save it for later, Greenberg."

"But it says, 'The ancient lands of the Hebrews, promised them by YHVH, the God of our Fathers, must be returned to

Israel, taken back from the Palestinian scourge by any means necessary.'"

"See what I'm talking about, Greenberg. You sound like
one of those Kahane nut cases. You keep reading those extremist interpretations of the Talmud while you're on duty, and I'm
gonna report you to Col. Mahron. You hear me?"

Samuel was an ultra nationalist, a supporter of the Messianic
Zionist settlements in the occupied territories. When on duty
and not training he preferred to read the interpretive works of
his rabbi. "I'm done with drills, Sir, why can't I read?"

"It's not that you can't read, but while you're in the army
you're not supposed to read extremist literature while on duty.
You know that, Greenberg, so stop giving me a hard time. Put
that shit away and standby for further orders."

Greenberg flipped his right hand up to his brow. "Yes, Sir, Lt.
Bernstein. Right away, Sir," he said mockingly, and sat back down.

Only three people were needed to operate a Patriot Missile
Battery, the Officer in Charge, a Communications Specialist who
operated the radar systems and a Technical Control Assistant who
fed radar information into the missile nose and initiated the firing sequence. Once the information was loaded it was ready to
fire.

After the missile left its firing tube the TCA would keep it on
track to the target by sending radar signals to an antenna in the
tail fin. At Mach Five the solid fuel rocket of a PAC-3 Missile
would cover a mile per second. Once located and targeted, it
would take less than a minute for a Patriot to destroy any airborne
target within fifty miles of Jerusalem.

The Golden Dome

The Old City of Jerusalem

ANNALISA SET THE ALTIMETER for the forward-looking Terrain Following Radar and turned on the autopilot. She heeded Duke's warning, holding onto the stick while keeping a close watch through the canopy for sudden elevation changes or surprises.

Three-quarters of an hour later she was approaching the Dead Sea and the Judean Mountains. She eased the nose down getting as close to the water as possible to avoid any down looking radar. She knew that as soon the F-15 rose above the hills she would be visible, but at seven hundred miles per hour she also knew she would cover the last twenty miles in just over a minute.

Her plan was to sight the golden dome above the porcelain-blue octagonal mosque on Temple Mount and use it as the hub of a wheel she would fly above the Old Walled City, home to many of the holiest sites for Christians, Jews and Muslims. Annalisa pulled back on the stick and the nose of her jet lifted. At that moment the satellite phone in her lap began to ring. "Jake, is that you?"

"Yes, it's me. I'm just a few minutes outside Tehran, but they don't seem to have me painted as a hostile target, at least not yet."

"I'm approaching the golden dome," she said with uncertainty. "Should I call in?"

"Yes, go ahead and announce yourself. I'll check in with Duke. He should be over Makkah by now."

Annalisa activated the radio transceiver at her neck and made contact with Israeli officials. "Ben Gurion International, this is Saudi Royal Air Force Eagle Two, come in please?"

"Eagle Two! Eagle Two!" screamed the reply in agitated English. "Who are you and what the hell are you doing above Jerusalem? We have activated interceptor aircraft and air defense missile batteries. If you do not proceed at once to BGI then you will be shot out of the sky. Do you understand, Eagle Two?"

"I understand, Ben Gurion, but you need to know that I come in peace. If you try to shoot me down then I will detonate a three-megaton thermonuclear warhead that will destroy the city of Jerusalem. Do you copy, BGI?"

She could not believe what she had just said. *Who am I?* She asked herself in surprise at the confidence with which she had communicated with the airport official. As she looked down on the city of a million people, many of whom were staring up at the blue and yellow symbols on the stabilizers of her aircraft, she received another call from BGI. "Eagle Two, Eagle Two, are you one of three Saudi jets hijacked from Jeddah two hours ago?"

"Roger that," was her reply.

"Are you aware, Eagle Two, that a nuclear detonation has occurred in the desert between Medina and Riyadh in Saudi Arabia?"

"Copy that," she replied. "I have exactly the same size nuclear weapon on board my aircraft, but I do not want to detonate, do you copy Ben Gurion?"

"We copy Eagle Two."

"I will be back in three minutes to tell you more," Annalisa continued, "but in the meantime please confirm with your intelligence sources that I do have a very powerful nuclear weapon on board my aircraft."

"We already have, Eagle Two, but understand, our interceptors will be in the air and you will be tracked by our missile batteries at all times. Do you understand, Eagle Two?'

"Copy that, BGI. Please standby for further transmission in three minutes. Over and out."

She reached down for the cell phone that was still on. "Jake, did you hear that? Did you hear me?" But there was no response. *Oh my God*, she thought to herself, *have the Iranians already shot him down?*

"Jake!" she shouted into the phone, "are you there?' She waited a moment longer then screamed, "Jake Eastwood, are you there, because if you're not I'm gonna..." but before she could finish she heard his voice.

"I'm okay, Annalisa. I'm okay. I've been talking with Duke. He's on the line with us now. Talk with him while I make the call to Jeddah."

"How ya' doin' there, pretty girl?" Duke asked in his best Carolina drawl. He was trying to inject a calming levity into a critical situation.

"I'm okay, Duke, how about you?"

"Got a lot of company on my tail. All three of those boys that were here when I arrived have locked on to me and I've had to put a little pressure on them to back off. Now we're all just flying around up here like old friends, two thousand feet above Makkah. How 'bout it girl, you makin' any new friends over there?"

"Looks like two missile batteries have locked on and several interceptors are on the way, but otherwise I'm good."

"Well, Jake's in some pretty deep shit over Tehran. One of their jet jockeys was about to take a missile shot at him till he was told by their ground control that if he didn't return to base that they would shoot him down. Guess it's like Jake said, those Mullahs play hard ball."

"I'm back" Jake said, " and we're all hooked up by phone line with ground control at each airport along with several media outlets so that everything I say will be heard by everyone at the same time. When I bring you into this conference call you're going to hear a lot of questions from a whole lot of people. Better let me do the talking. If you need to communicate with me do it through your aircraft radio. Understood?"

"I understand, Jake." Annalisa checked to make sure she had not turned off the transceiver around her neck.

"Copy that," Duke added. "Go ahead and bring us on line."

"Okay, here we go," Jake said as he connected them to the international conference call. There was a great din of voices clamoring for information all at the same time and Jake had to shout them down so that he could speak.

"This is Eagle One at two thousand feet above the city of Tehran. My colleagues are also flying over major cities in the Middle East. Eagle Two is now over Jerusalem and Eagle Three is wheeling above the city of Makkah.

"It has been confirmed by your governments that each jet has on board a three megaton thermonuclear weapon capable of destroying everything within a five-mile radius of ground zero. This means there are now fifteen million people at risk of being incinerated in nuclear fireballs within the next hour.

"But the outcome of this operation has yet to be determined. If it is Alpha and you agree to our demands, then we will leave in peace. But if it is Omega then we will detonate in one hour. That is all the time the governments of Iran, Saudi Arabia and Israel have to consider and agree to our demands and save these cities."

Jake could feel the frustration through the phone of the military pilots and missile batteries that were now targeting their aircraft. *If only they could get us into a fair fight,* they must be telling themselves and going over in their minds what they would do. Jake understood. It was the nature of their training. He had been in the same situation many times before on the scene of pirate hijackings in Malaysia and Somalia and kidnappings in war torn environs while an agent with the CIA.

Jake went back on line with the media and into the frenzy of rapid-fire questions. Eventually he was able to explain why each nation had been targeted and listed the demands for the Saudis,

Iranians and Israelis, just the way Robert had explained it to him back in Paris. Then he gave each nation the ultimatum. They had one hour to agree or face the loss of millions of their citizens.

"By my time it is 1045 hours. If I do not have a positive response from all three governments by 1145 hours then we will detonate. Do you copy, Ben Gurion International?"

"We understand," came the reluctant Israeli reply.

"Do you copy, Khomeni International?"

"Yes, we, understand," the Iranians responded.

Jake was almost shouting into the satellite phone, "Do you copy, Aziz International?"

"Yes, Eagle One, we copy."

"You have my number. I am expecting a call no later than 1145 hours. If I do not hear from you by then," and he paused not sure what to add. "Over and out."

Jake felt exhausted as he let go of the satellite phone. He had made it clear to the media that once he got off the phone he would not answer again unless he recognized the number of the airport control towers that he had been speaking to. It was much more strenuous than he had imagined. He was exhausted and sagged back into his pilot's seat when a radio transmission came in.

"Eagle One, this is Eagle Two. I feel Robert's spirit here in the cockpit with me, Jake. Do you copy? Over."

Jake used the back of his right hand to wipe perspiration from his forehead then reached down to activate his transceiver. "I'm looking forward to that glass of Merlot. Don't be late. We have dinner reservations."

Annalisa called Duke. "Are you okay?"

"Yeah, but I've got some angry bees on my tail," he replied. "Must be that Captain Wahib and some of his pilot buddies we tagged this morning. Can't say as I blame them."

"Copy that," Jake said in a tired voice. "Let's take a break now and wait for our hosts to give us a positive reply. Over and out."

Annalisa could not see them, but based on three blips on her Threat Assessment Radar she knew that Israeli interceptors were flying above. And there was also the low hum from two missile batteries as they tracked her around the Old City. "Stay calm, boys, just stay calm and maybe all of us will make it home in time for dinner."

But Annalisa had no idea of the fury welling up inside an expatriate American with his finger on the trigger of a PAC-3 missile targeting her aircraft.

A Binding Resolution

Washington, D.C.

AT 3:30 AM EASTERN Standard Time the news broke in America, including a satellite feed of nuclear-armed jets flying above Jerusalem, Tehran and Makkah. CNN in Atlanta, the BBC in London and Al Jeezera in Qatar were the first outlets to broadcast pictures and convey the demands of the NDR to the rest of the world.

Every television in America was tuned in listening to analysts and announcers trying to interpret the meaning and potential impact of these live events taking place in the Middle East. Leaders of every nation were meeting with their military and financial advisors calculating the potential outcomes and effects on their economies. In Washington, D.C. a small group of men were secretly conferring in the Situation Room of the White House hoping to agree on a resolution to resolve the crisis.

"My king wishes you to know," the Saudi ambassador announced to the others, "that even though one of our senior foreign officials may be involved in this treacherous plan the Saudi government has nothing to do with this conspiracy. How could it even be thought that we would destroy the most holy site in Islam along with millions of pilgrims and all the citizens of Makkah. This is preposterous," he added with a flourish.

"I agree," the President said in a conciliatory deal-brokering tone. "Everyone here understands the Saudi government had nothing to do with this. But have you located Abdullah bin Ghazi, the man we believe is the mastermind of these events?"

"We are looking everywhere for him. If he is in our country then we will find him. Not a grain of sand will be left unturned in our search."

"And the nuclear detonation that occurred in the An Nafud desert region of your country," the President continued, "what can you tell us of that?"

"Nothing!" the embassy official shouted. "We know nothing of how or why a nuclear weapon was detonated there. There was a call to a police station east of Medina from some goat herders. The man said three Saudi jets were seen flying very low over a desert mountain valley, that something fell from one of them and a parachute opened. Then there was an explosion and his sons and father disappeared. This is something we must ask bin Ghazi when we find him, but until then..." and he threw his hands in the air.

"It was a warning," the Israeli official announced calmly, "a simple warning. They want us to know they possess viable nuclear weapons."

"I agree," the Iranian envoy interrupted. "It was a warning to us all and may I suggest that the solution to this is very simple. They have demanded we concede, but not that we follow-through. The Ayatollah suggests we simply concede publicly to diffuse this situation. Later we shall discover these people and deal with them."

"If they are found in my country," the Saudi official added, "they will be publicly beheaded in Makkah."

All eyes turned to the Israeli Ambassador. He stared at each of them for several seconds before throwing his hands in the air. "Is there any other choice? I ask you, is there another option?" He sat back and smiled to himself. "But I tell you, once we concede there will be public outcry for the reforms these people have demanded. And I believe this is part of their mad strategy."

The President smiled to himself before speaking recognizing the Israeli Ambassador may be right. "Then we have consensus," he said with relief. "Israel, Iran and Saudi Arabia will publicly concede to the demands to diffuse this extremely dangerous situation and then we, along with the rest of the world, will investigate these events to find out who is behind this unprecedented nuclear threat."

He looked up at the bank of world clocks on the walls and spotted the times for each nation. "We still have twenty minutes, gentlemen, but there is much to do. Please take advantage of the secure phone lines in this room to call your governments so they may inform the pilot flying above Tehran that all three nations have agreed to the demands. He appears to be their leader."

Within minutes calls were made to Israel, Saudi Arabia and Iran. Then the President and three ambassadors went upstairs to the Briefing Room to face a gauntlet of haggard media representatives gathered at the White House.

The Sound of Fury

Jerusalem, Israel

THE TACTICAL CONTROL ASSISTANT for the Patriot Missile Battery on Beit Zait listened on his radio to the demands given by Jake Eastwood to the Israeli government. He could barely contain his rage. Without orders Samuel Greenburg began transferring radar data into the nose section of the PAC-3. All that remained was for Lt. Bernstein to give the order to fire and within twenty seconds the Saudi jet flying above Jerusalem would be blown out of the sky.

Greenberg gave little credence to the possibility the aircraft might actually have a nuclear weapon on board. *Impossible,* he thought to himself as he considered when to fire his missile and where the wreckage of the invading aircraft might fall. He smiled to himself. *If I wait until it turns back to the East it should drop into the Arabic section of the city, or even further into the West Bank.*

While Bernstein communicated with the Battalion Commander on a radio outside the vehicle Greenberg stood up and looked toward the western horizon. He heard the slow roar of a jet engine laboring to maintain airspeed while in a turn. "There it is," he whispered, spotting the blue and yellow stabilizers in a clear sky above the Old City.

"Greenberg." It was Bernstein shouting up at him. "It has been confirmed by U.S. intelligence services that the Saudi jet is carrying a nuclear weapon. But whether or not it can actually detonate, they aren't sure. Our orders are to treat this with kid gloves, do you understand? So, don't program any data inside the nose of the missile. We can't take a chance on an accidental firing. They're even pulling the interceptor aircraft back."

"What the hell are we gonna do, Lieutenant?"

Bernstein shook his head. "Looks like we're going to concede to their demands for the moment. If not, Jerusalem could be blown away."

"Concede!" Greenberg screamed his face contorted in rage. "Never!" he shouted while saliva flew from his mouth. "We can't give in to them. We never give in to terrorists. I didn't come all the way over here to give in to terrorists."

Bernstein was shocked at the outrageous reaction of his Tactical Control Assistant. "Calm down, Greenberg, " he yelled back. "It's just a verbal concession. Once this nuclear business is over and they evaluate the demands we'll go back to business as usual. But in the meantime we have to follow orders, now bring the threat level from red down to standing alert. Can you do that for me, Greenberg?"

"Sure, Lieutenant," the TCA replied caustically. "I can take care of it."

"Make sure there's no targeting data in the nose of the missile, understand?"

"Yes, Sir, following orders, Sir," Greenberg responded with a growl.

There was something discomforting about the look in his eyes that gave the Lieutenant cause for concern. He went immediately to a phone in the rear of the vehicle to speak with the Communications Specialist to make sure Greenberg wasn't given any radar tracking data unless the alert level went back up to red.

"What do you mean he's already programmed the data into the missile? Who authorized that?" he screamed at the top of his lungs, "I sure didn't!" Berstein ran around to the Fire Control

Center just in time to be knocked to the ground by the force of an anti-ballistic missile firing from its tube.

"Holy shit, Greenberg!" he screamed as he fell backwards. "What have you done? What have you done?"

A Calm Before the Storm

In the Sky Above Jerusalem

ANNALISA FELT ODDLY CALM as she wheeled above the city.
"It's going well," she whispered to herself sensing that Robert's
plan was on the verge of success and that no one would have to
die in this extraordinary adventure.

Down on her left she could see old Mount Moriah, the location
of the City of David, Solomon's Temple, and Herod's expanded
Old City that was now divided into quarters. *One of the oldest cities
in the world*, she thought, a*ttacked and captured over forty times, even
destroyed twice*, she recalled from previous readings, *but not this time.*

She thought about walking hand in hand with Jake along the
Via Dolorosa, the street on which Jesus had carried his cross on
the way to the crucifixion. Her heart swelled with admiration for
the man she loved. *My own knight in shining armor* she was thinking when she heard a strange high-pitched beeping.

"Oh my, God!" she screamed out loud, as she realized what was
happening. A missile was speeding toward her at hypersonic speed.

"Jake, Jake," she screamed into the radio. "My God, they've
fired a missile at me, Jake. What do I do? What do I do?"

"Are you sure, Annalisa?" he answered.

"Listen!" She held the satellite phone near the Threat
Assessment Radar. The high-pitched beeps were getting closer
together. Jake was helpless. He had selected Jerusalem for her

target because he believed Israel would be the least likely to fire a missile knowing for certain that a detonation would follow.

He could hear the maddening high-pitched beeps screaming over the satellite phone and then they stopped. "I've turned off the Threat Assessment Radar, Jake, so it won't know..." Her words faded away. "I can't do this to all those innocent people down there.

"I love you, Jake, " were her last words and then there was silence.

Samuel Greenberg stood up inside the turret of the Fire Control Center and looked out into the bright blue sky. He watched the missile track toward the F-15 that had just made a turn toward the West Bank. From this distance he wouldn't need to send any more radar information. The missile had locked on its target and would not miss.

"Greenberg!" the Lieutenant screamed as he climbed up the side ladder to the turret. "My family lives in Jerusalem, you asshole, all of my family and you may have just..." He began administering a ferocious beating to the head and shoulders of his Technical Control Assistant. "My wife and kids, you son of a bitch!"

Greenberg held his hands above his head and shouted with a snarl. "It's God's will! I did it for Israel! Don't you believe in the manifest destiny of Israel?"

At that moment there was an explosion in the eastern sky, but it did not turn into a fireball. There was no nuclear detonation. The two men watched as both stabilizers blew off the tail of the jet, but it continued to glide on an easterly course.

"Good Lord!" the Lieutenant screamed. " Looks like someone's trying to steer that thing toward the hills." Just before the fuselage struck the ground a white canopy shot out of the dying aircraft only a few hundred feet above the horizon.

Bernstein looked back down at the soldier cowering in the turret. He opened a leather holster strapped on his hip and reached for his pistol, a 1903 Colt 45 Automatic that was his grandfather's personal sidearm during World War II.

"Get your sorry ass off my missile platform. You're under arrest, Greenberg, for insubordination, disobeying a direct order and putting the lives of a million people at risk all because of your stupid fanatical beliefs." The Lieutenant could barely contain himself. "Shit," he screamed, "I ought to blow your ass away right now and save the government the expense of having to put you in jail for the rest of your miserable life."

A Moment of Silence

Tehran, Iran

JAKE FELT THE AIR sucking from his lungs. *What happened?* he screamed to himself. *Why did the Israelis shoot her down?* The battle hardened veteran of many campaigns on behalf of the CIA and New Democratic Right felt chest heaving sobs welling up inside.

"Eagle One, Eagle One, this is Eagle Three, do you copy?" After a moment of silence without a response Duke called again. "Jake, do you copy? Are you still there?"

Already on this mission Jake Eastwood had lost his best friend, Robert Faircloth, the trust of his long time friend and colleague, Nalum Taylor, and now the woman he loved, Annalisa Bertolla. He was trying to clear his mind and consider his options.

"Eagle Three, this is Eagle one." Jake spoke in a trembling voice, knowing the entire world was listening on the satellite phone link. "You know what just happened."

"Yeah, they took her down. I think it's Omega time," Duke said flatly.

"She turned it off, Duke. She turned off her Threat Assessment Radar. She knew that if it was off the auto detonator couldn't detect an incoming missile."

There was another long moment of silence. Duke finally responded. "She was right about that, Jake. No detection, no detonation. She saved Jerusalem's ass with that move."

An Israeli Apache Attack Helicopter was already airborne, in route to the crash site. Within minutes it was hovering over the burning wreckage of the Saudi F-15 aircraft. "This is Apache One," the pilot reported. "The jet is on fire burning from nose to tail. No sign of the pilot."

The copilot slapped the top of the pilot's helmet to get his attention then pointed to the top of a nearby hill. The helicopter pilot looked to his left and saw someone standing with hands in the air. "We have the pilot in sight!" he shouted with excitement. "I repeat, we have the pilot in sight!"

He pulled up the collective control, changing the pitch of the rotors, pushed the left tail rotor pedal forward and the powerful Apache lurched toward a parachute crumpled among the rocks. Hovering less than a hundred feet away he reported, "The pilot is standing right in front of me hands raised in the air. He appears willing to surrender. He's removing his flight helmet and.... "

"Holy shit, it's a woman! I repeat the Saudi pilot is a woman. Do you copy?"

"We copy, Apache One. This is Colonel Mayer, Director of Security at Ben Gurion. Can you land and take that pilot into custody?"

"It's pretty rocky here, Sir, but I believe I can land. She's holding her right hand up to her ear, with her thumb and finger extended, like... " he paused, "like she wants to make a phone call. She's waving us over. She has her hands together now like she's praying, or pleading, or something."

"Apache One, get on the ground and get her on the radio as quickly as possible. We have to find out if there is a radioactive crash site out there," he shouted.

"Landing now, sir. We'll get her on the horn."

"Think she ejected?" Duke asked.

"Don't know," Jake answered. "Haven't heard anything from the Israelis."

"It's possible she did. Maybe she's okay."

"Hold on, Duke, I'm getting something on my radio. Be right back."

"Eagle one, Eagle One, this is Colonel Mayer, Security Director at Ben Gurion International. Your pilot is alive. I repeat Eagle Two is alive and well. She is receiving medical attention at the crash site. She may have a broken leg from a parachute landing among rocks in the Judean Hills, but she is okay. I repeat, Eagle One, your pilot is down and safe and we will have her on the radio in a few minutes. Do you copy, Eagle One?"

Silent sobs were pounding in Jake's chest as he tried to control his voice long enough to reply. "Copy that, Ben Gurion. Will hold for confirmation." Then he went back to his satellite phone. "She's okay, Duke. The Israelis have her. She may have a leg injury but she's okay."

"Good news, Jake, but they'd better get a 'HAZMAT' team to that crash site pretty quick because they have a lot of nuclear trash to clean up."

Jake thought at this point it would be good to let the Israelis and the rest of the world know what may be there. "Yeah, it'll be a big clean-up job, Duke." Then an angelic voice called to him.

"Jake, I'm okay, Jake. I'm fine. There's no reason for Omega. I repeat," and she screamed over the radio, "negative Omega. The Israelis agree to Alpha, all of Robert's demands, if the Iranians and Saudis will do the same."

Jake pushed back hard in his seat stunned at her announcement. "Are you sure, Annalisa? Need confirmation before we can..." He wanted to say *abort the mission* but quickly reconsidered.

"Jake, I dropped the belly tank before I ejected. Thought it better to break apart on the ground than risk a fire setting off the charges. Did I do the right thing?"

He thought for a moment and was pleased with her quick thinking. "You did exactly right. That containment vessel is pretty rugged and probably held together when it hit the ground, but those cordite charges would have burned in a fire and exploded."

Another voice interrupted, but this time on the phone line. "Eagle One, this is Yitzhak Meir, Prime Minister of Israel. I'm told that you once met my grandmother."

Jake was shaking his head in disbelief. "Yes, Sir, I met her in New York at a function in 1978, just before she died." *And if they know that info about me,* Jake thought, *they're hinting they know a whole lot more.*

"She was a fine person, Eagle One, a great diplomat for Israel, but now to the business-at-hand. I speak for the Kinneset, and all of Israel, when I say that we accept your conditions. And further, I have been informed the Iranians and Saudis also agree to this extraordinary opportunity for moving the peace process forward in the Middle East. Your plan, however frightening, has had a profound impact."

"Not my plan, Sir. It came from Robert Faircloth who recently died in Iraq pursuing the cause of peace." It felt wonderful to proclaim to the world through the satellite phone link that Robert was the true hero behind the plan. He was the one who had faith that it would work.

"Well then, we will remember this man and your pilot, Eagle Two, as heroes of Israel. One saved Jerusalem and the other may yet bring peace to the Middle East."

The Prime Minister couldn't have said anything more to fill Jake's heart with pride than praising Robert and Annalisa. All that remained was to land and refuel outside Tehran and for Duke to do likewise in Jeddah. Then they would fly their jets to Kuwait and surrender. But he recalled that he was also to meet Annalisa at the U.S. Air Base.

"Sir, I need to speak to Colonel Mayer again about a private matter."

"Ay, yes," the Prime Minister answered, "dinner reservations at a certain location. She has made it clear that if she is late it could result in a detonation and we don't want that to happen. Plans are being made for transporting Eagle Two. She will be there in time for dinner. Do you understand?"

"Copy that, Sir, over and out."

Veramar

Berryville, Virginia

NALUM TAYLOR, LEADER OF the New Democratic Right in America, sat in a green leather chair inside his home in Northern Virginia. It was a modern French Chateau built next to the family vineyard bordering the Shenandoah River. It had taken thirty years to cultivate the delicate vines at Veramar that now produced some of Virginia's finest Cabernet Francs and Riesling/Vidals. He was saddened at the prospect of having to pass it all down to his son and his wife, but felt relieved the whole affair of Peaceful Eagle would soon be behind him.

He was staring at a 52" digital screen monitoring satellite broadcasts of the events taking place in the Middle East. Media experts on varying subjects from oil and politics to nuclear weapons were being interviewed. Their interpretation of events and their meanings were being replayed, over and over, every half hour.

The CNN announcer was speaking gravely. "The United States has just announced the 18th Airborne Corp, including the 82nd Airborne Division at Fort Bragg, North Carolina, and the 101st Airborne Division at Fort Campbell, Kentucky, have been alerted for deployment to bases in Saudi Arabia. If needed they will assist the Saudis in securing ARAMCO's oil and gas production facilities, pipelines and ports."

The announcer put a hand to an earpiece to receive a message from his director in the control room. "I'm also receiving a report from our correspondent in Beijing that in response to the Americans, the Chinese have announced they will alert two infantry divisions for possible deployment to Iran to secure their investments in the oil fields and pipelines of that country.

"And this just coming in... under emergency authority from the Security Council at the United Nations, there is word that an international security force has been authorized for possible movement into all countries along the Persian Gulf to help secure those facilities.

"My God," he exclaimed into his microphone. "It seems the entire Middle East is about to be reoccupied by foreign powers over concern for the oil production fields and facilities." He looked up at the camera with a puzzled expression on his face. "Who could have predicted this?"

Not me, Nalum thought to himself. *I seriously miscalculated Jake's commitment to our original plan. But with the death of Robert Faircloth everything seemed to change. Didn't see it coming*, was his last thought before his personal assistants entered the room.

"Mr. Nalum, we are ready to leave," Muri announced.

"Everything is done, then?" Nalum asked.

"Yes, all paper and electronic trails have been severed and destroyed. We have been very thorough, Sir."

"Very well then, it's time for you and Gordo to leave for Dulles and catch your flight to Jamaica." He looked up at the huge Caribbean man. "Gordo, you must help look after Muri. He is a fine fellow and a rich man. Both of you are," he added with smile. "I've created Swiss accounts for each of you and deposited two million dollars in each as monies due for your fine service to the New Democratic Right."

Nalum rose for a final handshake and a gripping hug from the two young men that had demonstrated a genius for creating computer software and hardware applications on behalf of the NDR. Nalum stepped back and looked at his protégées. "You have served well, my friends. Now go and enjoy the fruits of your labors in this brave new world that Robert, Jake and Annalisa have created for us."

Muri bowed his head at the mention of Jake's name. "He was my adoptive father so that I could remain in this country after my mother died. And the two of you nurtured me here. I will never forget my debt to each of you, Mr. Nalum."

"Nor I," Gordo added. "It has been an honor to serve with you."

Nalum's voice choked with emotion. "Go now, please, before it is too late. Leave this country and do not return for quite some time. Do you understand?"

"Let me assist you with your coat," Muri said as he raised a grey wool topcoat to Nalum's shoulders. It seemed especially heavy with the 38 Caliber Smith and Wesson that Nalum had asked be placed in the side pocket.

After the overcoat was securely around him Nalum waved his hand as if to dismiss the two men. "Go now, and have a good life. This is a direct order, now leave me."

Muri backed away and bowed deeply, a last gesture of respect to the leader of the NDR. Gordo also bowed. The two young men turned away and left the vineyards of Veramar. They would never see Nalum or America again.

Nalum turned back to the television screen to view more satellite images beaming from Iran and Saudi Arabia. At Khomeni International outside Tehran, a lone F-15 sat at the end of a runway while a fuel truck filled it with jet fuel. There was no trickery, no scheming to capture the aircraft or its weapon. The Mullahs wanted nothing more than to rid them selves of the nuclear threat.

At Aziz International north of Jeddah, two American agents walked slowly up to an F-15 while it was being refueled. Duke raised the canopy so that he could speak with them. "Close enough, boys," he shouted as they stood near the front of his jet.

"You really got a nuke in that belly tank?" Agent Weller asked.

"A big one," Duke answered crisply. "Enough to blow this airport and the entire city of Jeddah into eternity." Then he held up the detonator. "See this green light? All I have to do is squeeze this handle, then a red light will come on and less than a second later fission and fusion."

Doug Jackson took a step forward. "Mr. Disisto, is there anything you can share with us about how all this happened, names of major players, how it was financed, anything like that?"

Duke looked curiously at the FBI agent. *He must be the inside man and he's letting me know that I can never go home again.* "Sorry, gentlemen. I'm sworn to secrecy. That information will go with me to the grave."

"You really gonna fly that jet to some neutral country," Weller asked, "and turn it over to their government, the weapon, too?"

"Roger that. It's part of the plan. The U.S. should regain control of both remaining nuclear weapons within a few hours. So be patient and don't go cowboy on us. This thing's about to work itself out, looks like everybody's gonna be a winner."

The fuel truck began backing away and Duke looked down at the two agents for a final comment. "Gotta go, boys. Maybe I'll see you someday in Paris." As the canopy slipped down he turned the switch for the APU to wind up and restart his engines. The two agents backed quickly away from the front of the jet so they would not be sucked into the turbines.

"That guy's got one big set of cahunas," Agent Weller said in admiration.

"He should," Jackson responded. "He's an American fighter pilot and you don't get 'em any bigger than that."

Death of the NDR

Berryville, Virginia

THE CNN ANNOUNCER CLEARED his throat and continued. "The Russians have just announced they will also make troops available for deployment to the Gulf as part of the United Nations Stabilization Force, the UNSF, as it is now being called."

Nalum sighed heavily and walked outside into the cold morning darkness. "Jake, my boy," he whispered aloud to no one there, "looks like this plan of yours is about to accomplish something good and useful, but unfortunately I will soon be exposed as complicit. Perhaps it is time for me to do the honorable thing and hopefully spare my son and his family some extreme embarrassment."

The NDR leader walked over to a stone and mortar wall that bordered the patio at the back of his home. He leaned into the cold granite and looked out toward the Shenandoah River. "This is the price of what we do, significant risks for great rewards, and sometimes even greater personal sacrifice."

He patted the right side pocket of his topcoat and thought of his wife who died the year before, recalling their run-away honeymoon to an old motel at Topsail Beach, NC, and the Calabash Style seafood dinner they had shared on their wedding night. He was just a Marine corporal at Camp Lejeune, but it was not long before his well-connected father-in-law secured a slot for him at Officer's Candidate School. With the retired Major General's connections he had risen quickly in the ranks, with the best of assignments that led him into contact with many influential leaders in Washington, D.C.

Nalum remembered the day he'd resigned his commission and went into government service with various agencies, eventually leading the American intelligence community through a difficult transition after the Iran-Contra era. And finally, as a well-respected government administrator, he was selected to run in the number two slot on the Republican Presidential ticket. Vice-President of the United States was a position he never imagined he would occupy and he enjoyed the power even more than the prestige.

He reached for the revolver inside his coat pocket, studied the silver-plated weapon then turned the pistol toward his face. He could taste the steel of the barrel in his mouth as he recalled the fragrance of lightly fried shrimp and oysters, dipping them in cocktail sauce and pressing them to the lips of his beautiful young wife. He took a last breath, exhaled, and watched the mist disappear into the cold morning air, then twitched his index finger and the pistol fired.

Richard Delano Harrington, former Vice-President of the United States of America, code-named, Nalum Taylor inside the New Democratic Right, fell backward on the patio. Early morning workers in the vineyard heard the gunshot. They ran to the back of the house and found his body splayed among the wicker furniture. He was bleeding profusely from his mouth and the top of his head. There was no hope to save him.

Flight 723 to Karachi

"LADIES AND GENTLEMEN, I have some incredible news," the captain of Flight 723 announced over the aircraft intercom. "We have just received an emergency transmission that nuclear weapons have been flown over three major cites in the Middle East; one over Jerusalem, another over Tehran and the other over Makkah in Saudi Arabia."

The cabin filled with the shocked voices of passengers. "How could this happen?" they exclaimed. "Who would do such a thing?" "My mother and father," a woman's voice wailed from the rear of the Boeing 757. "They are on hajj to Makkah."

In the first class cabin a small Pakistani man stared out the window. *What has happened?* He screamed inside himself. *Three jets with three nuclear weapons, what has happened, Jake?* Abdul Khan sank into his seat as a stewardess leaned over and addressed him. "Sir, are you all right? Do you need assistance?"

Abdul Khan looked up at the pretty young woman and shook his head. "No," he croaked, "but I know many people in those cities and it is hard to imagine…" His voice broke and fell away as he curled up and tucked a clean white pillow under his chin. "I will be okay," he said while trembling in his seat. "I will be okay."

The stewardess reached down and touched his shoulder. "All of us feel the same way. We cannot imagine such a thing. It must be the terrorists. They have somehow gotten their hands on nuclear weapons. But where will it end?" she asked as she stood up and moved on to the other First Class passengers.

Khan stared out the window and considered what he must do. *If I go home to Karachi, it is only a matter of time until they find me. Where can I go?* He sat up in his seat with a curious expression on his face. *To the Swat Valley of my ancestors.*

Once known as the Switzerland of Pakistan, the Swat Valley of the Hindu Kush Mountains had been taken over by the Taliban and was now considered a lawless region on the northwestern frontier. *I must take all my money and hide there. As long as I have money the old tribal leaders will protect me as they have the Taliban. Oh, my,* he thought to himself, *Abdul Khan joins the Taliban to save his own miserable life.*

"Ladies and gentlemen," the Captain announced, "I have an updated report. All is well. The Israelis have shot down the aircraft flying over Jerusalem and captured a woman pilot. There was no nuclear detonation."

Oh my God, Khan thought fearfully. *The Israelis have Annalisa. They will torture her. They will find out about me.*

"There is more good news," the Captain continued. "Demands were made of each country for a peaceful settlement in the Middle East and all three nations have agreed. Peace may be breaking out in the Middle East."

There was clapping and cheering throughout the cabin from the First Class section all the way to the rear of the aircraft. "And who knows," the Captain continued. "If peace can be made in Palestine then peace may come to Pakistan and Afghanistan."

The clapping and cheering filled the cabin as all of the passengers were rejoicing in the possibilities. But one man sat squirming in his First Class seat unsure of what to do with the feelings of exhilaration that suddenly filled him with hope for the future. He pressed his hands together, raised them to his lips and closed his eyes.

"I never met you, Robert Faircloth," he whispered to himself, "but surely you were a good and wise man. May Allah bless your wisdom and courage," then he looked back out the window with renewed hope.

Bin Ghazi Must Die

Jeddah, Saudi Arabia

THE HEAD OF THE General Intelligence Directorate and the NCTC agents met at the penthouse elevator of Le Meridien Hotel. Prince Ali ibn Saud, a cousin to the king, had been contacted by bin Ghazi hoping to confidentially explain events from his position.

Ali listened patiently then consulted other members of the Royal Family. An hour later he dutifully called the GID and told Colonel Hatani where Saudi's UN Ambassador was hiding. The agents were to meet the prince at the elevator doors on the top floor.

"Sa'eeda," the royal prince said in greeting.

"Sa'eeda," Hatani responded respectfully to the prince. "These are the two American agents."

"Ahlan wa-Sahlan," the prince said in greeting to the Americans.

The colonel looked at the two agents, "The prince says 'Welcome.'"

"Thank you," the agents mumbled, confused why a Harvard educated prince would speak to them in Arabic.

"The greetings are traditional," the prince said, "but now I will speak in your language." He turned to face the colonel. "Bin Ghazi is expecting only me and that I will be alone. Please, let me greet him and explain that you are here only to ask a few questions. Then you may take him into custody."

The Colonel looked over at the two Americans. "There is no way for him to escape. This elevator and that staircase at the end of the hall are the only means to leave. He is trapped, yes?"

"Seems to be," Agent Weller said, not sure that it was a good idea to let the prince get to him first.

Jackson nodded. "Sounds okay to me."

"Very well then," the prince said. "I will greet bin Ghazi. After a few minutes I will come to the hallway and invite you into the room. Is that satisfactory?"

"Yes," the Colonel said emphatically, letting the two Americans know there would be no more discussion.

The prince walked halfway down the hall then turned to face the door. He knocked gently. "Bin Ghazi, it is I, Prince Ali ibn Saud, here to greet you, my friend."

The door opened slowly. "Aasalaamu Alelkum, ibn Saud."

"Wa-Alelkum Aassalaam," the prince responded calmly. "May I come in?" The prince entered the penthouse suite and for the next several minutes the three intelligence agents stood outside by the elevator doors unaware of what was being said in the suite.

"Our King sends you greetings," the prince said. "He is aware of the great sacrifice you are about to make. And he wants you to know that he is a man of his word. He will take care of your family. Your wives and children have been gathered. Even now they are being transported to a new location where they will live in comfort for the rest of their lives."

"Then it is time," the man stated emphatically. "I must repay my debt for all that King Khalid has done for me and my family." He smiled to himself. "The death of Abdullah bin Ghazi should close the door on this investigation and protect the House of Saud."

The prince stood and bowed in respect to the man who had always served his king faithfully. "Il-Hamdu-Allah."

"Yes, thanks be to God," the man repeated, then stared at an open door to the balcony of the penthouse suite. "Go now, and tell the Colonel and the Americans to knock on my door so that I can finish this business."

"Ma'a Salaama."

"Farewell to you, too, Prince Ali."

The prince walked out of the suite and left the door slightly open. He looked down the hall at the three men waiting by the elevator. "He is ready to talk with you, Colonel, and also the two Americans," then waved his hand for them to come forward.

There was no one to greet them in the main room of the suite. The two agents searched the bedrooms while the Colonel stayed in the living area. He spied a long grey dishdashah lying outside on the floor of the balcony. He rushed over to pick it up, saw the royal emblem embroidered on the front then peered over the edge of the balcony.

"Gentlemen," he called urgently to the American agents. "It seems bin Ghazi is through talking. Look there." Twenty-five stories below the body of a man lay facedown on the concrete parking lot, blood pooling around his head.

Hakim Abdullah Faisal

Aziz International, Jeddah

A PRIVATE JET WAITED inside a hangar at the airport. Four women and nine children had been escorted aboard. A tall portly clean-shaven man in a white shirt, red tie and dark blue suit ascended the stairs to the cabin.

Ali ibn Saud stepped out to greet him. "Sa'eeda, Abdullah bin Ghazi."

"Oh, no," the man replied. "Abdullah bin Ghazi died tonight, did you not hear? He fell from a balcony at his hotel. But I understand your confusion. I am his cousin, Hakim Abdullah Faisal. I've been told many times that I look like my wealthy relative."

"My apologies, Hakim," the prince acknowledged with a knowing smile. He pulled out a small leather attaché. "I have travel documents for you and your family."

"Also, the King suggests you visit a skilled surgeon while you are away to alter your appearance, so that you will not be confused with your cousin. It might cause you and your family undue embarrassment if you are recognized as his relative."

"The king's wish is my command. I will see to it as soon as I arrive in London."

"Well then," the younger prince said as he descended the staircase, "King Khalid wishes you and your family good health on your extended stay in England."

The Evening News

New York City / Kuwait

MEDIA COVERAGE OF THE near disasters in Israel, Iran and Saudi Arabia was unrelenting. Oil speculators had driven the price beyond two hundred dollars a barrel with no ceiling in sight. The G-20 leaders of the world's largest economies met in emergency video summit and recommended that trading on all world stock markets be suspended to prevent speculators from driving up the prices of basic goods and services. National economies teetered on the edge waiting for any encouraging news that might stabilize and diffuse the threat of military occupation of the oil-producing nations in the Middle East.

Stephan McCallister, a senior network correspondent in New York City was beginning his evening commentary, lending his sage character and baritone voice to the unfolding events of the day. He had been schooled in journalism in the 1950s, and was a young protégée of the peerless Walter Cronkite. The man with perfectly coiffed white hair and deep set compassionate blue eyes had taken his place at the news desk to speak to the nation and the world.

"Good evening, my fellow Americans and citizens of all the nations of the world. As the nuclear clock has ticked within a quarter second of Armageddon, we must step back from this outrageous world we have created and ask ourselves poignant questions.

"Throughout history there have always been angry men, ambitious men, fanatical men with pathological obsessions, but only in the last few decades have weapons of incalculable mass destruction been available to them.

"The genie is now out of the nuclear bottle granting wishes to nations large and small, both good and evil. All of us knew, and we must not pretend we did not know, that one fateful day an enterprising group of fanatics would somehow gain access to these weapons, and not understanding their majestic destructive power might use them frivolously against perceived enemies.

"As in the story of King Solomon who once held the fate of a child in his hands we often ask ourselves, what if both women had been so stubborn and foolish that neither had conceded to the other? Would Solomon have allowed his man to cut the child in half? Today the child was nearly destroyed.

"Had it not been for the extraordinary courage of one woman, willing to sacrifice herself in a lone effort to prevent a nuclear disaster, we would be living in a different world tonight. Temple Mount and the Old City of Jerusalem would have melted into an unrecognizable dome of limestone. Tehran would have been shattered by five hundred mile per hour winds and burned from the face of the earth. And Makkah, with nearly three million pilgrims from all over the Muslim world, would have become grim testament to the proliferation of nuclear weapons.

"But I tell you, we are all part of God's creation and the gifts of reason and compassion He bestowed upon us must now be brought to bear. If ever there was a moment in human history to deny the maniacs such weapons, it is now.

"People of good reason, leaders of the world, nations of integrity, I implore you. If we learn nothing more from these recent events it is that the spread of weapons of mass destruction must be contained. The nuclear genie must be returned to its bottle. Nuclear stockpiles must be severely reduced and eliminated whenever possible.

"The people of this world must be protected from the fantasies of extremists. If not then we are doomed to repeat this scenario. Next time we may not be so lucky, the fanatics might succeed. This is Stephan McCallister wishing all of us a brighter future."

The camera cut back to the news anchor. "Thank you, Stephan, for those sobering words," then he glanced down at his teleprompter and continued. "The Security Council at the United Nations is in session tonight considering what must be done to ensure the integrity of nuclear stockpiles around the world, and what can be done to calm tensions in the aftermath of this unprecedented event in the Middle East. Here in America, Homeland Security has placed the nation on its highest level of alert and it's expected to remain so for weeks to come.

"In other news tonight, we are saddened to learn of the death of former Vice-President, Richard Delano Harrington. It was reported that he was in failing health and depressed over the loss of his wife just over a year ago. His body was discovered early this morning on the patio of his home at the family vineyard at Veramar. He will be remembered as one of our nation's most brilliant and controversial Vice-Presidents."

The Rock

Kuwait

THREE EXHAUSTED AMERICANS WERE sitting at a table in the bar of the Officer's Club at The Rock, a section of the Ali Al Salem Air Base in Kuwait assigned to U.S. Air Force personnel. Jake Eastwood, Annalisa Bertolla and Duke DisSisto had survived Robert's nuclear peace ultimatum and were waiting for the Kuwaiti authorities to arrive and formally accept their surrender.

They were watching a replay of the evening news from America when Jake's eyes opened wide. He pointed toward the huge digital television above the bar where a dated picture of Nalum Taylor showed prominently on the screen. All three were stunned at the news of the NDR leader's death. Annalisa looked at Jake. "What's going to happen to us? Without Nalum how are we going to…"

Duke leaned back in his seat. "Yeah, Jake, I don't think this was part of Robert's plan. Got any ideas?"

Jake and Duke had refueled without incident and flown directly to the air base in Kuwait. U.S. Air Force personnel worked alongside both men to ensure the blasting caps and compression detonators were safely removed from the remaining warheads. No one on base seemed to know how to treat the two men. Were they terrorists or heroes? The opinion of the military personnel on The Rock was leaning toward bodacious hero status.

Late that afternoon a private jet from Israel landed at the base with an injured, but adrenalin fueled American woman on board.

She had arrived as planned for dinner with Jake and Duke at the 'OC' and a glass of California Merlot. Annalisa was squeezing Jake's forearm gently with one hand while holding a glass of wine in the other, and if it were in her power she would never let go of him again.

As Jake continued to stare into the television screen four men walked briskly into the bar. On the left was the American base commander, Air Force Colonel Steven White. Beside him was the American Ambassador in Kuwait, Roger Robertson, smartly dressed in a dark linen suit with fresh white shirt and a yellow tie.

Just behind the Americans were two men in elegant flowing Arabic attire. One of them had a Kuwaiti flag sewn on the front of his gutrah and the other had an impressive emblem embroidered on the front of his dishdasha.

Jake and Duke rose from their seats. "Please sit down, gentlemen." The colonel spoke softly while waving his hands downward.

The U.S. ambassador addressed them. "As you know we are all guests here in Kuwait. This means the disposition of your status is in the hands of the Kuwaiti government. So, may I present Prince Saleem, representative of the King of Kuwait."

"I bring you greetings from my government," the prince said nervously. "What happens next is a very delicate matter. It has taken much time to arrange. Final preparations have only just been completed." He turned to the man standing beside him. "For this may I introduce Prince Ali ibn Saud, personal envoy for the King of Saudi Arabia."

The Saudi prince smiled and bowed deeply. "Like Prince Saleem, I take care of many important and delicate matters for the royal family. That is why I am here, to assist you." Without commenting on the incredible events of the day the prince went directly to the business at hand. "You have heard of the passing of your former Vice-President, Richard Harrington?" he asked them.

"Yes," all of them said together. "We just heard on the news."

The prince looked over at the colonel, the American ambassador and the representative from Kuwait. "My conversation with our guests must now remain confidential. I hope each of you will understand."

"Of course," the two Americans responded. They turned away and walked out of the bar.

"I will wait outside, ibn Saud," Prince Saleem said.

The Saudi prince bowed slightly and when he was alone with the Americans he spoke quietly. "You must know that your friend, Mr. Harrington, was an honorable man or I would not be here."

"Calls were made from his home early this morning to certain members of the Saudi Royal family. And so, we have arranged through private channels that the Kuwaiti government allow us to transport you to a classified location where you will remain in comfort for the next several months. After that, you will be free to relocate to a place of your choosing."

"But where are we going?" Annalisa asked.

"Into the lap of luxury," the Saudi envoy responded with a sweep of his hands. "Perhaps you have heard of the Burj Al Arab Hotel in Dubai?"

"Sweet, Jesus," Duke said in amazement. "You mean the one built on a man-made island out in the gulf, that looks like a huge sail."

"Yes," the prince responded with a smart head nod. "Every comfort will be provided Mr. and Mrs. Eastwood in the Royal Suite on the top floor." He smiled at Jake and Annalisa. "And for you, Mr. DiSisto, a large sumptuous suite of your own."

"Sounds expensive," Duke said shaking his head.

"It is a small gift from those who wish to anonymously express their gratitude."

"And after three months, then what?" Jake asked.

"You will be free to go anywhere in the world you wish with your new identities and appropriate travel documents. May I suggest Canadian, or perhaps Australian papers? You will also have access to your new Swiss bank accounts which have been generously deposited with the balance of funds from Peaceful Eagle."

"Ninety days," Duke said. "Considering the alternatives, Jake, guess I can pull some time in Dubai. What about you and Annalisa?"

Jake looked into the eyes of the woman still gripping his arm. "And after that, I'm thinking about a nice stretch of beach just east of Havana." He turned back toward Duke. "Where will you go after Dubai?"

"Me," he said thoughtfully. "I'm thinking about a little sheep ranch just north of Galway. I hear it's really pretty and green in Ireland."

"Well, then," the Saudi prince said with open arms. "My jet is waiting."

About the Author

RICHARD FOLSOM IS FROM Fayetteville, NC. He lives with his wife on the Pamlico River in Beaufort County, NC. He earned BA and MA Degrees from East Carolina University, has worked in education, business and industry and now writes full-time.

Richard enjoys hearing from readers at:
r*ichardfolsom11@gmail.com*
Personal responses may be limited.

Other Books by Richard Folsom

The Pareto Spread
A PREQUEL TO *The Project*... an action-packed thriller that tells the story of Robert Faircloth, drafted into the New Democratic Right by his old friend, Jake Eastwood. The NDR believes 20% of the people in America are causing 80% of the problems. The covert paramilitary group wants to reset the moral compass of the nation by eliminating the most egregious offenders of a traditional set of values and beliefs known as 'The American Way.'

Indian Wood: A Mystery of the Lost Colony of Roanoke Island
More than a historical murder mystery and well researched tale of the 1587 'Lost Colony of Roanoke,' it is also a story of the Lumbee Indians of Robeson County, NC, and their claim to be descendents of the Lost Colonists. Who killed the professor that may have discovered a link between the Lumbees and the Colonists? The person that can unravel the professor's new theory may be able to solve the mystery of the Lost Colony.

Waiting for Kerouac
To be released in 2013... a story of the Folk Music Revival of the early1960s. The transition from the Beats of the 50s to the folkies of the early 60s is told through the eyes of Maggie O'Neal, the 'Flower Lady' of Greenwich Village. The story reveals her relationships with many of the young folk performers that created the soundtrack for an entire generation of young Americans.